DADDY'S HOME

"Do you know him?" Rich asked, reluctantly lowering his rifle.

"Yes, he's my—ah—your—" Flair couldn't seem to say the words as she looked over her son's head to the man still sitting quietly on his horse, taking in the situation.

Caden Maxwell tipped his hat to her, pushing it farther up his forehead, revealing his face, exposing his greenish-brown eyes. "It's been a long time, Flair."

"Yes," she whispered, brushing her drying hair away from her face.

She hadn't remembered Caden being so handsome to look upon with his angular jaw, small nose, and finely sculpted lips. He wore more than a day's growth of beard and his clothes were dusty and sweat-stained, telling her he'd been on the trail a few days.

Caden cut his eyes over to the boy. "Is it all right if I get down off my horse?"

"Of course," Flair answered. "Rich, take his horse over to the barn, unsaddle him, and give him water and oats."

Flair watched as Caden dismounted. Had she forgotten how tall he was, how broad his shoulders and how slim his hips were? Her hand crept up the front of her robe and she held it together at the base of her neck.

"Does he have a name, mister?" Rich asked as he took the reins from Caden.

"I call him Max."

"Hey, that's part of my name." He looked back up to the porch at Flair. "Isn't it, Mama?"

TODAY'S HOTTEST READS
ARE TOMORROW'S SUPERSTARS

VICTORY'S WOMAN (4484, $4.50)
by Gretchen Genet

Andrew—the carefree soldier who sought glory on the battlefield, and returned a shattered man . . . Niall—the legandary frontiersman and a former Shawnee captive, tormented by his past . . . Roger—the troubled youth, who would rise up to claim a shocking legacy . . . and Clarice—the passionate beauty bound by one man, and hopelessly in love with another. Set against the backdrop of the American revolution, three men fight for their heritage—and one woman is destined to change all their lives forever!

FORBIDDEN (4488, $4.99)
by Jo Beverley

While fleeing from her brothers, who are attempting to sell her into a loveless marriage, Serena Riverton accepts a carriage ride from a stranger—who is the handsomest man she has ever seen. Lord Middlethorpe, himself, is actually contemplating marriage to a dull daughter of the aristocracy, when he encounters the breathtaking Serena. She arouses him as no woman ever has. And after a night of thrilling intimacy—a forbidden liaison—Serena must choose between a lady's place and a woman's passion!

WINDS OF DESTINY (4489, $4.99)
by Victoria Thompson

Becky Tate is a half-breed outcast—branded by her Comanche heritage. Then she meets a rugged stranger who awakens her heart to the magic and mystery of passion. Hiding a desperate past, Texas Ranger Clint Masterson has ridden into cattle country to bring peace to a divided land. But a greater battle rages inside him when he dares to desire the beautiful Becky!

WILDEST HEART (4456, $4.99)
by Virginia Brown

Maggie Malone had come to cattle country to forge her future as a healer. Now she was faced by Devon Conrad, an outlaw wounded body and soul by his shadowy past . . . whose eyes blazed with fury even as his burning caress sent her spiraling with desire. They came together in a Texas town about to explode in sin and scandal. Danger was their destiny—and there was nothing they wouldn't dare for love!

GLORIA DALE SKINNER

MIDNIGHT FIRE

ZEBRA BOOKS
KENSINGTON PUBLISHING CORP.

ZEBRA BOOKS are published by

Kensington Publishing Corp.
850 Third Avenue
New York, NY 10022

First Printing: August, 1994

Printed in the United States of America

Prologue

South Alabama: 1878

Swinging doors hit Flair in the back, pushing her farther into the crowded saloon. She stumbled forward, tripping on the hem of her skirt. Her breaths came in shallow little gasps as she regained her footing and quickly moved to the side of the doors. Loud voices, laughter, and a lively tune on the piano shuddered through her. Her gaze darted fitfully around the smoky room, scanning each corner. Slowly, she backed up until she felt the wall behind her.

How was she going to find a husband in the midst of these drunken cavalrymen?

Her hand trembled as she reached to brush away a strand of hair tickling her heated cheek. There were more men in the saloon than she'd ever seen in her life. Her eyes grew wide with shock as she looked upon the faces of the strangers. She saw tall men, short men,

husky, lanky, neat, and dirty men. There were
soldiers with hats on and those with them off.
Some sat, others stood. A few of them leaned
against the bar. Before her were clean-shaven
men and some with mustaches and beards.
Fear and panic welled up inside her, choking
her. She must have been out of her mind to
think she could do this.

The stifling heat of the late August evening held smells of liquor, tobacco, horse,
leather, and sweat in the windowless room.
Gas jets mounted on the walls gave the room
a pale yellow glow and added to the overpowering warmth inside. She felt hot, faint. Her
stomach seemed to be caving in on her back.
What had made her think she could find a
man willing to marry her in this maddening,
disreputable crowd?

Her gaze continued to dart frantically from
one end of the room to the other. The voices
sharpened, the faces grew larger, the laughter
intensified, the piano played wildly. She had
to get out before she fainted from the heat,
her anguish, and overwhelming despair. She
had to get out before anyone saw her. She'd
rather face her father's wrath, the humiliation, and the town's gossip than approach
one of these men about marrying her.

With a desperate flash of energy Flair pushed

away from the wall, burst through the swinging doors, and fled into the darkness.

Caden Maxwell rubbed the back of his neck and looked around the room to see if anyone else had observed the slight-built young woman walk into the saloon, hover frightened against the back wall for a minute, then rush out again. She was pretty, carried herself well, and her dress had a freshly pressed look.

It appeared no one else in the saloon had noticed her. She looked a little young to start selling herself; maybe, fifteen or sixteen, he thought. Certainly younger than most of the women he'd been with. But he wasn't one to judge. His uncle had taken him to his first whore when he was sixteen. That had been five years ago and there'd been a steady stream of painted-faced, red-dressed women since. If this young, pretty lady was out to make a few dollars for the evening, he was interested. He'd been drawn to her sweet face and big blue eyes. Besides, he wanted to know what had her acting and looking like a rabbit caught in a briar patch.

Caden pushed through the swinging doors and stepped outside. He stopped and took in a deep breath of the fresh air. *Damn, it felt good to get out of that hot, noisy room.* He hadn't realized how light-headed he'd become. He breathed in deeply again, trying to clear the ringing in his ears.

The heavens cast a bluish light on the midnight sky, obscuring the moon and most of the stars. With the little light afforded him, he looked in both directions, but saw no one on the deserted street. The young woman seemed to have disappeared as easily and as quickly as she'd entered the saloon.

He took off his army issue hat, brushed his hair back with his hand, and resettled it on top of his head. He blinked a couple of times, wondering if he'd imagined the young woman. His ears were buzzing from the whiskey he'd consumed since his platoon arrived in town late that afternoon. And his sight wasn't as clear as it would have been had he not been into the liquor. No, he decided, shaking his head as he loosened the kerchief around his neck. He'd had a few drinks over the last four or five hours, but he wasn't drunk enough to see a woman who wasn't there.

Shrugging his shoulders, he started to walk back into the saloon when a voice in his head told him finding the young woman would be far more interesting than fighting for elbow room at the bar or a gaming table. *Why not?* He wiped his mouth with the back of his hand, then pulled on the waistband of his dark blue trousers. He'd had enough to drink.

Once again he peered down one side of the street, then the other, looking for her and wondering how she could have gotten away so quickly? Deciding that to the right would have been the most logical direction for her to take, Caden headed down the boardwalk. Not ten steps away from the saloon a soft crying reached him. He stopped. His chest constricted tightly. He hadn't heard a woman cry since his mother died. He rose up on his toes to keep his spurs from clinking and followed the sounds of gentle weeping.

A short way down the boardwalk he came upon a narrow alley and cautiously stepped inside. Darkness engulfed him. He stood quietly a few seconds, hardly daring to breathe while his eyes adjusted. Slowly the pale outline of her dress became visible. She leaned against the side of the building, her face buried in the crook of her arms.

It wasn't like him to feel so compassionate toward anyone. Why should he care if the woman cried? But as he watched her he knew the reason. She reminded him of his mother and he hadn't thought about her in a long time. It wasn't that she looked like his mother, for surely she didn't with her golden blond hair and small build. It was the weeping.

Her quiet sobs tore at his heart and forced him to recall the last time he'd heard his mother cry. He remembered going to her bedroom door in the middle of the night and finding it ajar. He peeked inside and saw his mother wrapped in his father's arms, her shoulders gently shaking, her face hidden in his broad chest. His father whispered softly telling her there would be more children for them, but there never were. Within a few minutes she'd stopped. An overwhelming need to comfort this young woman the way his father had comforted his mother flooded him.

Stunned by this sudden feeling, Caden wiped his eyes, then his mouth with the back of his hand. Damn, he must have had too much to drink. These warm tender feelings were foreign to him. He stood quietly, willing the desire to comfort her to go away, but it didn't. He had to stop her tears.

"Miss," he called to her softly.

She gasped and spun around to face him. From over his shoulder hazy moonlight filtered through the narrow alley and shone on her wet face. Frightened, she backed away from him.

He didn't want to scare her more than he already had, so he hurried to say, "I heard you crying and came to see about you. Are you all right?"

She sniffled and wiped her reddened eyes with the tips of her fingers. "Y-yes. I'm fine."

He didn't have a handkerchief so he untied the yellow kerchief from around his neck and gave it to her. She hesitated, but finally took it and wiped her eyes again. He saw that his first impression of her had been right. She was young.

"I saw you come in the saloon and look around, then hurry out again. What's a pretty young lady like you doing out this time of night by yourself?"

"I—I—have to get home."

Caden looked down into the bluest eyes, the prettiest face he'd ever seen. His heart melted into a desperate caring. Whatever she needed, whatever she wanted he would get it for her. "I'll be happy to see you home, but first, why don't you tell me why you were crying? I may be able to help."

Her bottom lip trembled and tears collected on her long lashes as she whispered, "No. It doesn't matter now. I've decided I can't do it. It was a stupid plan."

He stepped closer. Caden didn't know if it was the drink making him feel so soft-hearted. He only knew he wanted this beautiful young woman to need him the way his mother had needed his father so many years ago. "Can't do what?" he asked, inching a little closer to her.

A gulp sounded in her throat. "I—I heard a troop of army men were in town for a day or two. I went into the saloon tonight hoping to find a h-husband."

"What?" he asked, thinking the whiskey had soaked his mind. He blinked rapidly, trying to clear his eyes, trying to stop the roaring in his ears, the quaking in his stomach. Surely he'd misunderstood her.

She sniffled again and dabbed at her eyes, but appeared calmer. "Don't worry. I told you I realized it was a foolish thing to do." She lowered her head. "It's just that—" She stopped.

Caden didn't have much experience dealing with women. He'd bedded his share of them, but he didn't usually do a lot of talking to the women he visited. Letting instinct lead him, he placed two fingers under her chin and tilted her head upward. She lifted her lashes, and Caden looked into eyes lighted by moonlight and brightened by tears.

"Just what?" he asked.

Meeting his gaze without flinching she said, "I didn't know what else to do. My pa's going to kill me when he finds out. I know he is."

Caden shook his head. "No one would kill someone as pretty as you. Least of all your pa."

"Yes, he will. You don't know what's happened." Her voice held a note of resignation.

"Tell me," he whispered softly.

"I'm—I'm going to have a baby, and the father won't marry me. He told me he's going to marry s-someone e-else."

She faltered for a second, and Caden swallowed hard. What kind of man would do something like that?

Suddenly she continued in a rush as if she had to vindicate herself. "When I heard cavalrymen were going to be in town tonight I slipped away from the house. I was hoping to find a soldier who might be willing to marry me. We—Papa doesn't have much, but we're not poor. I'm his only child so I'll inherit the farm someday." She lowered her head again. He watched her hands make fists as she pulled them up tight to her chest. "I told you it was a stupid idea. What man would want to marry a woman who's already with child for a piece of land?" Another sob broke past her lips. "No one would want me after what happened."

With tentative hands he reached for her, but she backed away, frightened again. "It's all right," he said gently. "I'm not going to hurt you."

As if sensing he meant what he said, she allowed him to draw her into his embrace. He held her lightly, barely touching her as she sniffled a few moments before drying her tears on the front of his army shirt. Her explanation cleared up a lot of questions. She was hoping to find a man who would give her baby his name in exchange for the promise of land when her father died. It was a courageous plan, but as she'd already realized, a foolish thing to do. He'd ridden for two months with some of the men in that saloon, and he wouldn't want to see her married to any of the ones he knew.

Letting out a loud sigh and shaking his head, a rush of anger attacked Caden as he softly patted her back. He wanted to get his hands on the man who had seduced this young woman and refused to marry her when she turned up pregnant.

Caden breathed in deeply and smelled the freshly washed scent of her hair. Nice, he thought and closed his eyes, enjoying the feel of the woman in his arms. An idea struck Caden and he studied over it.

He knew his uncle wouldn't like what he was about to do. In fact, Shelton would be furious. But then, Shelton was always angry about something. His attitude over this wouldn't be anything new or different.

After a few minutes Caden took hold of the young woman's shoulders and set her away from him. He looked down into her eyes and said, "A woman's worth isn't measured by her purity or the land she inherits. You remember that. Now come on, let's go find a preacher."

"A—a preacher?"

"I'm going to marry you."

One

South Alabama: 1888

"It's that man again, Mama. Want me to get the shotgun?" the boy asked as he came running into the kitchen of the two-story farm house.

Flair squeezed her eyes shut for a moment before she turned away from the cook stove to face her nine-year-old son. This was the second time Douglas had come over. Earlier in the week he'd been waiting on the front porch when she and Rich returned from the south field where she had been letting him practice shooting. She had taken the rifle from Rich and threatened to shoot Douglas if he didn't get back on his horse and leave.

Looking down into Rich's determined little face she realized she shouldn't have threatened Douglas with the rifle in front of her son. Flair let out a sighing breath. She might as well talk to the man and find out what he wanted. It was obvious he wasn't going to give up until she listened to what he had to say.

Forcing a smile to hide her uneasiness, she spoke softly to her son. "I don't think I'll need the shotgun, Rich. Mr. Eagerton shouldn't be dangerous."

She picked up the hem of her apron and wadded it around the handle of the iron skillet. The bacon hissed and sizzled as the grease sloshed around in it. Carefully she pushed the hot pan to the back of the wood stove. She lifted the lid and checked the boiling pot of potatoes and snap beans before turning back to Rich.

"I want you to stay in here and set the table for me. If you get through with that before I get back, spread some molasses on a loaf of bread for Samp and Booker and get their supper basket ready."

Rich twisted his lips, wrinkled his forehead, and scrunched his nose, making an ugly face. "I don't want to stay in here, Mama," he complained, pulling on the fasteners of his suspenders. "I want to go outside with you while you talk to that man."

"I know." Flair's heart softened as she looked into her son's dark brown eyes. He desperately wanted to grow up fast and be the man of the house. She brushed his dusty brown hair away from his forehead and gave him a light kiss on the tip of his nose, which he quickly wiped off. "But I need you to take care of things in here for me." She looked toward the door. "Not out there. I won't be long, and I expect all your chores to be finished by the time I come back."

"All right," he answered grudgingly.

Flair untied her apron as she headed for the front of the house. She threw the small piece of material onto a square-back side chair as she passed through the small dining room. Thank God Rich had remembered Douglas and hadn't invited him inside. He deserved no kindness from her. Her stomach was jittery as she opened the front door and stepped out on the porch. Why after all these years had he decided he wanted to talk to her? She wanted nothing to do with him.

Douglas, sitting on his horse at the hitching rail, dismounted when she came out. It made her feel a little better knowing he was unsure of her and had played it safe this time by staying in the saddle until he saw whether or not she'd come out with a gun.

Not wanting him near her son, she hurried down the steps and walked over to the neatly trimmed shrubbery that lined the front yard, forcing him to follow her away from the

house. It angered her that she had to speak
to him at all.

April sunshine filled the late afternoon sky
with puffy white clouds and the air with a
comforting warmth. Taking a steadying breath
Flair denied the threat she felt at his presence. She looked up at Douglas and asked,
"What are you doing here?"

Douglas's gaze left her face and roamed up
and down her petite figure. A grin appeared
slowly on his thick, oval-shaped lips. "It's nice
to see you again, too," he said in a mocking
tone. "My my, Flair. Time has been good to
you. You're more beautiful now than you
were ten years ago." He took off his hat and
laid it on the shrubbery.

Unaffected by his flattery, Flair folded her
arms across her chest and fixed him with a
stern stare. With every moment he was there
tension mounted within her. She hadn't forgotten how he'd treated her, how he'd
shamed her and ruined her life. "I have supper cooking. What do you want?"

He tilted his head and shrugged lightly.
"Just a little friendly conversation." He pushed
his coattail aside and slipped his hands into
the pockets of his trousers. "It's been a long
time since we've been this close. I'm enjoying
looking at all the changes in you. You've—filled

out quite nicely. And I do believe your eyes have gotten bluer since I last saw you."

Flair might have laughed if she hadn't been so distraught by his visit. He'd always been good at flattery and sweet talk, but she wasn't sixteen anymore. There had to be a reason he'd shown up after all these years, and she knew of only one thing they had in common.

Determined to show her lack of interest in him she answered, "I don't want, nor do I have time for friendly conversation. Now for the last time, state what you are doing here?"

Douglas threw a glance back to the house behind him. "We have a fine looking boy, Flair. I hear his name is Rich."

Flair stiffened perceptibly. Her heartbeat raced. The sun suddenly felt too warm on her cheeks, her eyes too dry. She'd stopped worrying that Douglas would try to see his son years ago. She fought back panic that wanted to rise within her and kept her breathing and voice normal as she said, "I have a fine looking son. If that's all you have to say I'd like to get back to my supper."

This time he looked into her eyes. "No. That's not all I have to say. But we can go inside and finish the conversation there, if you like."

He made a move toward the house, but Flair stepped in front of him, blocking his way. The long-sleeved blouse she'd put on that morning had warmed her against the April breeze, but now she felt uncomfortably hot. "You're not welcome in my house, Douglas. I don't want anything to do with you, and we have nothing to say to each other."

He stepped back, placing his hat on his head, covering his closely cropped, dusty brown hair. "You're wrong, Flair. We have a lot to talk about. I'm not surprised you're still sore at me. I didn't do right by you when I didn't marry you."

Fury exploded inside her and she shook. "You didn't do right by me when you forced me down on the ground." She stopped abruptly. No, she wouldn't let him draw her into this conversation. He had no right to make her relive that time in her life. Her stomach clenched as tight as her hands at her sides. She didn't want to go through this. He had no right to show up now and upset her life. Flair fixed him with an icy glare and said, "I don't care about that anymore, Douglas. I haven't for a long time."

He smiled. "So you've forgiven me."

She laughed bitterly. "For what you did to me. Never. But you can see I didn't let it ruin my life."

Nodding again he said, "No reason for it

to." He paused. "I guess you heard my wife died."

She had, and was sorry to hear of someone so young dying. "Yes," she answered from a tight throat. "I would have sent condolences but didn't feel it was appropriate under the circumstances."

"I guess you also know we never had any children."

A small grain of fear rolled up Flair's back, suddenly chilling her. She strove for control. She wanted to lash out at him and ask him how he dared show his face on her land? How he dared to talk so casually as if nothing had happened between them? Instead, she remained calm because if she let go of her temper she'd try to scratch his eyes out. "Douglas, none of this has anything to do with me."

"Oh, but it does." He paused and looked around the lush greenery of the countryside. "I came over here to ask you to marry me."

Her eyes widened, her muscles relaxed. A hysterical little laugh sounded from her throat before she managed to say, "You must be crazy."

Douglas chuckled, too. His dark brown eyes flashed merrily at her and that made her more enraged. He wasn't the least bit concerned about invading her life. But then, he never had been. What he wanted was the only thing that had ever been important to him.

"No, I'm not crazy. Why should I be? We were in love once. It makes perfect sense."

"In love?" she exclaimed, choking on the words, shocked by his announcement, but not surprised by his ego. "I loved you, but you only used me!" Her temper neared the edge and she fought for control.

"That's not true, Flair. You knew how I felt about you. I would have married you, but you know my father had his heart set on me marrying Jean so we could merge the two properties one day. I had to marry her."

Flair held up her hands to stop him. "Get off my land. I don't care about any of this. I don't care about you or what you think. Just leave me alone." Calling upon her reserve strength she looked him in the eyes. Her voice was gravelly with outrage as she said, "I want you to leave. And if—"

"I can't do that," he interrupted.

"If you come back on my land I *will* shoot you." Her voice was steadier this time. She knew she meant it.

The smile remained on his lips and in his eyes. "Do you really think you frighten me, Flair?"

"I mean for you to leave me alone."

"That's fine. I'll leave *you* alone for now, but what about my boy?"

"He's my son," she said with mounting fury that showed in her voice.

"Whew, Flair. When did you develop a hot temper? You used to be so—easy to talk to."

Flair hated what his words implied. "So easy to manipulate. So easy to force me to the ground," she said with conviction.

The amusement left his face. "Now wait a minute. I didn't force you to do anything, and you know it. We both wanted it."

"No, I didn't want it. I begged you to stop." She caught a sob in her throat. All the feelings of that night came back with jarring reality. She felt the cold ground on her buttocks and the back of her legs. She bore the pressing weight of his body, fought his groping hands and fervent kisses. She bucked and kicked against legs that spread her knees. Flair shuddered. She didn't want to remember that time in her life. The pain was too great.

"You agreed to slip out of the house and meet me down by the pond, remember. You must have known what I wanted. Why else would you meet me? That night you said you were pregnant I told you I didn't force you to do anything."

He blamed her for what happened. Just as

he had that night many years ago. "Kisses," she whispered, tormented by the past. "I expected a few kisses." She paused, suddenly feeling shaky, weak-kneed. Her throat hurt from holding back her tears of anger. She wanted to walk away and leave him, not say another word to him, but knew it was best to have this out with him now so he wouldn't come back. She had to do this for Rich's sake. "I told you, none of that matters now. You know I have a husband. My son has a father. You're ten years too late."

"You say you have a husband. I've checked around town. No one's ever seen him."

"He doesn't live here."

"That's odd, isn't it? Married people usually live together." He took a step toward her. "Where is your husband, Flair?"

Her stomach jumped. She wanted Douglas to go away and leave her alone, leave her son alone. "Th-that's none of your concern."

"I spoke with Reverend Henderson about what happened. He said he was awakened in the middle of the night and asked to marry you and a soldier. He didn't want to do it because he was afraid of what your father would do to him. The soldier pulled his gun and forced him to marry you. Is that true?"

The only good thing that had happened to her during that painful ordeal was meeting the tall, dark-haired soldier with brownish-green eyes. Moved by the fond memory of the young soldier, she managed to nod once.

"The reverend said that two days later, your father came to see him and he confirmed that he'd married you to a cavalryman who left town the next morning."

Anguish and misery settled over her, weakening her. She asked, "Why are you going over all this? The whole town has known the story for years. It's over. It has nothing to do with you."

His eyes hardened. Contempt showed in his voice as he said, "It has to do with *my* son."

"No!" she challenged immediately, lifting her chin a little higher, taking a step toward him. "Caden Maxwell and I have a son. You have no claim to him."

His voice grew louder. "If this Caden Maxwell has a wife and son, why hasn't he been back for you?"

Her strength faltered. The sun was too hot. She shielded her eyes with a trembling hand. "I—I don't know. I guess the army keeps him busy—traveling."

"Where was he headed when he left?"

"They—He was on his way with a brigade to capture some renegade Indians. I don't—" Flair stopped, realizing she'd let Douglas draw her into conversation and answer his questions. "How many times do I have to say it. None of this is any of your concern," she reminded him.

"You know what I think?"

"No, and I don't want to know," she countered quickly, wishing he'd go away, wishing the sun wasn't so hot, wishing he wouldn't force her to remember the past. It was behind her. She'd lived through it and she was a different person. She was stronger. Caden Maxwell had given her what she needed to hold her head up and carry on with her life.

"I think he's dead," Douglas said callously. "I don't believe you have a husband any more, Flair. I don't believe the boy has a father."

Perspiration dampened the back of her neck. "You're wrong." *He had to be.* "And my son has a name. It's Rich. I suggest you use it when referring to him."

He lowered his voice, saying, "Let me put it to you as plain as I can. Rich is my son and I want him. I want you to marry me, Flair, and both of you come live with me."

Flair backed away from him, disbelief filling her. "You must be mad. I told you I have a husband. Rich has a father."

Douglas nodded, advancing on her. "You're right. Me. I want you to marry me, Flair," he spoke softly, slightly smiling. He picked up her hand and held it between both of his. "You know I always had feelings for you. It will be good between us. You'll see."

She jerked her hand away and rubbed it down the front of her skirt to get the feel of him off her skin. "Don't touch me." Anger and fear brought to life emotions she'd hidden in order to survive.

"Rich needs a father. I'll give him everything he wants. I'll teach him to ride and hunt. I'll teach him how to be a man. You can't do those things for him."

"I'll teach him to ride and Booker is already helping me teach him to shoot and hunt."

Aggravation clouded his expression. "I don't want that Negro teaching my boy anything."

"If you'd wanted your son you should have done what was right ten years ago when I was a naive sixteen-year-old." Her words were choked past a tight throat. "I wouldn't marry you even if I weren't already married, and I'll never let you near my son." The last words were hissed from her mouth.

Douglas grabbed her upper arms and dragged her up to his chest. She struggled to free herself, but he held fast. He lowered his head, placing his face close to hers, their noses almost touching. She squirmed against the bruising force of his hands.

"I'd like to do this the easy way, Flair, but I'll be tough if I have to. I aim to get my son."

She tried to pull away from him, but it only made him squeeze her tighter. His fingers dug painfully into her muscles, but she refused to cry out.

"Why?" she pleaded when she realized he wasn't going to let her go. "Why are you suddenly so interested in Rich?"

"That's a fair question." His voice softened, but he didn't let her go. "I need an heir. I'm almost forty years old. By the time I could marry and have a son the age of Rich I'll be over fifty. I don't want to wait that long to have a son I can start teaching about the farm." He moved his face closer to hers. "And why should I when I can have my son and you, too."

"Let go of my mama or I'll blow your head off."

Flair snapped her head around and saw Rich standing on the porch holding the double-barrel shotgun. She gasped.

Douglas laughed and let her go. "See, that boy needs a father to teach him a few things. And I aim to be that man. I'm not giving up." He reached into his pocket and brought out a folded piece of paper. "See this? It's the note you sent me ten years ago telling

me of your condition and asking me to meet
you. If I have to, I'll take you to court to get
my son. With no husband to dispute my
claim, I think the judge will see things my
way."

"No." An inexplicable pain tortured her as
she recognized the note.

"Oh, yes. I kept it all these years." He
eased the paper back into his pocket. "Think
about what I've said. I'll be back. I'm going
to get my son. The only thing left to talk
about is whether you come with him." He
turned to Rich. "You did a good job of taking care of your mother. You can put that
shotgun down now. I'm leaving."

Douglas didn't move. Neither did Rich. He
kept the barrels aimed at Douglas's chest and
said, "I'll put this down when you ride out
of here, mister. Not before."

Douglas glanced at Flair as if he expected
her to speak to Rich. She remained quiet,
shaking. He chuckled again, shook his head,
and headed for his horse.

As soon as he mounted, Flair picked up
her skirt and hurried up the steps to stand
beside Rich. "Don't come back, Douglas. I
think you can see you're not wanted here."

He looked into her eyes and said, "You
know I'll be back." He whipped his horse
around and galloped away.

Flair relaxed a little as she watched the horse kick up dust from the dry earth. It had been years since she'd worried about Douglas. She'd thought he'd forgotten about her and what had happened between them. *Dear God, what was she to do?* Did he really intend to use that note to take her son away from her, or was he just trying to frighten her?

"Mama?"

Flair swallowed hard, her son's voice bringing her back to the present. She could ponder what Douglas had to say and all the emotions he revitalized later. Right now she had to deal with her son. She turned to him.

Rich placed the butt of the shotgun on the porch and grabbed hold of the barrel. He looked up at her. Her heart constricted as she saw that Rich had his father's dark brown eyes and light brown hair.

Douglas was right. She hadn't heard from Caden Maxwell since he rode away from the farm that morning after having words with her father. Now looking at her son's face she wondered if she had the right to deny him the opportunity to have a father. Douglas had wanted no part of her or the baby she was carrying. Could she even consider marrying him after what he did to her? Her mind went back in time to the night Douglas forced her to the ground and the argument she'd had with him two months later. She remembered crying several nights later and being held against a broad chest and tenderly comforted. She remembered the black eye her father gave the soldier when he told him they were married. Flair knew she would have received that beating if the young man hadn't married her.

"Mama," he said again.

"You disobeyed me," she said softly, finally garnering her strength.

"I know, Mama, but he turned you loose, didn't he?"

Rich looked so innocent with his expressive brown eyes, softly rounded cheeks, and sprinkle of reddish-brown freckles across his nose. He wanted her to be proud of him and she was. She easily forgave him and smiled. "Yes, but I could have handled him very well without your help. I don't want you to make a habit of disobeying me."

Her son's eyes lighted and his face beamed with a smile. Obviously, he was pleased to have gotten off so lightly. "No, ma'am. I won't."

"Good."

"What did he want, Mama?" Rich asked, lifting the shotgun off the floor and placing the shaft under his arm.

Flair tensed. She'd never lied to her son,

and she couldn't start now. "He wants something that belongs to me. I won't let him take it away from me." Her tone sounded so cold and bitter it frightened her. She wrapped her arm around Rich. He didn't like cuddling since he'd gotten older, but she needed to touch him and reassure herself that Douglas couldn't separate them. "Don't worry," she said in a softer tone as much for her own peace of mind as her son's. "I won't let him."

How could she tell her son that horrible man was his father and now that Douglas's wife had died leaving him without an heir, he wanted to claim Rich?

"Come on, we need to finish supper. Booker and Samp will be coming in from the fields any minute now and we won't be ready. I'll finish everything inside while you go to the back porch and pour them a jar of fresh milk."

As they walked back into the house, Flair's stomach continued to quake. Her hands trembled as she took the shotgun from Rich and replaced it in the corner behind the front door. She didn't want him to know how upset she was. She needed to get things back to normal as soon as possible. "I think I'll whip up a sweet cake for us. It should be ready to come out of the oven about the time we're finishing supper. How does that sound?"

Rich grinned up at his mother as he licked

his lips. "Mmm. I'll tell Booker as soon as he comes to wash. He'll be happy about that."

She laughed as she watched her son take the milk bucket and head for the back porch. She loved her son and she would never let Douglas get his hands on him. She'd managed for nine years without his interference. And, because of a handsome young soldier she was given a second chance. She was sure her father would have turned her out once he discovered she was pregnant if Caden Maxwell hadn't found her crying in that alley and married her. As it was, her father agreed she could continue to live there. He accepted her marriage, but she wondered if he ever forgave her. One thing she always appreciated was that he never took his disappointment in her out on Rich. He'd loved his grandson.

She'd promised herself that she'd never be taken in by a man again. And she hadn't. Since her father died, three different men from town had made the ride out just to offer their services should she need help with anything.

Caden Maxwell. She thought of him again as she slid the skillet back on the burner. What had happened to the young man who'd risked her father's wrath and trouble with his officers to marry her? Even though he'd told her father he'd return for her some day, she knew he never would. Over the years she'd wondered if he'd been killed.

The bacon started hissing and popping. She lifted the lid and checked the potatoes and beans. There was no way around it. She needed Caden Maxwell again. She needed to find him and prove to Douglas that she was still a married woman.

The only thing Caden had told her about himself was his name and that he lived on a cattle and horse farm near Richmond, Virginia. She'd named her son after that town. There was only one thing to do. She'd mail a letter to Caden in Richmond and hope that someone there would know where to locate him. If she still had a husband, Douglas's note would be worthless to him.

Booker licked the crumbs from his lips and sighed. Miss Flair's sweet cake was the best tasting food he had ever put in his mouth. He liked the molasses and cornbread they had most evenings, but it didn't even come close to being as good as the cake. It was so light and fluffy it melted in his mouth. He picked up the large slice with his hand and took another bite. From the corner of his eye he saw his father slowly cutting his dessert with a fork.

He wrinkled his forehead as he looked over the table to the gray-bearded man who sat opposite him. "This is too good to eat so slow, Papa. I don't know how you stand it."

"No," Samp answered. "Good sweet bread is to be treated like a good woman. Slow and easy so's you can savor the taste."

Booker wiped his lips with his tongue, then with the back of his hand to dry them. Maybe it was an omen that his father had mentioned women tonight. He'd wanted to talk with him about that very thing for weeks now, but didn't know how to broach the subject. The topic of women hadn't come up between them often.

He looked out the open window and saw that dusk lay on the horizon. His mind went back in time to that day several months ago when he drove Miss Flair into town. He was waiting by the wagon for her just like she told him to do when the prettiest young woman he'd ever seen walked by him. He couldn't take his eyes off her, and she was taking her time with him, too. She'd given him a shy smile before hurrying to catch up with the white woman she was walking with. Booker sighed and leaned back in the chair, throwing his hands behind his head and locking his fingers together. He sure wished he knew her name and where she lived. He hadn't been able to stop thinking about her.

"You got something on your mind, son?" Samp asked as he pushed his empty plate away and propped an arm on the table.

"How long have we worked for Miss Flair?"

Samp pulled on the lobe of his ear and seemed to study the question. "Since her pa died. 'Bout three year ago, I reckon."

Booker realized he hadn't asked the question the right way. He wanted to know how long they'd been at the Bowen farm. "How long did we work for her pa?"

"I guess I started working here when you were about this high." He looked at Booker and held his hand up to the height of the chair back. "How old did I say you are?"

"We figured I'm about nineteen years."

Samp stared up at the ceiling in the small room and seemed to ponder again. Finally he said, "Yeah, yep, that'd be 'bout right. I'd say we been here maybe thirteen, fourteen years."

"Right after Mama died?" Booker questioned.

Samp rubbed his bearded chin and glanced back at his son. "What's on your mind, son? You ain't asking what you want to know. You asking what you already know."

Booker's palms felt sweaty and his chest tight. He spied a couple of crumbs of cake left on the tin plate and lifted them to his mouth with the tip of his forefinger. Then he planted his feet firmly on the floor and his hands on his knees as he leaned forward and asked, "How am I ever going to find me a woman to have me a son like you did if I don't ever go anywhere to meet women? I haven't been into town more'n a dozen times in the last year." Getting it all out gave him a great sense of relief. His chest felt lighter. He leaned back in the chair.

"Well, son you got yourself a point there." Samp nodded his agreement, but didn't offer a solution and that bothered Booker.

After a moment or two of silence Booker pushed back his chair and rose. He walked over to the small table in front of their sofa. He picked up the tattered Bible and carried it back and laid it in front of his father. "I guess the Good Book will tell us. You said it had the answer to everything. You find it for me."

Samp's aging brown eyes grew wide. "Well, son, I don't rightly know where it says in there how to find a woman."

"You told me David had more'n a hundred wives, Solomon, too. It must tell us how they found 'em."

"Well, now them men were kings. Things are different for kings." He pulled on his ear lobe again. "Besides, that was hundreds of years ago. We can't have that many wives now-a-days.

Exasperated, Booker said, "I only want one."

Samp slid the oil lamp over, struck a match, and lit it. He opened the Bible and carefully and slowly leafed through many of the pages. Booker remained standing, silently looking over his father's shoulder, wishing he hadn't laughed and rejected Miss Flair's offer to teach him to read.

Finally, Samp closed the Bible and said, "It must say how they got all them wives in those words I can't read."

That wasn't what Booker wanted to hear. He thought for a moment, then asked, "How'd you find Mama?"

"I done tole you that story a hundred times, son. We both worked for Mr. Eagerton on that big farm of his. Miz Eagerton didn't mind that me and your ma took up together until she got too big with you to do her work. That's when Mr. Eagerton tole both of us we had to leave. I guess we worked for five or six different farms before Miss Flair's pa gave us this job."

Booker knew the rest of the story. His mother came down with lung fever and never recovered.

Without giving the thought full consideration Booker asked, "Do you think Miss Flair will read the Bible for us and tell me what it says?"

Samp ran an open palm over his gray hair, then rose from his chair and started stacking the empty plates in the supper basket. "No need for us to worry her with this. Give me time to think about it. I'll see what I can come up with. Now, hand me that plate. I best take these dishes back to Miss Flair so she can wash 'em and get to bed. You know she ain't gone rest until every plate in that kitchen is clean."

Two

Virginia: 1888

"You're crazy, Cade. You can't make it down that ledge without falling and killing yourself."

Caden squinted from the glare of the sun. He looked up at the foreman who hadn't bothered to get off his horse. He didn't like the fact that Jake had made a determination without assessing the situation. He simply assumed it couldn't be done, so Caden did the usual thing and took Jake's words as a challenge.

"Watch me."

He turned away from the foreman and looked over the side of the steep cliff again. A young bull looked up at him with big brown eyes. He didn't know how the calf had made it to the bottom without breaking its neck or its legs. What he did know was that bull would be worth a lot of money to the

Maxwell Farms when he was grown. Besides, he wanted to prove to Jake he could do it.

"You're a hell-of-a risk taker, Cade," Porter said, shaking his head with disbelief as he beat his sweat-banded hat against his leg, sending dust flying.

Caden ignored the cow hand's praise and whipped the rope off his saddle. He circled it around his waist twice, then knotted it three times. Sweat popped out on his forehead, trickled down his face, and dripped onto his shirt.

"Use your head, Cade. Even if you make it down, you'll never get back up with that bull. You can't hold onto him and the rope, too," Jake added when he saw Caden was serious. "We'll just count it as a loss and pick another calf."

Glancing up at the foreman, Caden said, "I want this one." He threw the other end of the rope to Jake and hit him in the chest with it. "Tie that around your horn." He turned to the two cowboys standing beside him. "You two guide the rope as I go down. Don't let the rope go slack. Rodman, you're the largest, so you stand in front. Porter, get about two feet behind him." He grabbed an extra rope from Rodman's saddle and fastened it to his belt. He looked over at Jake again. "You ready?"

Jake hesitated but finally said, "Ready," then started backing up his horse.

When the rope stretched tight, Caden took his first step over the edge and started walking down the cliff. The sun beat on his back and shoulders. Sweat rolled down his neck. Rocks and gravel shifted beneath his feet every time he put a boot on the dried earth of the cliff side.

He knew the reason Jake hadn't wanted him to attempt the rescue. Jake didn't want Caden to do better than him at anything. After Caden came to work at his uncle's farm it didn't take him long to realize Jake often provoked him into doing things just so he could prove he was better at it, or as Jake thought in this case, that it couldn't be done. But Jake didn't challenge him as often as he used to. Caden had learned quite a lot over the years, and the twelve years difference in their ages had started to show on Jake. And it didn't bother Caden to point it out whenever the opportunity arose.

Caden breathed a sigh of relief when his foot touched bottom. Down was easy. Going up with a hundred pounds of bull strapped to his shoulders wouldn't be. He looked up the thirty-foot drop from the ledge and saw the two cowboys. He waved to them.

Porter turned back to Jake and said, "He's down."

Now, came the hard part. That bull wasn't going to want to be lifted up the side of the mountain. He had to work fast before the calf had time to realize what was happening. Caden took the extra rope from his belt and quickly made a lasso.

After three strong twirls of the rope in the air he let it go and lassoed the calf's neck. The young bull bellowed and strained against the binding. Caden pulled the struggling animal to him and grabbed him around the neck and under his flank and threw him to the ground. The calf bellowed again and struggled to stand while Caden wrapped the rope first around his hind legs, then his front hooves.

In one easy motion Caden lifted the calf under his belly and settled him around his neck and upper shoulders. Caden's broad shoulders accepted the weight of the calf's body. The animal's heat seared him as he settled the warm belly against the back of his neck. Next he wrapped the rest of the rope around his chest a couple of times, then tied the loose end to the calf's hind legs, securing the animal on his shoulders. The weight was cumbersome, weakening.

Caden placed his gloved hands on the rope tied around his waist and yelled, *"Pull!"*

The rope tightened and Caden placed his foot on the side of the cliff. When his other foot left the ground there was no doubt he had an extra one hundred pounds on his back. The bull squirmed and made a noise that sounded more like a sheep than a cow.

With his third step, Caden felt the tug of the rope on his arm muscles. Beneath his leather gloves, the rope burned into his hands, singeing them with pain. His cotton shirt was little barrier as the cording dug into his waist. His wrists felt as if they might break if he didn't let go. The weight of the calf pulled him backward, but still he held tight to the rope, straining his arms, sapping his breath, taking one step at a time.

From above him he heard Porter and Rodman grunting and groaning as they helped guide him and the rope up the cliff. Once, his boot slipped on loose rock, but he managed to catch himself with his other foot without losing a step. Sweat continued to roll down his face and neck, drenching him with the moisture. His arms and legs weakened.

He didn't want to look up and see how much farther he had to go for fear he'd realize he wasn't going to make it and give up. The pain in his arms became unbearable, still he put one foot ahead of the other, determined not to lose.

All of a sudden, the rope went slack. Caden slammed into the side of the cliff, knocking his knee and his head. The calf bellowed as the force of their weight slung them backward. Caden grunted with pain as he bounced off the rocky earth and hit again before letting go of the rope and grabbing hold of a jutting rock to stop and steady them. The calf mooed and squirmed, choking him. The first jolt against the mountain had stunned him. Caden heard shouts of alarm above him, but for the moment all he could do was be still and catch his breath and wonder what went wrong.

"What the hell happened!" he yelled after a moment or two. He chanced a glance upward and his hat fell off. The wind caught it and swept it over the ledge where the bull had been and down into the canyon.

"Jake said something spooked his horse," Rodman called down to him. "He says to cut the calf. You won't make it up."

Anger and determination filled Caden. Jake didn't want him to make it. "Hell no," he muttered to himself. Not after he'd made it more than half way up. What could have spooked the horse with Jake on it? The foreman was the best horseman on the farm. Jake could go to hell. He wasn't giving up. "Hell no!" he shouted to the men above him.

The bull was squirming, its hooves digging into his skin, its weight pulling him down. He was losing strength fast. The hit against the mountain had taken a lot out of him. He couldn't wait any longer.

"All right, on the count of three let's try again!" he yelled up to the men.

"This is foolish, Cade. Cut the damn calf!" Rodman yelled back to him.

He refused to listen. "One. Two. Three."

Without further thought, he swung away from the side of the cliff and caught himself with his foot. Caden gritted his teeth and with the same determination he had before starting the climb. He didn't allow himself to think, only to move. He concentrated on putting one foot in front of the other until he made it to the top.

When he stepped on level ground Caden's knees almost buckled beneath him. One of the men cut the ropes holding the bull and slid the animal off his shoulders. With his last ounce of energy he fell against his horse and held on to the saddle, gasping for breath, wet with perspiration. Rodman took care of the calf while Porter removed the rest of the rope from his waist. He opened his canteen and took a long drink before wiping his forehead, neck, and face with his shirt sleeve.

"Hey, Cade that gave us all a hell of a scare," Jake said as he came walking up. He clapped Caden on the shoulder and grinned. "I don't know what happened," Jake continued. "Baron isn't usually skittish."

Caden's right hand closed into a fist. He wanted to knock that grin off Jake's face. Not for a minute did he believe Jake's horse was spooked.

"I know." He stared boldly at Jake.

"I should have known that once you set your mind to it you'd get that calf up." He gave Caden a nasty smile before walking back to his horse.

Caden would have tackled Jake if he'd had the strength to fight him. Instead, like his father had taught him, he held his anger in check.

He was breathing hard, and covered in sweat, but the work day had barely started. He grabbed hold of the horn and lifted himself into the saddle. "Get that bull back in the pen and get back to work," he called to the cowboys, then spurred his horse and rode away.

Caden's knee bothered him as he walked down the stairs of the two-story ranch house that evening. His hands were chafed, his shoulders and chest sore, and he had the makings of a good-sized bruise on his forehead. His gaze swept past the gilt-covered crown molding and highly polished banister as he stepped onto the wool rug and made his way to the parlor where his uncle waited.

As he entered the large sitting room Shelton looked up from the papers he held in his lap. The once wide-shouldered, robust man was thin, pale, and shaky. His evening jacket drooped on his shoulders, the neck of his white shirt too big for his sagging skin. His thick brown hair seemed to have grayed overnight and lost its wave when the disease the doctor had called muscular dystrophy had made an invalid out of him a year ago.

"Good evening, Caden. You're five minutes late."

"Hello, Shelton. I hope you had a good day," he answered without bothering to tell him he had a lot of dust to wash away.

Their routine hadn't changed much over the past several months. Not since his uncle's illness had confined him to a chair. Caden walked over to the D-shaped sideboard and took the top off a crystal decanter. His uncle liked a shot of bourbon in the evenings before dinner. Caden poured himself a Scotch.

"I heard about what you did today. It was

a damn fool thing to do, but I approve. A man should never show his fear. When a job needs to be done, he should just do it."

One thing about his uncle that hadn't changed was his frank attitude and his no nonsense approach to everything. Keeping his back to Shelton as he replaced the tops on the decanters Caden said, "I'm surprised Jake told you about the incident with the bull."

"He didn't."

Caden whipped his head around to look at the older man.

With shaky hands Shelton laid the papers on the Sheraton worktable beside his chair. "Jake isn't my only source of information for what goes on around here since this illness grabbed hold of me and won't let me out of this damned chair." His hand trembled uncontrollably as he pointed a crooked finger at Caden.

"I never thought he was."

He picked up the glasses and walked over and handed his uncle the bourbon which he held tightly between both hands. Shelton eyed Caden's drink disdainfully as he did every night. The first drink Shelton ever gave him was homemade rot-gut whiskey. It wasn't until later in life that Caden discovered he preferred the smoother taste of Scotch. His uncle's cold stare at his drink served as a reminder to Caden that Shelton thought Scotch was a weak man's drink. Strong men drank whiskey—straight.

Caden walked over to the Sheraton oval-back sofa and sat down on the plush rose-colored velvet. As he'd gotten older Caden realized that even though he lived in Shelton's house, there were some things Shelton couldn't force him to do. He knew there were times he had to take a stand against his formidable uncle. And even now in a wheel-chair, Shelton Maxwell commanded a presence most men never achieved.

Shelton's hands shook and trembled as he carried the glass to his mouth and took a drink. Smacking his lips appreciatively, he glanced back up at Caden. "Risking your life to go after that calf proves you care about this place. I've been watching for things like that."

Caden didn't know how Shelton could doubt his love for the farm. He had always worked twice as hard as any of the other hands. He had to. Shelton demanded it of him, and Caden didn't want any of the men to think he wasn't doing his share just because he lived in the large ranch house rather than the bunkhouse Shelton had built for the farm hands.

"I've had a lot of time to think recently.

More time than any man should have, and I've been making some plans. After what happened today, I decided to go ahead and discuss them with you."

That surprised Caden. Shelton didn't usually talk anything over with him. "What do you have in mind?" Caden asked as he pulled on the tight collar of his shirt. He much preferred his open-collar work clothes to the jacket and cravat he always wore to dinner.

"Emmett, sorry doctor that he is, has convinced me I need to get my affairs in order."

Caden tensed. He knew the muscular disease was bad. His uncle had continued to lose strength and mobility. But his mind was as sharp as ever. "Shelton, we don't have to talk about this now. You're not—"

"Don't interrupt me." His strong voice boomed across the room. "And for heaven's sake don't pity me. I'd rather die than see pity in your eyes. What I have to say has to do with you. Not me."

Caden remained quiet. He relaxed and lowered his gaze to the faint flower pattern in the velvet material of the small sofa. His moment of softness disappeared. Shelton would always treat him like the youngster he was seventeen years ago when he first came to live at the ranch. He never had fond feelings for his uncle, but he didn't like seeing him deteriorate slowly day by day, able to do less and less.

"Although I still have my wits about me at this time, if not my legs, Emmett has assured me that won't last forever." Shelton slapped a hand against his thigh before continuing. "I never cared for your father. You know that, and you know why. I promised Pearson I'd take care of you. But I also told him you'd have to prove yourself before I'd treat you like my own. He agreed to that."

And all Caden had to do for that honor was risk his neck for a bull calf that would be important to the farm one day? After all these years, didn't Shelton know Maxwell Farms was his life. He had always loved every inch of it. But he knew Shelton didn't want to hear words like that, so he said what his uncle would approve of. "You know this place always comes first with me."

"I think I do." Shelton drank from his glass again. "Since I never married, and Pearson died leaving only you as his heir, you're the only heir I have."

"I don't think your sister would approve of you saying that."

"Pauline?" He laughed, almost shaking the liquid out of his glass. "Well, it's for damn sure I don't want her puny-ass son to get his hands on this farm. God forbid that should happen!"

Caden chuckled.

Shelton smiled, obviously pleased with Caden's reaction to his derogatory comments about his other nephew.

"I want you to take over the farm."

Caden sobered and sat forward. His pulse raced. This was the day he'd worked so hard for.

"That's not all I have to say. You have a few things to take care of first."

He should have known there was a catch. Caden sat back and propped one leg over the other. He continued to stare at Shelton.

"I'd like to see you settled before I make my departure from this world. I want to know that you're going to have a son to take over for you one day. I want you to find that woman you married ten years ago, divorce her, and marry William Hanks's daughter."

Caden showed no emotion outwardly, but inside his stomach roiled. His leg ached from the bruising crash against the hillside. Caden cleared his throat. "Are we back to that, Shelton?"

"It appears we are." His eyes didn't waver. "If you don't do as I ask, I'll leave everything I have to Jake."

"Jake?" Caden wasn't sure he'd heard him correctly.

"That's right. He started working on this farm when he was still wet behind the ears, and he's been a good foreman for fifteen years. I'd trust my life to him. He's always done everything that I've asked him to do."

Caden was afraid to take his glass to his lips for fear his hands would shake as badly as Shelton's. No way in hell would he let Jake inherit Maxwell Farms. The divorce didn't bother him. Hell, he hadn't thought about the woman he married in a long time anyway. But he damn sure wasn't going to marry Jenny Hanks. The only thing she knew how to do was giggle and bat her eyelashes at him. Caden found it ironic that the man who'd never married and had children was so bent on him marrying the right kind of woman and having a son.

"I know you weren't happy when I returned from the army and told you I was married. But—"

"Happy?" he interrupted again. "Hell, I nearly threw you out of the house. To think you wanted to go back for her and bring her here." Shelton shook his head irritably.

The callous way he'd dismissed that time in Caden's life still rankled. It had taken him a long time to forget about the petite young woman with tear-filled blue eyes. Gritting his teeth to hold in his anger, Caden picked up where he left off. "I never let that interfere with my job at the farm when the army released me."

"I know, but you never did what I told you to do either, and that's always bothered me."

Hearing Shelton admit that was like winning a small victory. It gave Caden a great deal of pleasure. He never filed for divorce, even though Shelton insisted time and time again. He had to show his uncle that he had some control over his life. If Shelton had told him to leave the horse farm and never come back, he would have. His father had taught him to respect his elders and his family.

Over the years, Caden had held his temper many times when he would have liked to tell his uncle to go to hell. But the respect his father had taught him meant too much to him. One way he could stand up to Shelton without being disrespectful was to stand up for himself. He had to obey Shelton's wishes in dealing with the horse farm, but he had to prove to his uncle that he couldn't control his personal life, so he'd never asked for a divorce. He kept thinking he'd hear from his wife some day. He'd told her how to get in touch with him, but she never had.

He sipped his drink again. "Divorce is a scandalous thing, Shelton," Caden finally said.

"I've raised eyebrows in this county before. Doesn't bother me." Shelton finished his drink and set the glass on the table beside him.

"What's important about all this is that I want to make sure you have a son to take over the farm, should anything happen to you."

That made sense, Caden thought. "I have no problem with getting the divorce. I don't have a problem with remarrying. In fact, I've found it very easy to be married all these years, so that shouldn't be a problem either."

Shelton laughed, then wiped his mouth with his handkerchief. "Women. They're only good for one thing, and it's not cooking. Many a man knows how to cook."

Ignoring Shelton's comment, Caden said, "I pick my own wife." Caden didn't bat an eyelash. He knew Shelton liked a show of strength even though he didn't like to be crossed.

The older man seemed to study that idea for a moment. "I guess I can live with that, as long as she's a woman of good standing in the community. I'll speak to Rutherford. The divorce should be started right away. The sooner the better. Now tell me, do you remember the name of the town that woman lives in? Do you remember her name?"

A faraway feeling stole over Caden. Oh yes, he remembered. He remembered a gentle hug, the smell of freshly washed hair, and eyes so blue he could almost see through them. He remembered a soft voice and a smile of gratitude given to him just before he rode away. A quickening stirred in his loins. No, he might have put thoughts of her aside for a long time, but he hadn't forgotten her.

"Yes. I know where to find her." His voice had turned husky so he took a sip of his Scotch to clear his throat of the tightness.

He'd had a lot to drink that night, but he remembered telling her he lived on a horse farm near Richmond, in case she needed him. She'd never tried to get in touch with him. Why? Did she have her baby? Was she still alive?

Shelton was right. It was time for a divorce. But he wouldn't agree to Rutherford getting in touch with her. He'd go. He wanted to see her again. He wanted to know what had happened to her and what she'd been doing all these years. And, he was a bit curious about her child, too.

Three

The back door was locked. While Rich sat on the front porch working on the arithmetic problems she had given him, Flair lay back in the wash tub soaking in the barely warm water. Sunday afternoon was the one day she allowed herself the luxury of a full bath. The rest of the week she washed from the pitcher and basin in her bedroom.

Earlier in the afternoon she'd walked the half mile down the road with Rich to the pond on their land. He didn't like to wash in the tub, but considered it a treat to be allowed to play in the shallow water for an hour or two. When it was time for him to get out, she'd hitched up her skirt, secured it inside her waistband, and waded up to her knees in the cool water to help Rich soap his hair and rinse it clean. She loved the way the sunlight sparkled and shimmered off his freshly washed hair.

She also allowed him free time to play in

the water for being so good about his lessons. She was determined to see that Rich learned as much as possible from the books she bought for him at the mercantile. It pleased her that he was eager and bright, and she was learning some things from the books, too.

Flair hadn't sent Rich to regular school classes for two reasons. One, they lived seven miles out of town, and she didn't think he was old enough to make that ride by himself each day. But she admitted to herself that gossip was the main reason she taught him at home. After all these years it hadn't stopped. Everyone still wondered about her hasty marriage and the husband who never returned to claim his wife and child. There were still whispers when she walked down the street, when she shopped at the mercantile, when she went into the feed and seed store on the outskirts of town. She didn't want Rich subjected to the teasing and bullying he'd get at school from the other children. Any pain she'd suffered from the gossip, her father's rejection of her affection, or the loneliness was all worth it when she thought of her handsome young son.

Flair scooted down in the tepid water, savoring the feel of it washing over her skin. She took her time and splashed it on her face, under her arms, and behind her ears.

She ducked her head under the water, soaped her hair, then rinsed it with fresh water from a pitcher she'd set by the tub. Even after she'd finished her hair she was reluctant to get out of the water until it was stone cold.

The front door burst open and hit the wall. "Mama! Mama! It's him," Rich shouted. "He's coming back!"

Rich came running into the kitchen at a breakneck speed and skidded to a stop in front of her. Flair quickly covered her breasts with her arms and slid farther into the soap-filmed water. "Who? Mr. Eagerton?"

"Yes. It looks like him to me." His eyes were wide with alarm, his round cheeks had reddened and his freckles stood out like glowing embers. "I saw him in the distance. He's riding this way."

Flair sighed heavily and gritted her teeth. "I wish he'd stay away from us. I've tried to make it clear we want nothing to do with him."

"Don't worry, Mama, I'll get rid of him." Rich pivoted and headed back the way he'd come, his boyish strides taking him quickly out of the room.

"No, Rich! Stay away from him," she called as she rose from the water and grabbed the cotton sheet and started drying herself. She heard a noise in the living room and knowing what he was doing, she quickly added, "Don't get the shotgun, Rich. Just keep him outside until I can get dressed and get out there."

She heard the door bang shut. She wasn't sure if Rich had heard her or that he'd obeyed her if he had. With nervous hands she reached for her pantalets and stepped into them, wondering what else she could do to keep Douglas away from her son. Talking wasn't doing the job.

Flair slipped her arms into her robe and wrapped it around her damp body as she hurried into the living room to look out the window. She realized she wouldn't have time to dress when she heard the horse approaching. That would leave Rich alone with Douglas, and that was the last thing she wanted. He might decide to tell Rich that he was his father. She'd have to confront Douglas with her wet hair and well-worn robe. Taking a deep breath for courage, she belted her robe tighter and threw her wet hair over her shoulders to her back, trying to comb it into some kind of shape with her fingers.

Her only hope in keeping Douglas away from Rich was proof she was still a married woman. She'd sent a letter to Caden Maxwell in Richmond, Virginia three days ago when she was in town, but what could she do until she heard from Caden—*if* she heard from him. And what would she do if she found out she was the widow Douglas wanted her to be? There was also the problem of the note she'd written Douglas. How could she deny that if he chose to take her to court?

As she opened the front door she heard Rich say, "Don't get off that horse, mister, unless you want a pocket full of buckshot."

Holding her robe together at the neck, she stepped out onto the porch. Startled, Flair gasped with surprise. His hat rested low on his forehead, shielding his eyes from her. With the late afternoon sun behind him the rest of his face was shadowed, but she knew him. She would have recognized him anywhere. She could never forget him. How could she after what he had done for her?

It wasn't Douglas who had ridden up to the hitching rail. The man was Caden Maxwell. Her heart jumped up in her throat, her breathing became shallow and labored. Knots of apprehension formed in her stomach. The saints were with her. Caden was alive.

Flair stared at him, unblinking, afraid he'd disappear if she closed her eyes. She tried to swallow, but couldn't. She wanted to move, but couldn't. She needed to speak, but couldn't. She couldn't get past the fact that the man she'd most wanted to see was before her in living form. He was a Godsend.

For a moment she thought he must have received her letter, then remembered she'd only posted it three days ago. He couldn't possibly have received it. Why had he come? What had brought him back to Alabama? It couldn't be coincidence that he showed up just at the time she needed him in her life. It might have happened once, but she couldn't believe it had happened again. Fate didn't smile on people twice.

"You better start talking, mister."

Rich's young, but effective voice brought Flair out of the stupor she'd fallen into as she stared at her husband. She noticed Rich still had the shotgun trained on Caden's chest.

She rushed up behind her son and put one hand on his shoulder and the other on the barrel of the gun and pointed it away from Caden.

"Rich, please put the gun down. You can see he's not the man you thought he was. He's another." Her voice sounded husky and somehow unreal. She picked up Rich's school book from where he'd dropped it and laid it in a chair.

"Do you know him?" Rich asked, reluctantly lowering his weapon to the floor.

"Yes, he's my—ah—your—" Flair couldn't seem to say the word husband or father as she looked over Rich's head to the man still quietly sitting on his horse, taking in the situation.

He tipped his hat to her, pushing it farther up his forehead, revealing his face, exposing his greenish-brown eyes. "It's been a long time, Flair."

"Yes," she whispered on a breathy note, brushing her drying hair away from her face.

She hadn't remembered Caden being so handsome to look upon with his angular jaw, small nose, and finely sculpted lips. He wore more than a day's growth of beard and his clothes were dusty and sweat-stained, telling her he'd been on the trail a few days.

Caden cut his eyes over to Rich. "Is it all right if I get down off my horse?"

Rich looked up at her for an answer, and she realized she was twisting the lapels of her robe between her hands. She placed her hand to his back and gently urged him forward. "Of course. Rich, take his horse over to the barn, unsaddle him, and give him water and oats."

Flair watched as Caden dismounted. Had she forgotten how tall he was, how broad his shoulders and how slim his hips, or had she never known these things about him? Her hand crept back up to the front of her robe and she held it together at the base of her neck. Her wet hair seemed heavy on her back. What did she remember about this man? His name. Where he was from. Where he was going. The color of his eyes. Yes, that piercing color that wasn't quite green or brown but a strange mixture of both was unforgettable. The way he'd held her and comforted her while she cried.

"Does he have a name, mister?" Rich asked as he took the reins from him.

"I call him Max."

"Hey, that's part of my name." He looked back up to the porch at Flair. "Isn't it, Mama?"

She looked at Caden, wondering if he minded that her son carried his name. "That's right," she said in the strongest voice she'd managed since Caden's arrival. "Now take the horse on over to the barn and do what I said."

Caden patted Max's forehead, then let his palm slide downward. "Rub his nose a couple of times like this, Rich, and he'll follow you without any trouble," Caden said as he showed him how to pet Max.

After a moment or two Rich led the horse away. Caden watched him for a moment before turning his attention back to Flair. In four easy strides he climbed the steps. He was much taller than she remembered. He stood before her, boldly searching her face. Flair found herself backing away from him.

"I'm surprised to see you," she said, trying to hide the rush of fear that pierced her.

He reached up and took his hat off, revealing a head full of thick, dark-brown hair that had been banded and creased by his hat. Some of the ends curled upward, others folded down but all of it had a soft wave. His intriguing eyes stared into hers, refusing to release her from his hold. "How have you been, Flair?"

His voice seemed to ask so much more than the polite greeting suggested, but Flair was afraid to open up to him.

"Good," she answered without explanation. "You couldn't possibly have received my letter. I only posted it a few days ago."

His gaze didn't leave her face, his friendly expression didn't change. "I don't know anything about a letter, Flair. You wrote to me?"

She liked the deep richness of his voice, the slow drawl of his words. She liked the way he said her name. She liked the fact that he'd called Rich by name and not by son or boy as other men had. She had to moisten her lips and swallow before she could speak again. "I sent it to you in Richmond, Virginia. That's all I remembered about where you were from."

A light seemed to catch in his eyes and he nodded. "Is that where Rich got his name?"

"Yes. He's Richmond Maxwell."

He nodded again but she could see by the narrowing of his eyes and the tilt of his head that the news shocked him. She saw that he tried to hide it by looking away from her and over to where Rich was disappearing around the corner of the house. He knew she was pregnant when they married. Did he not realize that gave her son his legal name? She wondered what he had expected, then remembered ten years had passed. She supposed it was natural he should be a little shocked to see that he had a nine-year-old son.

"Looks like we have a lot of things to discuss." His gaze swept down her. "Why don't I go help Rich with Max while you put that shotgun away and get dressed."

She had forgotten the shotgun propped against the porch chair. "Oh yes. I'm sorry about this," she said, picking up the gun.

"Nothing wrong with being careful."

He turned to walk away, but she called to him. "Caden." He faced her. "Don't tell Rich your name."

He questioned her with his expression, but remained quiet as he resettled his hat on his head.

Flair brushed a drying strand of hair away from her face and pulled on the lapels of her robe again. There was no reason to be nervous around this man, no reason to apologize. She hadn't forced him to marry her ten years ago. She hadn't even asked him to. Relaxing a little she said, "I told Rich that Caden Maxwell was his father."

His gaze locked onto hers. "Does he think I'm dead?"

"No—no. I mean, I don't think so. We haven't talked about you in a long time." Her throat was suddenly so dry again she could hardly speak, her chest so tight she could barely breathe. "I've always told him the truth. You left with the cavalry to round up renegade Indians and never returned. If you don't mind, I'd rather explain everything to him after we talk."

"All right. I understand."

Flair watched him walk away before hurrying into the house and up the stairs. She tried to calm herself as she dressed. Her body shook and her fingers trembled as she tightened the strings on her day corset. She had no reason to be so strained. She'd wanted to hear from Caden. For heaven's sake, she'd written to him and asked him to get in touch with her! *What was wrong with her?*

But Flair knew. From the moment she'd

seen him sitting so casually on that horse she'd been attracted to him. "No," she whispered aloud as she slid a dark gray stocking up her leg and fastened it to the suspender on the bottom of her corset. After Douglas she'd vowed never to be attracted to or taken in by a man again. And she wouldn't. She wouldn't even think of Caden as a man, only as someone to help her keep Douglas away from her son.

When her blouse was buttoned and her skirt fastened, she quickly ran a brush through her long wet hair before winding it into a tight chignon at the back of her neck.

Maybe he'd somehow heard that her father had died and had come for the land. She'd promised it to him upon her father's death. Yes, that must be it, she reasoned. Why else would he just show up after ten years? A pain of sorrow stabbed through her. She had no choice but to let him have the farm. But, did he want his wife and the young boy he'd given a name to go along with it?

"Oh, God," she whispered as she hurried down the stairs and back into the kitchen. What would she do if Caden had come back expecting a wife? How could she tell him that she still needed his name but had no intentions of becoming a real wife? He'd think her an idiot!

While she waited for Caden and Rich to return, she bailed her wash water out of the tub and poured it into the back yard. She usually took the time to water the flowers and shrubs with the water, but not today. After dragging the wash tub out on the back porch and mopping the wet floor, she turned her attention to the stove.

She added new wood and stoked the embers into flames. Caden would need more than a light supper. Ordinarily, she and Rich would have bread and jam with a glass of milk on Sunday night. Everyone enjoyed their day of rest and the light supper seemed to please Booker and Samp, too. She wondered for a moment what her two workers would think about Caden.

A quick look around the kitchen told her that a vegetable soup seasoned with crisply fried bacon would be the quickest, heartiest meal she could prepare. She set a kettle of water on the stove, then started peeling potatoes. While the soup cooked she would fry the bacon.

She worked with sure, quick movements, not allowing herself to think past getting through supper and putting Rich to bed so she could talk to Caden. If he'd come after the land which was rightfully his, what was she going to do? And what would she do if he wanted a real wife?

By the time Caden and Rich came through the back door, Flair had potatoes, beans, carrots, and onions boiling in the pot. Bacon sizzled in the skillet and Flair was cutting cabbage, the last vegetable to go into the soup.

"Mama, Cade said he'd take me for a ride on his horse tomorrow. Max is a stallion. Can I ride him? Can I?"

She gave Caden a quick glance. "It's *may* I ride him. Did Cade offer or did you ask him if you could ride?"

"No, ma'am, I didn't ask." His eyes blinked as he defended himself. "I was just telling him how much I liked his horse and he said he'd let me ride him sometime. I asked if it could be tomorrow." He turned his big brown eyes on Caden. "Isn't that right?"

Caden smiled and patted Rich on the shoulder. "He's telling the truth."

Flair swung away from the hot stove and grabbed a bucket.

"Oh, do I have to?" Rich complained before Flair had the chance to say a word.

His mother gave him the bucket. "Yes. That cow can't milk herself."

"All right," he complained as he opened the back door and shuffled out.

Flair forced herself not to look at Caden

as she scooped up a double handful of cabbage and dropped it into the bubbling soup.

"You must be tired and thirsty," she said, noticing that he looked as if he could use a good night's sleep. "If you'll sit down at the table I'll pour you a cup of coffee. It should be hot by now."

"I don't suppose you have anything stronger," he asked as he pulled out a barrel-back chair.

Flair thought for a moment. "Papa had a bottle of whiskey at one time, but I haven't seen it in years. He must have drunk it, or maybe he threw it away."

"Coffee will be fine."

A moment or two later she set the cup down in front of him, reaching wide so she wouldn't come close to touching him.

"Where is your father?"

Funny, it didn't hurt like it used to, like it should have when she thought about her father's death. She walked back over to the stove and cleared her tight throat. "He died three years ago."

"That's too bad."

His voice was kind, even. She appreciated that. "I thought you must have known. I assumed that was the reason you were here."

He sipped the coffee, then stretched his legs out underneath the table and hid a yawn behind his cupped hand. "No. Why would you think that?"

Flair busied herself at the stove, checking the soup and the bacon. Heat from the stove made her feel flushed. She lifted a piece of bacon out of the pan and placed it on a platter. "I promised you this land after my father died, remember?"

"I didn't know your father had died. And I'm not here to take your land."

The irritable edge in his voice left her no doubt he meant what he said, and he wasn't happy she'd suggested it. She put the fork down, turned away from the stove and faced Caden. Again she felt the pull of womanly attraction. Why? Why was he here? Why did his presence disturb her? She wasn't supposed to be affected by men. She'd hidden all those feelings long ago. She didn't want to be attracted to any man. And certainly not this one.

"It's yours," she said, fighting down the warm feelings that surfaced, determined not to be affected by him.

"No. It's yours and your son's." Caden remained firm on that point and continued. "What happened after I left you that morning?" he asked, his gaze lighting on her face. "Did your father give you any trouble?"

"Not too much. Thanks to you Papa didn't

throw me out. Our relationship was strained, but we didn't have too many problems." A pang of sorrow struck her. Even though that still bothered her, having Rich made everything she'd lost, everything she'd gone through worth the pain.

"Did you ever hear from Rich's father again?"

She stirred the soup and pushed the skillet to the back of the stove and turned to face him. "Not until recently. He—his wife died a few months ago. They never had any children. He's the reason I wrote to you. He came to see me a week or so ago. Actually he's come over twice. He wants to marry me and raise Rich as his own."

His lashes lifted and he sat up straighter. "You want a divorce so you can marry him?"

"Heavens no! Of course not. I could never marry Douglas." She picked up her apron and wiped her hands. "I don't want Rich to ever know that man's his real father. I wrote you a letter because I wanted proof that you were still alive. Douglas, and most everyone else in this town, has assumed you were dead because you never returned." She stopped when she saw that he rubbed his eyes. He looked tired and confused by what she said.

"Did you expect me to come back?"

"No—I don't know. I'm not sure what all I

thought back then." Her voice softened and her gaze fluttered across his face. "I was very grateful to you for giving me your name. There was a lot of talk. There still is, but the important thing is that you are alive. I don't know why you've shown up at this time but it's so very important to me that you have. I can prove to Douglas that I'm still married and Rich still has a father. He'll have to leave me alone." She smiled gratefully.

Caden shook his head. "We have a problem, Flair."

She walked closer to him. "What? I don't understand." Something was wrong. She saw it in his expression, heard it in his voice.

"I came to ask you for a divorce."

Four

Caden couldn't sleep any longer so he'd risen while it was still dark and slipped downstairs to make himself a pot of coffee. Last night, after he'd eaten the delicious soup Flair had made, his two weeks in the saddle caught up with him. Rich showed him to a bedroom upstairs, and he fell on the bed, clothes, gun holster, and boots.

He raked his hand across his cleanly shaven chin. Rich must have carried his saddlebags upstairs. They were lying on the chair when he woke up. He'd taken time to shave and wash his neck, but what he'd really needed was clean clothes and a soak in the river.

When the coffee was ready, he poured himself a cup and quietly opened the back door and walked out onto the porch. A slightly crisp chill in the air left him feeling invigorated. The sun was just beginning to break above the horizon. There wasn't a sound to be heard in the stillness of morning's first light. This was his favorite time of day, before the birds started chirping, before the bees buzzed, before the world awoke.

Caden walked down the steps and out into the dew wet grass. He needed this time to think before Flair came downstairs. He'd been too tired to say much of anything when he arrived yesterday. Maybe he should have taken a room in town and rested a couple of days before riding out to the farm, but the truth was, once he started the trip he realized he was anxious to find out what had become of the woman he'd married so hastily.

Three days into his journey he'd decided he should have taken the train to south Alabama. It would have been faster and a whole lot easier. But from his younger days as a cavalryman he'd remembered long rides in the saddle, sleeping out on the range, and experiencing nature—the sun, the rain, the moon and stars—as the manly thing to do when in reality it was no fun at all. He now knew it was more tiring than a hard day's work on the farm.

He sipped his coffee and looked up into the purple hue of daybreak and thought of the woman he'd come to see. Flair was even more beautiful than he remembered. Her eyes were such a clear shade of blue he could almost see himself in them. She'd smelled heavenly when he walked up on the porch yesterday afternoon and stood before her. Even though he was so tired he could hardly think straight, his lower body hadn't been immune to catching Flair right out of the bath water. That had made her extremely desirable. Dried wisps of her golden blond hair had caught the sunlight and shimmered invitingly, beckoning him to reach out and touch it, to tame it with his hand. He wanted to carry it to his face and bury his nose in its sweetness.

He hadn't remembered her delicate-looking features. A small, slightly pointed nose. Cheeks that looked as soft as the brush of butterfly wings. And lips beautifully shaped and temptingly full. Her build was petite, but she had enough curves and swells to turn any man's head.

However, there were many more things to admire about Flair than her alluring beauty—starting with her son. She'd obviously done a good job of raising him. That was evident in the way Rich had greeted him. He liked the fact that Rich wanted to protect his mother. Caden had also noticed how Flair had touched Rich with tenderness, how she spoke to him with affection, and how he spoke to her with respect. It was easy to see love between the mother and son. That thought caused him a moment of envy. She had someone who loved her and someone to love.

Caden sipped his coffee again and looked up into the sunrise sky. His parents had been dead a long time. He'd forgotten a lot of things about them, but he remembered that he'd loved them. They had loved each other, and they had loved him. His father had talked to him with the same affectionate tone Flair used with Rich, unlike Shelton who always used a demanding voice. He hadn't loved anyone since they'd died.

In his mind's eye, Caden went back to the time when his father lay on the bed dying, his body bruised and broken from the carriage accident. Caden knew the only reason he'd stayed with Shelton all these years was because on his deathbed, his father had asked him to stay with Shelton and, *be as good for him as you have been for me*. Had Pearson known how difficult that was going to be for his son? The strong impact his parents had made on his life had been all but eradicated by Shelton's constant harangue about weak men and never trusting or loving anyone but yourself.

Caden shook his head clear of those unbidden memories and returned his thoughts to Flair. She had obviously managed the farm since her father died. A quick look around the house and yard, the neat rows of a vegetable garden told him she hadn't let the place get run-down.

By all appearances Flair had managed to make a good life for herself and her son—and with no husband to help her. That pleased him. There was another thing to admire about Flair. She hadn't let one bad incident in life stop her from going forward. She'd taken it and made something worthwhile from it. Rich. And now when the true father of her son wanted her, she had the strength and courage to say no. He admired her for that, too, but could he help her this time? He had to have that divorce. He wanted Maxwell Farms. After putting up with his uncle for most of fifteen years, Caden knew he'd do anything to keep Jake from getting his hands on the farm. That thought brought him back to Flair.

Caden leaned against a fence post at the edge of a wooded area. He didn't want Flair asking why he hadn't returned for her when he left the cavalry. He didn't want her to know how his uncle had berated him for doing something so foolish as to marry a pregnant young woman in southern Alabama. But one thing was sure. He wasn't going to let Flair keep him from getting Maxwell Farms. He'd worked too hard for it all these years.

He had helped her. Now it was her turn to help him. He had to have that divorce.

He'd had a good reason to marry her that night. Even then he'd been drawn to her. She'd shown strength, courage, and determination in trying to do something to take care of herself and the child she was carrying. Yet, before it was too late she'd realized the foolishness of her actions and left the saloon before anything happened.

It had bothered him when she thought he was after her land. With two thousand acres to Maxwell Farms, a hundred horses, and several hundred calves born each year the last thing he needed or wanted was Flair's small vegetable farm. But he guessed it was natural for her to assume that was the reason he'd shown up at her door after all these—

The click of a hammer being pulled back sounded behind him and Caden went still. He faced the house, his back to the woods. Anyone could have come up behind him.

"Turn around nice and slow like," came the deep voice.

Not one to disobey a man with a gun trained on his back, Caden turned slowly and saw a black man holding a pistol aimed at him. Did everyone in Alabama greet strangers with a weapon, he wondered? For the most part he was an easy-going man, but he was getting tired of looking down the barrel of a gun.

"You want to tell me what you're doing here in Miss Flair's back yard?" the man asked.

Caden quickly sized up the man. Nineteen or twenty years of age, strong build. His black-brown eyes didn't waver from Caden's face. The man wasn't nervous or shaky. He was prepared. But sensing no real danger from him, Caden held up his cup and said, "Having coffee."

"That might be so, but who are you? What are you doing here?"

"I'm Caden Maxwell, and I'd appreciate you putting down that gun. As you can see, I'm not armed and I'm not going to hurt anyone." He kept his voice slow and even. To appear more relaxed than he actually was, he sipped his coffee again. He knew he couldn't be too careful with a pistol pointed at him.

The dark man's eyes widened. "You Miss Flair's husband?" He released the hammer with a resounding click and lowered the gun. He looked up and down Caden as if he thought he might recognize him. "You been gone a mighty long time," he finally said as he stuffed the gun into the waistband of his black trousers. He snorted agreeably. "Everybody 'round here thought you was dead."

Not surprising. Ten years was a long time. And he wouldn't be here now if it wasn't for his uncle and his ridiculous stipulation to becoming his heir.

"As you can see, I'm very much alive." Caden shifted his stance.

A shuffling noise came from behind the barn and another black man came running up to them, shoving his work shirt into his breeches and pulling up his suspenders. This man was older and of a husky rather than muscular build like the younger man. His hair and beard showed signs of graying, even though his movements were agile.

"What's going on here?" he asked. "Who's this?"

"I was 'bout to go in and start the fire in the stove like always when Miss Flair's back door opened and he came out," the younger man pointed to Caden. "That's when I went back for the gun and to wake you. But it's all right, Pa. This here stranger is Miss Flair's husband," he offered. "I guess he showed up sometime last night."

The old man looked from Caden to his son, then back to Caden, clearly shocked. He rubbed the back of his neck, then slid his hand around to rub his chin a couple of times. "Is that so?" he finally asked Caden, shaking his head a bit. "Are you Miss Flair's husband? Rich's pa?"

Caden chuckled. His admiration for Flair Bowen Maxwell grew. She'd actually pulled it off. They knew his name—considered him Flair's husband and Rich's father. He didn't know what he'd expected when he arrived in Alabama, but it hadn't been this instant recognition as Flair's husband. Many times after he'd left her that morning so many years ago he'd wondered what people would say, how they would react, how they would treat her, and if anyone other than her father would believe her.

"It appears the two of you know who I am. But I don't know who you are? Do you have a particular reason for prowling on my wife's land."

The younger of the men frowned and the older one spoke up and demanded, "Prowling? We ain't prowling. Not us. We live back behind the barn. Got our own place. Mr. Bowen helped us build it more'n ten years ago." He walked closer to Caden, pulling on the waistband of his breeches. "Name's Samp. This is my boy, Booker. We tend the farmland for Miss Flair. She gives us a place to live and a few dollars in our pockets."

That information let Caden know why the place seemed so well cared for. These two men were obviously dedicated to Flair. He nodded a greeting to the two men, then threw the last of his coffee onto the grass.

"I guess you'll be starting the fire in the cook stove from now on," Booker said.

Caden tensed. They assumed he was here to stay. They thought of him as the long lost husband who had come home to his wife. He wasn't about to get into trying to explain anything to these two men so he simply said, "For now, I'll take care of it."

The aroma of freshly boiled coffee hit Flair as she opened her bedroom door. She knew immediately that Caden had made it. She picked up the tail of her crimson-colored skirt and hurried to the kitchen, unhappy that he'd arisen before her. The wood stove was hot. The coffeepot sat to one side, but nothing else was out of place. Caden was nowhere in sight. Thinking he must have gone to the outhouse, she immediately put on her apron and started preparations for breakfast.

She removed the dish cloth from the flour bowl, added a scoop of butter and a dipper of milk, and started mixing the three ingredients, thinking about Caden. She hadn't been able to talk with him last night after he'd given her the news he'd come to divorce her. He'd been too tired. *Divorce*. She cringed, and her stomach knotted every time she thought about that. But, what could she have said to him, other than no? Caden had saved her life. It wasn't that she was ungrateful. She wasn't. She owed it to him to do whatever he asked.

But, she couldn't. She had to think of her son, too. And no matter what Caden had done for her ten years ago, what was best for Rich had to come first. She didn't know how to go about telling him, but she intended to stay married to Caden Maxwell until Douglas was satisfied she and her son were not available to him.

The back door opened and Caden walked in carrying an empty coffee cup. Their eyes met briefly before she quickly glanced away. She didn't like the stirrings of long forgotten romantic feelings and emotions curling inside her whenever she looked into his eyes. Douglas's treatment of her had cured her forever of indulging in those kinds of feelings.

"Good morning," she said, dipping her hand into the flour jar and sprinkled a generous portion of the white substance on top of the counter.

"Morning," he answered.

"I'm sorry I wasn't up in time to make coffee for you. I had no idea you'd be up so early. You were really tired last night." She poured the dough out onto the counter and rolled it in the dry flour.

"I guess I almost fell asleep in my soup bowl. I pushed it pretty hard to get here."

She grabbed a rolling pin and started flattening the dough. "All the more reason I should already have breakfast ready for you."

"I don't mind making coffee in the mornings. Would you like a cup?" he asked.

He walked up beside her and reached for the pot. She smelled soap and leather. Even though the stove had warmed the room, she felt heat from his body. He didn't touch her, but he didn't have to. She felt him. Not looking at him she shook her head. "Not right now. I have to be up awhile before I can drink it." She wished she wouldn't get that fluttery feeling inside when he was so close. There was no reason for it. She wanted to get her mind off the way he smelled, the way he made her feel when he was near, and when she looked at him. She was angry with herself for letting him disturb her so intimately.

Flair noticed he'd shaved, but he hadn't put on clean clothes. "I have some of Papa's old clothes if you'd like for me to wash those you have on."

He looked down at his sweat-stained clothes and dusty boots. "Thanks. I have other clothes.

It's just that they're as dirty as these from the trail dust."

"If you'll bring them into the kitchen, I'll wash them for you. It doesn't look like rain today so you should have clean clothes by the end of the day."

He nodded. "I'd appreciate that."

She was working the dough too fast and too hard. The biscuits wouldn't turn out well if she didn't slow down and do them right.

"Booker and Samp will probably be showing up at the door any minute now wanting their breakfast so they can go to the fields. I cook for them every evening, too. Neither of them has a wife. I don't mind. I have to cook for Rich anyway." Flair stopped. She was babbling like an idiot about something she was sure he wouldn't be the least bit interested in. What did he care about her life, her farm, or her son? He wanted a divorce!

"I met them outside. Booker was on his way to start the fire for you."

"Yes. I told him I didn't mind doing it, but he thinks that's part of his job. They're good workers."

"I can see that."

"So tell me, are you still in the army?" she asked.

"No. I was only in for three years." He paused. "My uncle had fought in the war. He thought it would be good for me to serve my time."

"And was it?" she asked as she picked up the tin cutter and started pressing the utensil into the dough, making little round circles.

"What? The army?"

She glanced over at him. He put the coffeepot back on the stove. "Yes."

He leaned a shoulder against the cupboard and stared at her. "Hard to say. The only way I figure it altered my life at all was by marrying you."

Flair snapped around to face him. His eyes had a teasing light in them but his voice had sounded serious. She didn't know which way he really felt about what he said. Their marriage had changed his life, but in what way?

"I suppose you've kicked yourself a thousand times for doing that," she said, then turned back to her chore. She picked up a deep skillet and wiped the inside with a glob of lard.

"I can't say that I have. The truth is I got busy with the farm and seldom remembered I was married."

Flair placed the biscuits into the pan. She could understand that. She'd felt the same way. How could either of them have possibly felt married when they'd never spent any time together, never touched, never kiss—Flair stopped her thoughts. What was she doing thinking that way? She brushed the back of her hand across her cheek. Just because Caden Maxwell was handsome, nice, and her husband was no reason to start thinking of kisses and caresses. She opened the door to the oven and shoved the pan of biscuits inside. A thought struck her, chilled her, defeated her. She knew why he wanted the divorce.

She shut the oven door, lifted her shoulders and chin, and looked into Caden's eyes. "You've met a woman you love and you want to marry her," she stated. She didn't know why that should bother her, but it did. If anyone merited their freedom Caden Maxwell did. He'd been a gallant young man ten years ago, and now, he had the right to happiness. He deserved to be married to the woman he loved. She knew and understood all that. However, she couldn't let those things keep her from the determination to see that there was no divorce between them until Rich was safe from Douglas.

Caden's facial expression remained passive. "My reasons aren't important to you. My uncle's lawyer is looking into the quickest and easiest way to accomplish the divorce. The only thing you will have to do is sign the papers when the time comes."

"I can't do that." She tried to wipe the flour from her hands and her apron.

"Flair."

"No, I'm sorry." She turned away from him. She hated telling him this when he'd been her salvation. It pained her to owe him and be unable to repay him.

He walked around her, forcing her to face him. "You don't understand." He stood dangerously close to her. "You don't have a choice in this."

"Yes, I do. I'll have to fight you," she whispered desperately.

Caden sighed audibly. "Flair, even with a divorce I'll still be Rich's father. He carries my name. That won't change."

"Mama!"

They both turned and saw Rich standing in the doorway. His little face went from red to white as shock settled in. His brown eyes questioned, widened, and teared before he turned and ran out of the house.

"Rich!" she called earnestly as she threw down her hand towel and started to follow him.

Caden caught her arm and stopped her. "Let me talk to him, Flair."

"No! Turn me loose." She struck out at him with a flour-coated hand. "I have to talk to him. I have to explain."

"It will be better if I do it," he tried to reason with her.

"No. He's my son," she argued in a scratchy voice filled with emotion, knowing she shouldn't have been discussing this in the house where Rich could overhear them. She was so angry with herself she shook.

Caden didn't let go of her arm. "Flair, listen to me. Sometimes boys don't want their mamas around and this is one of them. I think I can handle this better than you."

After taking a moment to think about what Caden said she knew it to be true. Rich hated for her to treat him like a little boy. She relaxed against Caden's hold. "All right."

"Now, do you have any idea where he might go?"

She moistened her dry lips and nodded. "To the pond about half a mile down on the east side of the house." She looked up into Caden's beautifully colored eyes and asked, "What are you going to tell him?"

"The truth. I'm his father."

Five

Rich was skimming rocks.

Caden stood behind the cover of a hardwood tree about twenty yards from the creek and watched him down by the bank, trying to come up with the right words to approach Flair's son. What had he been thinking to tell Flair he'd handle this for her? He didn't know anything about talking to a boy. He had no idea what to say to the young fellow. He must have been *mad, crazy* to have insisted! He didn't know anything about boys or their feelings.

But as he continued to watch, Caden knew he was lying to himself. He *did* know about young boys' feelings. He remembered the pain of losing his parents. And finding a father for the first time in life must have Rich feeling some of the things he'd felt so many years ago.

Early morning sunshine sparkled off Rich's light brown hair as it fell across his forehead with each toss of a rock. The legs of his black trousers and the sleeves of his white shirt looked too short for him. Spring obviously had the boy growing.

Most of the crispness had left the morning air, making the temperature comfortable. Rays from the sun filtered through the towering hardwoods and glistened off the water and glared in Caden's eyes. He heard an occasional tweet from the birds in the surrounding trees. A bee buzzed near his head and he swatted it away.

There were other reasons why he'd spoken up; the expression of shock and anger he saw in Rich's young face, the look of horror in Flair's eyes when she realized her son had overheard their discussion. He had caused their pain by coming back into their lives. He wanted to make it as easy for them as possible.

Caden listened to the plopping sound of the pebbles hitting the water. Rich had good aim, a good arm for throwing, Caden noticed. Skimming rocks wasn't an easy thing to do, and he found himself wondering who'd taught the youngster.

Chuckling ruefully to himself, Caden wondered why he became a different man when he was around Flair? His rough and tough attitude that he wore everyday on the horse farm deserted him whenever she was near.

Tenderness and compassion replaced them. He shook his head, clearing his mind of Flair—his wife. Now wasn't the time to get caught up in those kind of thoughts about her.

Since he didn't know anything about talking to a youngster, he would talk to Rich as if he were an adult, Caden decided. That might be better than trying to treat him like a child anyway. And maybe, at first, it would be better if they didn't discuss what he'd overheard in the kitchen. Caden thought it best to ease into that subject.

He pushed away from the tree trunk and started toward Rich. His boots crunched on small twigs, snapping them and rustled fallen leaves, making a lot of noise as he walked. He expected Rich to turn around when he approached, but Rich continued to face the water.

"You've got a good arm there," Caden said, coming to stand beside him. "Who taught you how to do that?"

The youngster didn't acknowledge him in any way. Rich bent and picked up several more small pebbles. After slipping the extra ones into his pocket, he hurled a rock out into the peaceful, shimmering water. It landed with one plop instead of skimming. Caden couldn't help but think Rich missed that one on purpose to contradict his praise.

Caden decided to try a different subject. "How many acres do you have on the farm? Looks like it's a big responsibility for you and your Mom."

Still no response.

"I thought we'd saddle my horse and take him out for a ride after breakfast. He doesn't like to be penned up for too long without any exercise."

Rich continued to ignore him. Caden's patience ran out. He planted his booted foot on a fallen tree limb and bent closer to the silent boy. Borrowing some of his uncle's tactics Caden kept his voice low, but firm as he said, "The way I see this, Rich, is that you have two choices. You can talk to me man to man, or you can talk to your mama and let her treat you like a little baby. Either way you'll talk."

Stopping his arm in mid-motion, Rich cut his big brown eyes around to Caden and mumbled, "I'm not a baby. Don't call me a baby."

With a strong swing of his arm and a quick flip of his wrist, Rich sent the rock skimming perfectly across the water, rippling the stillness.

Caden was impressed, but now wasn't the time to tell him so. "Then don't act like one.

When a man speaks to you, you answer. Don't sulk."

Rich faced him. His wide eyes held tears, his nose was red, his lips formed a trembling, disappointed pout. He folded his arms across his chest and stated, "I thought you were dead."

His words, the way he was trying hard to look and act tough tugged at Caden's heart. He knew Rich had reason to be upset, but he also had to learn how to handle the hurt. "I guess a lot of people round here thought I was dead, including your mama."

"Why did you take so long to come back to us?"

"I had a lot of things to do." The excuse was so pitiful Caden cringed. He renewed his anger against himself for telling Flair he'd explain all this to Rich. Just because Shelton wouldn't let him mourn over his parents' deaths didn't mean he shouldn't allow Rich the opportunity to come to terms with his sudden appearance.

"What kind of things? Where have you been? Why didn't you come for us?" he demanded in his child's voice. "We've been waiting for you."

Caden realized Rich needed to say some things and get them off his chest. Rich didn't understand why he was angry or why he was hurting. He must have felt like Caden had mistreated him and his mother by staying away so long. And if he'd been a real husband that would be true. *A real husband and father.* Caden shook his head. How could he explain to this nine-year-old boy that he only married his mother to give him a name? He couldn't. If Rich was to ever be told that, it would have to come from Flair.

"Some things are just too complicated to explain, too difficult for a youngster your age to understand."

"I can understand," he insisted, still trembly. "Mama says I'm smart."

Caden smiled to himself and rubbed his chin thoughtfully. He didn't doubt that. "I can see that."

"Didn't you want us?"

Sighing, he looked down at Rich and said, "Let me put it this way. Sometimes it's better to work from the present and go forward and not think about or worry about what happened in the past. That part of life can't be changed anyway."

Rich scratched his nose, sniffled, then wiped his eyes with a dirty hand, smearing his face with the dirt. He looked up at Caden. "What are you going to do? Are you going to live with us now, or are you going away again?"

What could he tell Rich? Why hadn't he

thought about Flair's child and how all this would affect him before he decided to ride into town and disrupt their lives? Because Shelton had taught him to only take care of himself and Maxwell Farms. He never had a reason to consider anyone else's feelings until now.

Caden straightened. "I don't have an answer for you right now. I have a home in Virginia just like you and your mama have this farm. I'll have to go back sometime."

"When you go, are you taking us with you?"

"Well—I—" Stunned by the question, Caden found it impossible to answer. It was natural for Rich to assume he'd be going with his father. Slowly an idea formed in his mind.

Why not take them with him when he returned to Virginia? Shelton wanted to know that Caden had a wife and heir before he died. Caden couldn't think of a woman in Richmond who stirred his blood like Flair. And Rich was a smart young man. Why not force Shelton to accept Flair and Rich as his family? Shelton's reaction came immediately to mind. It would be explosive. He wouldn't approve of Caden taking charge, keeping control of the situation, but this was one of those times he had to stand up to his uncle.

Caden smiled to himself. Yes, Shelton would

be livid. His illness hadn't kept him from being a strong and domineering bastard. He'd be outraged that Caden would bring his wife and son into his house. But Caden knew Rich could bring a lot of pleasure into Shelton's life if he'd let the boy do it. There was always the chance Shelton would throw all of them off his farm, but for some reason Caden had a feeling he wouldn't.

Not taking his eyes off Caden, Rich said, "You might as well go on back to your home today, because we don't need you here."

Caden had taken too long to answer Rich. He saw the sting of rejection in Rich's eyes. It shocked him that the youngster's words hit him hard. He hadn't expected to be affected by Rich's anger. He wasn't sure how to go about smoothing things over with him. Maybe all Rich needed was time to get used to the idea of having a father.

"You and your mama have done a fine job of taking care of each other. As far as going to Virginia with me, I'll talk to your mother about that. It's something we'll have to work-out between us."

Rich rubbed his eyes again, smearing the drying dirt farther down his cheeks. He looked up at Caden and said, "I don't want to go with you, but if Mama says I have to, I will."

Caden felt a tightness creep up on him when he thought about Flair. How was he going to convince her to go to Virginia with him?

There were a number of reasons why he shouldn't allow himself to be attracted to her. But there was something about this woman that made her special. He was intrigued by her and the truth was, he wanted her to go to Virginia with him. He wanted to get to know her better. He wasn't sure he was ready to cut her out of his life.

"A-am I supposed to call you Pa or Cade?"

A frisson crawled over Caden and shook him. He hadn't thought about that either. Of course the boy would expect to call him Pa. What should he tell him? The boy actually thought he was his father. He looked down into Rich's face with his big brown eyes, round cheeks, and slightly squared chin. The freckles across his nose made him downright fetching. But Caden knew how the boy felt. He remembered how expectant he was after his parents were killed and he went to live with his uncle. He'd desperately wanted a father, too.

"What do you want to call me?"

"Cade," he answered emphatically, a firm set to his lips.

Caden didn't know if he was relieved or

disappointed. He only knew that for now it
was right. He wasn't prepared to make Rich
any promises and it appeared Rich wasn't
ready to make any to him.

"All right. Cade it will be. Now we better
get back to the house. I think Flair will have
breakfast waiting for us. After we eat, you can
show me around the farm. Think you're big
enough to do that?"

Rich rolled his eyes heavenward. "Course I
am. Mama lets me go with Booker and Samp
when they have a lot to do so I can help."

"I bet Booker is the one who taught you
how to skim rocks, isn't he?" Caden asked as
they started down the path that led back to
the house where Flair waited. Even though it
was clear Flair loved her son more than anything, she had somehow managed not to
make a mama's boy out of him. Caden filed
that away with the other things he admired
about her.

Flair had given Booker and Samp a basket
filled with bacon and egg biscuits and sliced
bread covered with butter and cooked pears.
The two field hands would eat on the generous fare all during the day and still be hungry as wolves when they came in for dinner
late in the afternoon.

When they returned, neither Caden nor Rich said anything to her about what Rich had overheard. Both were quiet as they sat down to the small table in the kitchen and ate their breakfast. Flair was eager to know what they said to each other, but was hesitant to bring up a matter that seemed already to be settled. Instead, she and Rich answered Caden's questions about the farm.

After they finished with the meal Caden asked Rich to go out to the barn and feed and water his horse while he talked to Flair alone.

Flair stood on the back porch and watched Rich hurry down the steps and race toward the barn. She needed to get her thoughts together before stepping back inside to talk with Caden. She wanted to know what Caden had said to Rich to smooth things over so quickly. Right up front she'd tried to explain to Caden that nothing in her life was more important than her son. She'd do anything to keep Rich from being hurt by anyone.

"You've done a good job with him. He's a fine boy," Caden said, walking up to stand beside her on the porch.

"Thank you," she answered, and moved away from him. She didn't like that funny feeling that stole over her whenever he was near. "What did you say to him?"

Caden leaned against a post. His wavy, dark-brown hair had been combed away from his forehead, making him look younger. He held his hat in his hand. His well-worn, dusty trousers fit him a little too well, she noticed, and his eyes seemed to pierce her.

"Nothing much."

Flair didn't like being left out of the conversation the two of them had. She had a right to know. "You must have said something worthwhile. He seems settled now about hearing you're his father, and he wasn't when he ran out of here."

Caden shrugged his shoulders. "He needs some time to adjust, but don't worry about him. He's going to be all right," Caden said, side-stepping her question again.

She folded her arms across her chest, pursed her lips, and looked into his greenish-brown eyes. "You're not going to tell me, are you?"

He gave her a pleasing grin. "I think there are some things mamas don't need to know."

His smile affected her greatly. Her stomach muscles tightened and her breath lightened. Was he trying to get her to notice him as a man? Did he want her to find him attractive? Did he care how she felt about him? She took a deep breath. At twenty-six surely she was too old for fanciful notions of kisses and caresses. But looking at him now, she knew she may have put them behind her at one time, but they had come bursting forth when Caden walked up on her porch yesterday afternoon.

No, she reprimanded herself. She had been hurt by a romantic attraction once before. She had vowed it would never happen again. And it wouldn't, not even if the man was her very attractive husband.

Taking another deep breath, Flair pushed those thoughts from her mind and said, "Don't tease me, Caden. Rich is all I have. He's my life. I won't allow anyone to hurt him." Her voice sounded more desperate than she intended it to be, but there could be no doubt to Caden or anyone else what Rich meant to her or what she'd do for him.

She was still upset by what happened earlier that morning. If Caden wasn't going to tell her what they had said to each other she'd have to ask Rich. She couldn't simply assume he was going to accept Caden as his father, or that Caden would accept Rich as a son, especially when he had come all this way to divorce her.

"I understand that, Flair. As you just saw, he's a little upset, but he's going to be all right. I sent Rich out to the barn because I want to tell you about a plan I have."

"What? Your plan on how to divorce me without my consent?" she asked turning away from him to look out past the trees to the fertile farm land in the distance.

Caden straightened and took a step closer to her. "Eventually that will have to be done, yes. But for now I've come up with a plan that might work for both of us."

She eyed him warily, wondering what could work for both of them when they wanted opposite ends to the story. She hadn't been able to think of anything that would work, but she'd listen to what he had to say.

"All right, let's hear it."

"I'll stay here on the farm with you for two or three weeks. We can go in to town together, have some neighbors over if you want, or do whatever you think's best to get the word out that I've returned. We'll let everyone know that I'm alive. I'm back. We'll leave no doubt to this man named Douglas that you are still married."

Hope surged within her and she faced him. "That—that's wonderful for me, but what about the divorce you want?"

His eyes narrowed. "That's the second part of my plan. In exchange for me playing your husband for a couple of weeks and getting Douglas off your back, you and Rich will travel with me to my home in Virginia and stay there with me until the divorce is final."

Flair blinked slowly as she studied what he proposed. "What?" she finally asked. "You must be crazy." She picked up the hem of her apron and nervously wiped her hands. She moved restlessly on the porch. "I can't go to Virginia with you."

"Why not?" He leaned against the porch post.

Exasperated that he pretended not to know, she said, "Look around you." She spread her arm through the air, sweeping toward the countryside. "I have a farm to run. I supply vegetables to the mercantile, the saloon, and the hotel in town every week. That's how we make a living."

"I understand that, but Booker and Samp seem capable of tending the farm while you're away."

She flapped her arms to her side and walked to the other end of the porch. "Yes, they can tend the fields, but Rich and I are the ones who take the fresh picked vegetables into town every Saturday."

"Samp and Booker can deliver the goods."

"Maybe they can, but a bigger problem is what will it do to Rich to suddenly uproot him and take him to your home for a few months."

"I've already talked with Rich about that. He understands that things may not work out between us."

Flair raised her eyebrows. "That must have been some talk the two of you had."

Caden smiled.

Still not convinced, she said, "Look, I don't want to argue with you about this. I can't leave the farm." She pushed back a wayward strand of hair that continued to tickle her cheek. "When the documents are ready send them to me and I'll sign them."

Caden slowly shook his head.

"Why not? You don't need me in Virginia to divorce me, do you?"

"I don't right now, no, but in the future, I might. And look at it this way. It will be a good way to keep Douglas away from Rich." He walked over to her. The heel of his boots sounded loud on the wooden porch. He stopped in front of her and looked down into her eyes. "You don't have to make up your mind right now. There's time. Think about it."

Flair wanted to dispute his words but knew in all honesty she couldn't. If Douglas threatened to take her son again, she'd do anything. She'd hoped the reappearance of Caden would settle this for Douglas once and for all.

There were many things to consider. She realized she needed to think about his proposal. She couldn't forget Caden had married her. She owed him, although he'd been nice not to put it to her that way.

"You're right. I need time to think about this. I can't make a hasty decision."

He placed his hat on his head and fitted it snugly. "Take your time. Rich agreed to show me around the farm—if you don't need him for anything special this morning."

"No. Booker milked the cow. I'll feed the chickens for him while the wash pot heats."

"Don't worry about us," he said as he walked down the steps. "We may not be back until late in the afternoon."

Flair stayed on the porch and watched Caden walk toward the barn. He had a slow, purposeful gait with a slight swing to those broad shoulders. What was she to do? Getting Rich away from Douglas, if only temporarily, was tempting. But would it be fair to either of them to follow this man to Virginia only to be sent back when the divorce was final?

By mid-afternoon Flair had finished most of her chores for the day. She'd weeded the herb garden, hoed around three rose bushes, and washed the clothes. Booker had come by the house at noontime to report on the corn and tomato crop so she had him kill and pluck a chicken for her. It was roasting in the oven for dinner.

She walked outside to see if Caden's shirts were dry so she could put a hot iron to them before he and Rich returned. The day had been beautiful, with warm sunshine and blue skies. Birds chirped in distant trees, butterflies skittered along with the breeze, and an occasional bee buzzed by her head. As she suspected, Caden's dark brown trousers were still damp around the waistband, his socks still wettish. But his shirts and long underwear were dry. If the sun stayed hot the rest of the afternoon Caden would have a clean and pressed suit of clothes by nightfall.

After she took the last shirt off the line something made her carry it to her nose and breathe in deeply before throwing it over her shoulders with the others. The shirt smelled wonderfully clean. She rubbed the cambric between her fingers as she looked at its off-white color. The fabric didn't feel heavy or coarse like the inexpensive cloth she used to make Rich's, Booker's, and Samp's shirts. She lifted the fine cotton fabric to her nose again and buried her face in it, moving her head from side to side as she felt its softness, took in its freshness.

Flair closed her eyes and thought about Caden Maxwell. She couldn't deny that there was something romantic working between them. He looked too deeply into her eyes. She searched his face too often. What was she to do about those budding feelings of attraction? And what was she to do about his proposal?

She had to consider it. Doing what he asked was without question the right thing to do. She knew that. She owed him. She knew that, too. But could she and Rich leave the only life they'd ever known to go with Caden to Virginia, if only temporarily? As she asked herself the question, she realized it was in their best interest to go. If they were gone for a length of time maybe Douglas would find someone else to marry. Leaving her free of him once again. Yes, Caden's idea had merit she hadn't thought about before.

But there was another side to consider, too, she pondered as she slowly inhaled the cleanness of the shirt again. Her attraction to him. Would it grow, or would she find the strength to deny it existed? All these things had to be considered before she made a decision.

"Afternoon, Flair."

Startled, Flair jerked her head up and saw Douglas striding toward her. She cringed inside at the sight of him. She had been so deep in thought she hadn't heard his horse approach. Her hands made fists and wadded the expensive shirt she held. How could she have ever thought Douglas a handsome man? "You have no business on my land, Douglas. I've told you to stay away from here."

Douglas grinned as he stopped in front of her. "That doesn't sound very neighborly of you, Flair. Can't you at least say hello?"

"I don't feel neighborly." She threw Caden's shirt over her shoulder on top of the others. "Why do you keep coming over here when you know you're not wanted?"

He sniffed and made eye contact with her. "I'm determined to make you change your mind about me."

"That won't happen."

"You should be grateful to me. I've come to give you one more chance to change your mind about marrying me. I don't want to have to do anything, but I will." He pulled a piece of paper from his pocket.

A chilling fear stole over her. Hooding her eyes with her lashes, she looked up at him. "What are you saying? Are you threatening me?"

He chuckled. "Would I do something like that? I just want to remind you that I usually get what I want." His eyes narrowed as he looked down the length of her. "Remember? Now I want my son." He pushed his hat up farther on his forehead, showing skin that hadn't been darkened by the sun. "I'm not going to give up, Flair. Make it easier on both of us and marry me."

Why was she allowing him to say all these things to her? Feeling strength in Caden's return, she lifted her chin proudly and said, "You have no choice now but to leave me and my son alone. That note you carry no longer threatens me. My husband has come home, and he will swear Rich is his son."

The smile slowly died on his lips. His gaze searched her face for truthfulness. "I don't believe you."

"Look at the clothes on this line." She motioned to it with her head. "Those are men's clothes on it." She held up the shirt she'd just wrinkled and smiled. "My *husband's* clothes."

He grunted, his upper lip curling into a snarl of unease. "You can't fool me, Flair. They belong to your hired hands."

She thrust the shirt into Douglas's hands. "Since when do field hands wear expensive, well-tailored shirts like this?"

He took the shirt from her, wadding it in his large hand as he looked over it. "What kind of trick are you trying to pull?"

Flair inhaled the fresh air and smiled again. It felt wonderful, wonderful to best him. "Nothing. Come back around supper

time and I'll introduce you to my husband
Caden Maxwell. Rich's father."

"I'm his father." He struck his chest with
his thumb.

"No," she denied hastily, in the heat of the
moment, wanting so desperately for her words
to be true. "You're not his father. Caden is,
and we're going—"

Douglas threw the shirt to the ground and
grabbed her arms so forcefully it wrenched
her sockets. He held her tightly, bruising her
upper arms. He shook her so hard hairpins
fell out of her hair and loosened her chignon. Flair tried to stop him, to lash out at
him, but she couldn't free her arms.

"Don't ever try to convince me or anyone
else that boy isn't mine!"

He shook her again. Flair felt like her teeth
rattled in her mouth. "S-stop!" she managed
to scream.

She tried kicking and bucking to free herself but, her foot tangled in her skirt. She
cried out again for him to stop. When at last
he did, she tried to squirm away from him,
but he wouldn't turn her loose.

"I know he's my son." Douglas said in a
demonic tone. "And I intend to have him
with or without you!"

Flair felt dizzy, faint from the furious shaking, but determined to get rid of Douglas

once and for all. With ragged breathing she managed to say, "There's no way a judge will give you rights to Rich with Caden alive."

His fingers dug into her arms and Flair cried out as she heard the sound of a rifle shot crack through the air. Douglas jerked, blinked, winced. Sprinkles of blood flew from his arm and splattered her taupe-colored blouse. She gasped as she saw a dark-red stain appear on the sleeve of Douglas's white shirt. His grip slackened. His eyes widened in disbelief. She pushed away from him as they both whirled to see who had shot him.

To Flair's astonishment, not twenty yards away Caden sat calmly on his horse, his rifle still aimed at Douglas. Rich straddled the stallion behind Caden.

"Goddammit! You shot me, you bastard!" Douglas shouted as he looked from Caden to his arm and back to Caden again.

"I suggest you watch your language in front of my wife and son or I'll decorate your other arm in red."

"You're crazy!" Douglas held his arm in front of him. Blood continued to trickle down his sleeve.

"That might be, but you better think twice before you put your hands on my wife again."

Douglas turned a pale, furious face toward

Flair. "He's a damned maniac! He shot me! I'm going to have the sheriff arrest him."

A shot rang out again and hit in the dirt beside Douglas's boot. He jumped back. "I'm not through with you, goddammit," Douglas muttered to Flair.

Without another glance toward Caden, Douglas held his injured arm to his side and ran back to his horse and mounted. "I'll see you in hell for this!" he called to Caden as he kicked his horse in the sides and galloped away.

Flair felt nervous, grateful, fearful for what Caden had done. She was trembling. Her legs were so weak she could hardly stand.

Caden took hold of Rich's arms and helped him off the horse. "Go see if your mother is all right. I'll put the horse away."

Flair opened her arms to Rich and he ran into them and hugged her passionately. Her arms ached as she squeezed her son tightly. She felt chilled even though the sun heated her skin with perspiration. Over Rich's shoulder she watched Caden spur his horse toward the barn. Yes, she'd go with Caden to Virginia. The sooner the better. She had to get Rich away from Douglas.

Six

Caden leaned against one of the front porch posts watching the sheriff and his deputy ride away. The officers' arrival had upset Flair at first, but Caden noticed she'd relaxed when the sheriff agreed that Douglas shouldn't have put his hands on her. Both of them expected the sheriff to arrest him for attempted murder. Caden hadn't cared much for the sheriff's reprimand about how he should have fired a warning shot. He would do it again if he had to.

It was a still black night. The small slice of moon offered no comforting light. Even the creatures of the dark were staying quiet tonight. Caden could use a good stiff drink.

Shooting Douglas wasn't one of the smartest things he'd ever done, but it was satisfying. When he'd ridden up and saw the bastard shaking Flair he went mad for a few moments. Douglas was right when he called him crazy. Only at the last second did he aim for the man's arm instead of his heart. It hadn't helped when Rich told him that wasn't the first time Douglas had grabbed her. It was no wonder Rich had met him at the door with a shotgun. Today probably wasn't the first time Douglas had shaken her either.

The bastard!

Caden half expected the sheriff to arrest him for attempted murder. Now he knew why Flair was so frightened of Douglas, and why she wanted to keep him away from her son. A flash of understanding pierced Caden. His stomach tightened. He quickly thought back to ten years ago when he first met Flair. He had always assumed they were lovers, but now he wasn't so sure. Caden suddenly found himself wanting to know what had gone on between Douglas and Flair.

Caden propped his foot up on the railing and stared out into the darkness, rubbing his chin as he pondered. He was getting in too deep with Flair and her son. What happened between Flair and Douglas ten years ago had nothing to do with him. It wouldn't do him any good to develop soft feelings for her until he'd talked with Shelton. His uncle's threat to leave Maxwell Farms to Jake had to be taken seriously. He knew the chance he was taking by insisting Flair and Rich accompany him.

But a moment later Caden knew he couldn't lie to himself. He not only wanted Flair to come to Virginia with him to prove to Shelton that he could make some decisions for himself, he wanted to spend more time with Flair. She was working her way into his life.

The door opened and he heard Flair come out. He turned around and looked at her. Light from inside the house behind her illuminated her hair, making her look like a golden-haired angel against the midnight sky. The white, high-necked blouse and the dark skirt complemented her straight shoulders and small waist. Caden felt a stirring in his manhood. He wanted to take her to bed and make love to her. What man wouldn't? Not only was she beautiful, she was strong and competent, yet soft and gentle. Why shouldn't he want her as a woman?

"Is Rich all right?" he asked, knowing it had to be upsetting for him to witness the shooting.

"Yes, he's fine," she answered in a soft voice. She moved closer to him. "He didn't say much, but I could tell he thought you very heroic."

Caden's chuckle was more of a snort of incredulity. He shook his head. Shooting a man out of rage wasn't heroic. "I'll explain to him tomorrow that usually a gun is the last choice, not the first, when you're trying to settle something."

"We both understand that, and I want to thank you for helping me."

"I'm glad you're not angry with me about it."

She shook her head. "I'm not," she said, wrapping her beige shawl around her shoulder. "I've decided to accept your offer. Rich and I will go to Virginia with you."

"I'm glad you've changed your mind. Douglas needs some time to cool off."

She nodded and turned to go back inside. Caden didn't want her to leave, so he took hold of her arm and said, "Wait just a—"

"Ouch! Ohh!" she cried out as he touched her.

Tears sprang to her eyes. Her shawl fell to the porch and she cupped her upper arm with her hand and held it close to her side.

"Flair, what's wrong? I barely touched you."

She turned away from him, but he saw her wiping her eyes with her fingertips.

"It's nothing, really. I—nothing."

She was lying and he knew why. Douglas had obviously hurt her when he shook her. His anger was renewed. "Nothing wouldn't make you cry out and bring tears to your eyes. Let me see."

"No."

"Flair."

She looked up at him, blinking. "No, I'd have to take my blouse off for you to see my arm."

He smiled understandingly. "I promise not to look at your underclothes, Flair. I want to see how badly he hurt you. Now turn around and let me unbutton your blouse."

Slowly Flair relented and turned her back to him.

Caden's fingers felt stiff as he unfastened the tiny buttons. He'd never helped a woman undress before. The women he visited were usually already undressed when he arrived. He didn't know much about being gentle with a woman. Shelton had taught him that a real man got in and out quickly. Only a weak man would linger with a woman once he'd laid her. But even though he didn't know much about women, something told him to take his time and be gentle with Flair.

With her help, he eased the sleeve of her blouse over her shoulder and down her arm, leaving it to dangle around her wrist. She held the front of her blouse to her chest with her other hand. From where he was standing all he saw was a pale, beautifully rounded shoulder, soft looking skin, and the wide strap of her white corset cover. He gently touched her waist and turned her arm to the dim lamplight coming from the open doorway. Four finger marks of deep purple and black showed on her upper arm.

"The other arm?" he questioned in a husky voice.

"It looks the same."

Caden looked down into her eyes. "I should have killed the bastard."

"No," she answered in a whispery voice. "The sheriff might have let you get by with wounding Douglas, but he wouldn't let you get away with killing him."

Their eyes met and Caden swallowed hard. He wanted to take her hurt away. He wanted to touch her soft skin. He wanted to kiss her beautiful lips. But he didn't want to frighten her. From the expression in her eyes, he couldn't tell if she'd accept or reject an advance from him. Without taking his gaze off hers, he reached over and softly kissed her bruise. When she didn't pull away from him, he closed his eyes and allowed himself the freedom to drop more soft, little kisses on top of her shoulder.

He felt her breathing increase and his lower body hardened. He let his lips glide across the injured skin and gently kiss the black and purple spots. His hand touched her arm ever so lightly, yet a chill of desire spiraled through him. Caden wet his lips with his tongue and softly kissed his way back up to the crest of her shoulder. He placed little raindrop kisses over her cotton strap to the junction of her neck and shoulder. That warm spot made him want to pull her close and snuggle into her embrace. She smelled of rose water. He had to taste her. He stuck out his tongue and lightly licked the tender, tangy skin. He heard her intake of breath when he cupped her neck with his hand. Her subtle reactions to his touch set him on fire and he grew hard fast. The pulse point in her neck beat rapidly against his thumb. He felt his own body pulsating in rhythm with hers.

Caden moistened his lips again and gently let them glide up the column of her throat, over her jawline, across her chin. When his lips reached the corner of her mouth, she gasped. Whirling away from him, she fled into the darkness on the other side of the porch, pulling her blouse up on her shoulder as she went.

Flair trembled as she reached behind her back to fasten her buttons. She couldn't believe she'd allowed Caden such freedom to touch her, to kiss her. How could she have fallen victim to his gentle persuasion? Had she no shame? Had ten years ago taught her nothing? She had to stay away from Caden Maxwell. She had to.

"It's all right, Flair. It was only a kiss. You don't have to be frightened," he said, moving to the end of the porch where she stood.

"I'm not," she answered, thankful her voice sounded normal. "I trusted a man's kisses once, and I'll never do that again."

He touched her cheek with the backs of his fingers. "Do you want to talk—"

"Don't." She jerked her head away from his touch, causing him to interrupt his sentence. "Just don't touch me again and we'll get along fine together."

"All right, if that's the way you want it. I'm not going to force you to do anything you don't want to do."

Those words chilled her as she hurried back into the house. Force her? No, she'd die before another man forced her.

Booker sat in a straight chair in front of the unlit fireplace clad only in his breeches, patting his rounded stomach. He'd raised the front legs of the chair off the floor and rocked back and forth on the hind legs. His bare feet scrubbed on the wood floor, the slightly scratching motion feeling good to his soles.

The oil lamp sitting on the mantel burned low, casting a dim, shadowy light around the room. The open window brought in night air just cool enough to make him comfortable. He heard his father softly singing a song about the good Lord as he prepared for bed on the other side of the room.

Something was missing in his life, Booker thought as he rocked. His clothes were clean, his stomach full. He'd rested from the day's work. He wasn't ready to go to sleep, but what else was there to do? He and Samp had grown tired of playing checkers and throwing darts in the evenings, something they used to do regularly. A year or so ago he'd suggested they switch to playing cards but his father insisted the game was invented by the devil and wouldn't play with him. But Booker knew games were not what he needed when the day's work was done. He wanted the company, the companionship, the softness of a woman. He loved his father, but he needed things his father couldn't give him.

His thoughts turned to the woman he'd seen that day in town. He wondered who she was. Ohhh—she was a beautiful woman with eyes as dark as a midnight sky in the dead of winter. A more luscious looking woman he hadn't seen. He laid his head back and brought her face to his mind's eye again.

He guessed her age to be a year or two younger than his. When he'd looked at her and she'd smiled at him, his stomach felt like it turned over a couple of times, then tied itself in a knot. He thought for sure he'd go crazy if he didn't find out who she was and how he could go about seeing her again.

"You coming to bed?" Samp called to him.

Booker set the chair down straight. His father made a grunting noise as he lowered himself to the bed. The framing squeaked. "Not yet. I'm not sleepy." He rose. "I think I'll take a walk. You want to come along?"

Samp chortled, truly amused. "No. Morning comes too early for me as it is. I'll just stay here and rest my bones. Don't forget to let the windows down. I think I heard thunder."

Stopping at the open doorway Booker turned back and called to his father, "Pa, do you think Miss Flair will let me use the mare on Sunday?"

He heard Samp sit up in bed. "What do you have on your mind, son?"

"Nothing. I just thought I'd ride over to the Miller farm and talk with their workers. I get tired of talking to you all the time, Pa."

Samp grumbled something under his breath. Booker didn't know what he said, but he knew his father didn't believe he spoke the whole truth. He didn't want to tell Samp what was really on his mind. Booker wanted to find out about that pretty young woman he'd seen in town a few weeks ago. He was ready to do some serious courting and get himself a woman.

"Well what about it?" he called. "Do you think she'll let me use the mare?"

"I don't see why not. She don't ever go nowhere on it, 'cept into town on Saturdays. But I 'spect you better ask her husband now that he's back. I guess he'll be making that kind of decision from now on. Wouldn't surprise me."

Booker nodded to himself. His pa was right. He'd speak to the white man, and if he said no, he wouldn't push it. Not after what he did to Mr. Eagerton. No, Caden Maxwell wasn't a man he wanted to tangle with.

Seven

When the wagon rolled into town Flair knew word had gotten around the community that her husband was back. Caden pulled the horse to a stop in front of the mercantile. The boardwalk was crowded with people, the dusty streets littered with horses, wagons, and carriages. The only other time Flair could remember seeing so many people in town was the Fourth of July picnic held each summer. This Saturday, it seemed everyone wanted to see Flair's husband. Some of the men and women openly stared while others hid behind conversation, fans, and parasols as they stood together in small groups. No doubt they'd all heard about his altercation with Douglas and had come out to catch a glimpse of Caden.

Flair allowed Caden to help her down. His warm touch around her waist gave her comfort and strength to face the townspeople. In truth, they probably didn't expect her to be conventional. She hadn't been since she married Caden and had a child seven months later. Over the years her neighbors had remained polite but not friendly.

As her feet touched the ground she looked up into Caden's eyes. He gave her a smile and squeezed her lightly before letting his fingers slide from around her. A quickening started in her stomach. She wondered if it was from Caden's touch or the fact that she felt every eye in town staring at them. She had lived through the townspeople staring at her once before, and she would now.

"Don't worry," Caden said. "Everything's going to be fine."

She returned his smile and nodded.

Rich jumped from the wagon and ran over to Flair. He tugged on the hem of her short cape and asked, "Can I go inside and look at the marbles?"

Flair stepped away from Caden and looked at her son. There was no reason for her to be nervous, but she was. In order for their plan to work it was important that everyone believe she and Caden planned to stay married.

"It's *may* I go and yes, you may, but take a basket of these turnip roots and greens in with you." She reached in the back of the wagon and handed him a small basket. Rich took off toward the mercantile to deliver his produce and stare at the jar of marbles on the countertop inside.

Flair reached for one of the larger baskets, but Caden put his hand on top of hers. "I'll take care of this. Go on inside and do whatever shopping you need to do."

His large, warm hand completely covered hers. For a moment she wanted to leave her hand there and let his strength, his toughness seep into her skin. She glanced up at him. His eyes seemed to be challenging her but she didn't know why.

She slipped her hand from under his and moved it farther over on the basket handle. "I've been carrying these baskets inside since my father died three years ago, and I'll continue when you're no longer here." She lifted the basket from the wagon at the same time Caden took the basket away from her.

He peered down at her. "All you said is true. But you won't be carrying them while I'm here. Now get your shopping done."

The expression on his face told her there was no use arguing. She wouldn't win this one. She nodded and turned away. From the corner of her eye she saw three women staring at her, but she kept walking toward the store. It didn't matter what the people of the town thought of her. It never had. From the moment she'd realized she was pregnant, she'd done what she thought was right and best for her son.

Mrs. Simpson who'd taught her the six years she'd gone to school stopped her on the boardwalk and talked as if they were close friends. She asked about Rich and his schooling, and if there was any way she could help with it. Clyde Benjamin's wife joined them. When Caden walked up to the mercantile with two baskets in his hands Flair excused herself and opened the door for him. Caden put the produce down and went back to the wagon for more.

"Good morning, Mrs. Mead. How are you today?" Flair smiled at the gray-haired woman behind the counter.

"Morning, Flair," Mrs. Mead responded, but let her gaze linger on Caden as he walked out. "I don't guess I can complain." She looked Flair over as if expecting her to be different. "I heard your husband was back. I suspect you're right proud of that. It's been a long time."

No one knew more about how long it had been than Flair. She wished people wouldn't act like they knew what she'd gone through. They didn't. Swallowing her apprehension, she turned a bright face toward the store owner and said, "Yes. Caden will bring the rest of the baskets inside while I pick up a few things."

She touched Rich's shoulder as she walked by the marble jar, heading to the back of the store where the men's ready-made trousers were shelved to pick out a pair each for Booker and Samp. Spring was a good time to give them a new suit of clothes. She heard Mrs. Mead speak a greeting to Caden. His answer was polite but not friendly. Flair stayed busy looking through the clothes. She quickly settled on the sizes and picked up the other things she needed, including shaving soap for Caden, before walking back up to the front of the store.

"That husband of yours looks healthy enough. I guess he wasn't dead after all," Mrs. Mead said.

Flair supposed it was natural for the townspeople to assume he was dead when he never came back to claim his bride and son. And she had to admit she wondered what had kept him away all these years. Why did he suddenly need a divorce? Was it as she first thought, a woman? Or was there something else?

"No, as you can see, he's very much alive."

"It's a good thing he came back."

Not knowing exactly what the older woman meant by that remark, Flair simply said, "Yes."

She laid her supplies on the counter and said, "Could you please add these to my account?"

Mrs. Mead glanced down at the men's clothing, the shaving soap, the length of dark forest green material, and the sack of flour. She lifted her head and looked out the front window to Caden who was working in the wagon, then settled her gaze on Flair.

"Flair, you know I've always bought my produce from you, and your father before you."

The tremor in the woman's voice and the twitching in her eyes sent a warning chill of fear up Flair's back. She felt as if a cold hand had taken hold of her and wouldn't let go. "Yes. And you know I've always been grateful to—"

"Wait," she said, holding up her hand. She picked up the hem of her apron and twisted it between her fingers. "I—I have something to tell you that you're not going to like. I've been offered the same produce I buy from you for quite a bit less than what I have to pay you and I've decided to take it."

Stunned, Flair's eyes widened and her body stiffened as she tried to hide her shock. A twinge of panic bubbled inside her, but she forced it down. This couldn't be true. She needed the money she received from selling the produce. Flair took a step away from the counter, trying not to react too strongly until she knew what was going on. "But I don't understand. What's wrong? Mrs. Mead, I'm always on time, and I give you only the best and freshest vegetables from my garden."

The woman's bottom lip trembled and her voice wavered as she said, "I know all that. Don't think this wasn't hard for me. Your land makes the best sweet potatoes, greens, and corn anywhere in these parts, but I've got to think of myself." Her fingers worked nervously against the fabric of the apron. Her eyes shifted restlessly from Flair, to Caden, to Rich.

"With Mr. Mead dying last year and all, I've got to think of myself. I sure could use the extra money. Anyway, you have your husband here to help you now. He'll take care of you. And well—that's all I have to say." Mrs. Mead dropped the tail of her apron and squared her shoulders as she looked pointedly into Flair's eyes. "I'll be buying from someone else now."

Like a rush of wind it hit Flair what had happened. Anger surged within her, robbing her of breath. She didn't even try to calm her racing heartbeat. "By someone you mean Douglas Eagerton, don't you, Mrs. Mead?"

It was Mrs. Mead's turn to look surprised. "Yes. How did you know?"

Flair took a deep breath, trying to calm her pounding heart, smooth her breathing, steady her shaky legs. Douglas had told her he would get even. As if sensing something was wrong, Rich moved over to stand beside Flair. She laid her hand on his shoulder. She swallowed and moistened her lips. "Did you pick out the marble you want, Rich?" she asked, trying to sound normal. How could she when she knew how badly this news would hurt them?

The vegetables she sold to Mr. Riggs at the hotel and Mr. Cockran at the saloon barely paid her farm expenses. What she made from the mercantile gave her money for all the extras they enjoyed like new shoes and clothes and Rich's school books. Another chill shook her. Her hand trembled as she raked her fingers through her son's dusty brown hair.

Rich moved his head away from her and said, "They don't have any new ones, Mama. Guess I won't get one today."

She smiled even though her stomach churned with anxiety. "Maybe next time she'll have new ones. Now you run outside and tell Caden I'll be right there."

When Rich cleared the door she turned back to Mrs. Mead. She tensed so tightly she could hardly breathe. She didn't want to argue with the woman, but she couldn't accept this news without a fight. She deserved a chance to compete. Desperately, she said, "I need your business. I'll match whatever price Douglas has quoted you."

Mrs. Mead's expression relaxed into a sorrowful one. "You can't match his price, Flair. He's practically giving his stuff away. You know I wouldn't have accepted his offer if I thought you could do better."

The knot in her stomach tightened. She glanced out the window, afraid any moment that Caden was going to come inside and catch her falling apart. Flair fumbled with the bonnet ribbon under her chin. "Mrs. Mead, you know how important your account is to our farm. I depend on it."

The woman picked up her pencil and started writing on a piece of paper. Not looking up at Flair she said, "I feel better about this knowing your husband's back. He'll help you find someone else. Now I'll get all this written down. Do you want to wait while I figure this so we can settle up. Unless you want to buy more supplies today I think I'm going to owe you some money back."

Mrs. Mead didn't know that Caden didn't plan to be around for long. And Flair couldn't tell her. Even if she did, the woman's mind was made up. She wasn't going to change it. For eight years her farm had supplied the mercantile's produce and now Mrs. Mead was letting her go. The silence between them grew. Flair hated to accept defeat without fighting harder, but how could she when she understood Mrs. Mead's position? She glanced out the window again and saw Caden lift Rich into the wagon.

"No, I don't have time to wait. I have other deliveries to make. Just credit my account." She picked up her purchases and hurried out the door.

Caden met her at the wagon, took the things from her, and handed them to Rich. She remained quiet while Caden helped her onto the wagon.

"Are you all right?" Caden asked as he climbed up beside her. "You're looking kind of pale and trembly."

She moistened her lips and tried to breathe deeply. Her throat was too tight. "I'm fine," she lied, not wanting Rich or Caden to know what had happened until she'd had time to get herself under control. "The next stop is right down the street at the hotel."

Flair kept her back straight and her head forward as they started down the road, but from her peripheral vision she saw the open stares, the quick glances, and the nods of greeting as they rode past the people on the street.

* * *

Later that night Flair sat on the front porch swing, staring out into the darkness. Night birds chirped, crickets sang to their mates, and leaves rustled against the spring wind. An occasional squeak from the recently oiled swing was the only unnatural sound to disturb the peaceful night. The air was breezy and comfortable, but Flair still felt flushed with the heat of anger and she burned from deep-seated disappointment. Midnight sky blanketed the night with a soothing feeling, offering a measure of comfort. Flair unbuttoned her dark coppery-colored vest and the first three buttons of her blouse, hoping it would help cool her heated skin.

Mrs. Mead's news had been so devastating that when Mr. Riggs and Mr. Cockran had told her they'd accepted Douglas's offer she'd hardly blinked an eye.

After supper Caden had walked down to the pond for a swim while she put Rich to bed. It appeared she'd been able to fool Caden and Rich into thinking nothing was wrong while in truth she had worried all afternoon about who she could sell their summer and fall vegetables to.

If she went to Virginia with Caden what would Samp and Booker do with the summer crops? The only thing she could think to do was stay and find customers in a nearby town. If she did that, what would she do about Douglas wanting to take Rich away from her. She didn't think the note she wrote ten years ago would hold up in court if Douglas decided to try it, but it would hurt Rich if the story got around town.

Flair gently rocked the swing back and forth as she closed her eyes and remembered seeing Mr. Riggs stroking his long, gray-streaked beard. "I'm not saying it's fair, missy. I'm saying, I wouldn't have taken his offer if I thought you could match it and not lose money. I don't mind taking Eagerton's crop for nothing, but I can't do that to you. Your pa was my friend. Looks like your husband came back to town just in time."

A whistling sounded in the distance and Flair jerked her head up. Realizing her eyes were wet she quickly wiped them dry with the backs of her hands. She wouldn't allow herself to turn into a crying, foolish woman. Hadn't she learned years ago that crying didn't solve any problem? She had too many things to do, starting with trying to find a way to hold up her end of the bargain she'd made with the man fast approaching the porch.

"I didn't expect to see you out here." Caden climbed the steps and walked over to stand in front of her.

Flair touched her toe to the floor and started the seat to swinging. His wet, wavy hair had been smoothed away from his forehead. He'd left his clean white shirt unbuttoned to the waist. Her gaze strayed down the V of taut skin. She tried not to look, but even in the darkness she saw a patch of dark, curly hair that ran from the base of his throat to his waist. A wave of awareness drenched her.

"I'm not tired," she lied and realized she often told the man half-truths or simple little lies. She didn't mean to, but how could she blurt out that her whole world had been turned upside down because of his and Douglas's reappearance in her life.

"Mind if I join you?" he asked.

"N-no." She grabbed her burnished copper-colored skirt and moved to the other end of the swing, giving him as much room as possible. She didn't like the places her thoughts wandered to whenever he was close to her. She didn't want to feel those little prickles of desire that wormed their way into her being.

"I noticed we received a lot of stares in town today. By now most everyone knows I'm back."

"The townspeople had already heard. I'm

sure that's why there were so many people in town. What you did to Douglas isn't the kind of thing people keep quiet about," she responded softly as she looked over his shoulder to the night sky.

"A smart man knows better than to put his hands on another man's wife."

She wanted to say, "I'm not really your wife," but decided against stating the obvious and remained quiet. From where they sat on the porch she could see a few scattered stars, but not the moon. The night was dark, but a little light from within the house shone through the window. In the dim light she could see his face. He looked relaxed, content and that surprised her. He had no guarantee she'd give him the divorce.

"The trip into town and all the people, is that what's made you so quiet this evening?"

"Have I been quiet?" she asked. She'd thought she'd actually talked too much during dinner while trying hard to appear normal.

"Do stars twinkle?" he countered with a hint of a smile.

Flair laughed lightly at his attempt to lighten her mood. "I think you almost smiled at me." At her remark he gave her a full smile.

Her breath caught in her throat, her cheeks heated again. She was immensely attracted to him. "I didn't mean to be so quiet," she offered softly. "It's just that I have a lot of things to think about, to worry about."

"I suppose you do. Neither of us knew what problems our actions of ten years ago would create for us today."

"No. It took care of my problem at the time, and I've been so grateful to you over the years. The townspeople may not have gone out of their way to welcome me into their homes, but they haven't blacklisted me." Flair's voice ended in a whisper. How could she tell Caden how grateful she was in one breath and tell him she couldn't honor their agreement in the next? She owed this man. But how could she go away this spring and summer and leave her farmhands with nowhere to sell her crop? If she didn't stay and work something out she wouldn't have a home to come back to.

He reached up and wiped her eye with his thumb. "Are you crying?"

"No. Of course not." She'd smelled the freshness of clean skin as his hand moved past her nose. She moved away from his touch, farther into the end of the swing. The tender flesh around her eye tingled where he had touched her. It was as if she felt his thumb long after it was gone.

"Are you sure? Were you crying before I came up?"

"No, I haven't been crying." He was too perceptive, too attractive, too gentle. "I might as well tell you that I don't believe I can go with you to Virginia."

"We have a deal." His tone and expression hardened. Gone was the man who'd teased her about twinkling stars.

"I know."

"I don't let people welsh on deals, Flair. I expect you to keep your word."

"You don't understand. Some things have changed." She didn't want to tell Caden what Douglas had done. He'd shot him for grabbing hold of her. She didn't want him going after Douglas again.

"Not your word. You don't change that."

She looked at him in the semi-darkness. "I'm needed on the farm."

"I thought we'd settled that Booker and Samp could handle things here on the farm." He shifted in the swing, making it rock back and forth.

"They can take care of the farm, but who will take care of them," she answered, suddenly a bit angry at him. If he hadn't shot Douglas he might not have made good on his threat to hurt her. "I cook for them and do their wash."

"We'll hire someone to look after them. There's something you're not telling me. What's the real reason you've changed your mind and decided you don't want to go?"

Caden took hold of her shoulders gently, careful not to touch where she was bruised and forced her to look at him. Frightened by his action she said in a rush of words, "Douglas has taken all my customers away from me."

As if realizing he'd scared her, he let her go. "What do you mean?"

"Today in town they all told me. He offered them prices they couldn't afford to turn down, and I couldn't afford to match. Now I have no one to sell my summer crops to. I've got to stay here and try to get customers in other towns. I may have to drive into Mobile."

"Don't worry about that. Let Douglas sell his vegetables for a pittance. He deserves no better. I'll find other buyers for you."

His easy dismissal of what Douglas had done to her rankled. "You make it sound so easy." Her voice was heavy with irritation. She sat up straight in the swing.

"You'll go with me, Flair. I'll take Booker and Samp into Mobile, and we'll find someone to sell your crops to. Come what may you and Rich will go to Virginia with me at the end of next week."

Flair thought about trying harder to make him see her side, but remembered the reason she'd decided to go was to get Rich away from Douglas. Realizing she had to put her trust in him made her shudder. She rose. "All right. I'll explain everything to Booker and Samp. Good night, Caden." She hurried into the house.

Late in the afternoon of the next day Flair walked down the path that led to Booker's and Samp's house less than a fourth of a mile from her back door. In her arms she held the new spring clothes she'd bought for them and a basket containing their supper. The door was open so she knocked on the framing.

She had to admit to herself that she liked the idea of seeing another part of the country and doing something different for a change. But on the other hand she worried about what living at Caden's house would do to Rich. What would she do if he became attached to Caden?

Samp appeared in the doorway. "Afternoon, Miss Flair. Here, let me help you with all that stuff." He took the basket and clothes from her and set them down inside the house before stepping outside.

Booker came down the front steps behind him. "Afternoon, Miss Flair."

"Hello, Booker," she answered with a smile to the young man.

"I brought your supper and some new clothes for you. I've already hemmed the trousers, but if you think anything else needs to be done just bring them back tomorrow morning."

"You didn't have to come all the way down here to take care of this for us. We'd been up there for our supper in a spell," Samp told her as he rubbed the bottom of one bare foot on top of the other.

"I didn't mind because there's something I have to tell you." She raked her hands down the front of her dress. "I'm going away for a while."

"Where you going?" Booker asked, drawing his thick eyebrows together.

Samp gave Booker a small whack in the stomach with the back of his hand. "It ain't none of your business where she going. Now mind your manners."

Flair smiled to reassure Booker that he hadn't done anything wrong by asking. "Caden wants Rich and me to go with him to his home in Virginia."

"Forever, Miss Flair?" Booker asked.

"No, of course not. I couldn't leave my father's land—Rich's land." Deep feelings of home rushed through her. She turned her attention to Samp before she embarrassed herself by becoming weepy. She might not want to leave, but it was best she take Rich away from Douglas's reach until he cooled off.

"Do you think the two of you can handle everything while I'm away."

"Oh, yes ma'am."

"Yes'em, we can." They both spoke at the same time.

"Good. Things have changed around here and in town. I won't go into all of it right now because Caden will be discussing all this with you in the next few days. The next time I go into town I'll see if Mrs. Mead knows of anyone who can come in and care for the house and cook and wash for you while I'm away. If not, maybe Mr. Crockran or Mr. Riggs will be able to help me find someone who needs to work."

"Don't you worry about us, Miss Flair," Samp said, rubbing his hand over his closely cropped hair. "I can cook. Done it many times. Booker here can take our clothes down to the pond once in a while and wash 'em. No need to trouble yourself looking for someone."

"I don't know anything about—" Booker started but was caught in the middle once again by the back of his father's hand to his midriff. He gave Samp a "why did you do that" look but said, "Don't worry, Miss Flair. We'll take care of everything. No need to worry 'bout us."

"I know. I trust you both completely. I don't think I'll be gone past summer, but I'll send word later and let you know."

"Miss Flair," Booker asked, "Do you mind if we use the mare on Sundays while you're gone?"

"Of course not. Feel free to use the horse and the wagon anytime you need it."

A broad, excited grin flew to Booker's face. "Thank you, Miss Flair. We heard tell there's a church for us colored folks over by Wilson's pond. Thought we might go over there and have a look around."

A smile of satisfaction spread across her face. All of a sudden she felt better about leaving the farm in their care. "I think that's a wonderful idea."

Booker clapped his father on the shoulder and said, "Those new clothes sure came at a good time, didn't they, Pa?"

Samp rubbed his chin thoughtfully. "Yes sir, they did at that."

Eight

The house was quiet when he opened the door and stepped inside. Caden had ridden ahead of the carriage carrying Flair and Rich. He wanted time to talk to Shelton and let him explode before they arrived. On the long trip from south Alabama to Virginia he'd decided what he was going to say to his uncle. Shelton would be mad as hell but after he cooled down he hoped the sickly man approved of him taking matters into his own hands. Shelton liked a show of strength. And Caden couldn't help but think that after he got used to Rich, he'd enjoy having the nine-year-old boy in the house.

He started to call out that he was home, but decided against that. Instead he hung his hat on the tree stand in the corner and walked down the hallway, assuming Shelton was in his office at the back of the center-hallway styled ranch house.

When he rounded the corner of the doorway he stopped dead still. Jake sat behind Shelton's desk. Shock and anger hit him. He stiffened. Obviously Shelton wasn't in the house, or Jake wouldn't be so presumptuous.

"What in the hell are you doing in that chair?

Jake looked up from the paperwork in front of him and leaned back in the chair, placing his hands behind his head. He grinned. "Somebody has to do the work around here. Who else would you have suggested?"

An uneasy feeling crawled over Caden. He gave Jake a hard look. "Where's Shelton?"

Jake looked out the window and nodded. "Out there six feet under. He's dead. Sorry you missed the funeral," he said with no emotion in his voice.

Caden's heart seemed to stop. "What did you say?" he asked huskily as he stared blank faced into Jake's steel gray eyes, but he knew he hadn't misunderstood the foreman.

"Shelton died two weeks ago."

His brows drew together, but Caden managed to control any other show of emotion. His heart beat rapidly in his chest. A physical pain attacked his stomach as he strove to remain unaffected outwardly. "How?" Thank God he sounded normal as he asked the question.

Jake remained in his relaxed position. "A

couple of days after you left Silas took him out for a ride in the carriage. The skies were clear when they left, but a sudden thunderstorm came up catching them quite a ways from the house. Shelton got drenched before Silas could get him inside. He took a chill and fever that developed into a bad cough. Before we knew it he was gone." Jake straightened in the chair. "When it was clear he wasn't getting any better no one knew how to get in touch with you, not even Shelton. Rutherford told me to continue taking care of the farm until you or Pauline showed."

Caden turned away. Shelton was gone. Damn he wished he was alone. Some of the old feelings he'd felt when his parents died assailed him. He tried to shake them off, but couldn't. Shelton wasn't an easy man to work for or to live with, but Caden hadn't wanted him to die.

He swallowed hard, taking control of those unwanted feelings. Shelton would be the last person who'd want anyone to mourn his death. But the truth was Caden did. And it surprised him. The two of them had their problems, and Shelton had done a lot of things over the years that Caden didn't like, but he could count on Shelton to be consistent. He never changed, not even after he became ill. And consistent was one thing Caden had never been. He was always trying to be the man Shelton wanted him to be and seldom measuring up to his uncle's expectations. The last thing he could do for Shelton was handle his death like the man Shelton always wanted him to be.

He turned to Jake. Clenching his teeth, he said in a deadly quiet tone, "Get out of that chair. As far as I know I'm Shelton's heir. That's my chair."

"Maybe. Maybe not. Rutherford wired Shelton's sister. She and *her* son, Shelton's *other nephew*, should be arriving any day now for the reading of the will. Rutherford is holding off until everyone is present."

The contents of the will worried Caden, but he wasn't about to let Jake know that. What did it say? Had Shelton kept his promise? "I'm here and they're not." Caden took a step toward the desk, giving Jake a hostile stare. "Now get out of that chair."

"Whatever you say goes—*Bossman*." Jake placed his hands on the arms of the chair and rose. He casually walked past Caden and away from the desk.

Caden didn't want to leave Jake any doubt as to his position on the farm. Jake was worker. That was all. "There's a carriage on its way here. Go out and tell Benny to watch for it and to help the driver with the luggage when it arrives."

Caught off guard by Caden's sudden order, Jake cut his eyes around to Caden. "Who's coming?"

Caden turned a sardonic expression on Jake. "My wife and son."

Jake reared back his shoulders, an incredulous look on his face. "Dammit, Cade, you can't be serious."

"I'm as serious as I can be," he answered nonchalantly as he walked behind the desk and sat down.

"You're bringing that woman you married years ago here to Shelton's house knowing how he felt about her?" Jake's look was one of scalding fury.

"That's right." He lowered his eyes to the papers Jake had been working on, seeming to have no regard for Shelton's feelings.

"I can't believe you'd bring her here." Vehemence shadowed his words. "You were supposed to divorce her, not bring her back with you."

Caden didn't like being questioned or lectured by Jake. "You just said it. Shelton is dead. I'm in charge."

"But you didn't know that. If the pneumonia hadn't gotten him this would have." Jake paused. "Maybe that's what you had in mind."

Caden looked up at Jake with murderous eyes. "Watch your mouth," he said, barely keeping his temper under control. "My relationship with Shelton has nothing to do with you. Now, I believe you have work to do."

Picking up his hat Jake mumbled loudly under his breath, "It's your life."

"And my wife. You'd do well to remember that."

Jake looked at him contemptuously before he turned and walked out.

Caden let his shoulders drop as he heard Jake's boots retreating on the hardwood floor. He held his breath and listened until the front door opened and shut with a bang. Caden propped his elbows on the desk and let his head fall into his hands.

He realized he was shaking. What was he going to do if Shelton had left the farm to Jake or Pauline's son? Caden wiped his hands down his face. No, Shelton might have left the farm to Jake because of Flair, but he'd bet his life Shelton hadn't left Stewart more than a few horses.

"Mr. Caden, I was upstairs and heard the door slam. I didn't know it was you. Have you heard about Mr. Maxwell?"

He looked up at the robust, gray-haired woman who had been brave enough to work for Shelton. "Yes, Bernie. Jake was in here and he told me."

She walked farther into the room. Her eyes clouded with tears. "It was a hard thing to do—watching him suffer like that. No man should have to go like that. Once the fever hit his lungs, he didn't want to live any more."

Caden felt for her. He knew she'd loved Shelton like a brother, much more than his real sister. "Did he have any last words for me?"

Slowly she shook her head. "No, sir. Mr. Rutherford was the only one he asked to see. The lawyer spent a lot of time with Mr. Maxwell the last two days."

An inexplicable feeling of disappointment cut through him, but he quickly denied it. He shouldn't have expected anything from Shelton. His uncle had never needed him. No reason to think he would have wanted him by his deathbed.

Caden took a deep breath and looked up at Bernie, wiping all traces of sorrow from his face and his heart. "A carriage will be arriving shortly. You'll need to prepare two rooms. One for my wife and one for my son."

Dust flew around the carriage as they pulled up to the large two-story ranch house of Maxwell Farms. A fair-haired young man came running up to assist Flair. She held up her skirts and allowed him to help her down. She stood awe-struck as she scanned the gently rolling hills lush with greenery in the distance beyond the house. There were horses, more horses than Flair had ever seen, grazing on the hillside. A big white barn with black shutters stood behind the house. The sky was the most beautiful shade of blue she'd ever seen. It seemed fuller, richer, deeper than the light blue skies with their wisps of puffy white clouds over south Alabama.

Flair turned around, looking at everything her eyesight could take in. Why hadn't Caden told her Maxwell Farms was so big? The wealth of the place showed in the upkeep of the house with its gleaming coat of white paint, neatly trimmed shrubs, and vast garden of flowers. It was no wonder he didn't want her thirty acres of land. The more she looked, the angrier she became. He should have told her he lived so well.

Her gaze scanned the hillside again. She'd seen the signs but she'd ignored them. He rode an excellent horse. His saddle was made from the finest of leather. Caden's clothes were expensive and expertly made. He spoke like an educated man. Her hands made fists. She should have known his house would look like this. She'd been so caught up in her own problems that she'd failed to realize Caden Maxwell came from wealth.

"Mom, can I go to the fence and watch the horses, can I?" Rich asked, fairly jumping up and down with excitement.

"It's may I go and the answer is no. I think you should help our driver and this nice young man with our luggage."

She looked over at the short, stocky young man who was busy untying the bindings on their trunks and lifting them off the back of the carriage.

He gave her a wide, bright-eyed grin. "Oh, no ma'am. I'll take care of this for you. You let the boy go on and watch them horses." He turned to Rich. "Just don't you go over that fence. Stay on this side."

"I promise." Rich smiled up at his mother before he took off running.

Flair needed time to get her breath, to get herself together. She wished Caden had prepared her for this. Maybe he would have if she'd been a bit friendlier to him before they left. She and Rich had nice clothes for the town they lived in, but in a house like this she was afraid their clothes would be too simple.

"Come on in here out of that boiling sun," a woman's voice called.

Flair looked over to the front of the house

and saw a hearty-looking woman standing on the porch motioning for her to come forward. She wore a high-necked black dress with a gray bib apron.

"Go on," the young man said. "That's Miss Bernie. She takes care of the house. I'll have all this inside for you in no time at all."

"Thank you. Oh, and, could you keep an eye on Rich and make sure he doesn't cross the fence. He loves horses."

"Yes, ma'am I'll see to it."

The woman's face fairly beamed as Flair started toward her. "I'm Bernice, Mrs. Maxwell, but everybody here calls me Bernie."

"I'm pleased to meet you, Miss Bernie. I'm Flair Bowen—Maxwell." It was strange that even after ten years of marriage she still forgot her last name had changed because she'd so seldom had a reason to use it.

Bernie laughed huskily. Her rounded cheeks disappeared into her double chin and caused her banded collar to roll down. "I know who you are. Mr. Cade told me to look after you and see you get settled in. Course, I guess I'll start calling him Mr. Maxwell now that his uncle, God rest his soul, is dead." She placed a finger to her bottom lip and seemed to study the idea for a moment. "I need to ask him about that. I'm not sure what he wants to be called."

Flair realized Bernie must have been talking to herself because she had no idea what the woman was talking about. Apparently Caden's uncle had recently died.

"Mr. Caden told me all about how you would be staying here with your son. I have your rooms ready. Now come on inside. It's a long ride from town. I'm making fresh coffee for you. We'll give your son something to drink when he comes inside. Those young ones can take the heat better than we can. What's his name?"

"Richmond," Flair said, following the broad-shouldered woman inside. "But we call him Rich."

"Can't argue with a name that sounds like that." She chuckled again. "Guess everyone would like to be rich."

Flair stepped out of the hot sun and into the coolness of a large tiled foyer. At a glance her eyes took in the white-painted embossed wallpaper. The frieze underneath the crown molding had a gold-tipped medallion which matched the anaglyphic wall covering. A small sofa covered in a velvety flower print sat in a corner, a marble-topped rosewood end table stood beside it.

Bernie stopped inside an arched doorway leading off the grand foyer. "Wait here in the parlor. Take your bonnet off and just lay it on the table. I'll take care of it later. I'll be back in just a minute with something for you to drink."

"Ah—wait, Miss Bernie."

"Oh stop that proper nonsense," she waved her hand at Flair. "The only people who call me Miss Bernie are the hired hands around here. You and your son call me Bernie same way Mr. Maxwell, God rest his soul, and Mr. Caden do."

"All right, Bernie," she said, stepping into the parlor. "Do you know where Caden is now? I'd like to speak to him."

"He took off almost as soon as he got here. Said he had business to take care of but told me to tell you he'd see you for dinner at seven."

"Did he—I mean Mr. Maxwell, did he die while Caden was away."

Bernie nodded slowly. "A shame it was. Took a chill after he got caught out in the rain. Never recovered. God rest his soul. Of course, he'd been poorly for more than a year."

"I'm sorry to hear that." She couldn't take Caden to task over not telling her about his lifestyle when he'd just heard about his uncle's death. Even though she wanted to give him a piece of her mind she'd let it pass and do the best she could to fit into his household.

The housekeeper looked up at her with sorrow in her eyes. "I can't help but feel it was for the best. But we won't speak of such things right now. Tell me what you need and I'll get it for you."

Flair looked around the room. "Does Caden dress for dinner?"

"Oh my, yes. Mr. Maxwell, God rest his soul, and Mr. Caden always wear their best for dinner. I'll lay out your dresses for you as soon as Benny gets your trunks inside. When you decide which one you want to wear tonight, I'll have it pressed for you."

Flair's fears about Caden's household were true. "Thank you," she murmured softly.

"Now, I'll get you something to drink and you can rest, or look around the house or whatever you'd like to do before dinner."

Feeling as if Caden hadn't been honest with her, Flair untied the ribbons of her bonnet and took it off as Bernie hurried out of the room. A quick glance around the parlor showed her no expense had been spared to make the house beautiful and comfortable. The claret red walls were accented by wide baseboard and crown molding painted a pristine white. Flair ran her hand over the dusty rose velvet cushion of the settee and felt the excellent quality of the material. Beige marble topped all the tables and the mantel, too.

Flair walked around the spacious room looking over and touching the lovely accent pieces of crystal and china. She felt out of place yet comfortable in the house. She wondered how that could be. She and her father had always had nice things but not the beautiful woodwork, opulent brass, and gilt and crystal things that graced Caden's home. She had never dressed for dinner, in fact she always cooked it. What had Caden thought those nights when he sat down to dinner with her and Rich, the three of them dressed in the clothes they'd worn all day?

No use worrying about that now, she thought lifting her chin. Caden had adjusted and sat comfortably at her table. She would adjust to his. She only had two dresses suitable for dinner, her dark blue with two rows of white lace at the collar and sleeves, and her burgundy-colored skirt and white lace blouse with three satin bows at the neckline. She'd have to make do with those until she could make another. Thank goodness she'd had the presence of mind to bring with her the forest green fabric she'd purchased the last time she was in town. If she chose the pattern carefully, she would have enough material to make a plain skirt to go with her white lace blouse and a one-piece dress. And she might as well get started on it as soon as she had her refreshment and checked on Rich.

Flair walked over to the window and looked out at the green hillside. She worried whether she was doing the right thing for Rich. Her son's welfare had to come first. But had she taken him away from Douglas only to have him hurt by Caden when he divorced her? It was difficult to know the right thing to do.

"Caden, come in. I was wondering when you were going to get back in town, ole chap." Rutherford moved away from the dark mahogany bookcase where he was standing and walked over to a silver teapot sitting on a credenza. "I just had fresh tea brought in. Sit down and I'll pour you a cup. No doubt you're in need of it. Your presence here at my office tells me you've heard of Shelton's death." His pewter-colored goatee moved up and down with each word he spoke.

"I heard." Caden said with no greeting whatsoever. Dropping his hat in one of the wing-back chairs, Caden remained standing. He'd never liked the fact that the short, pale-faced Englishman called him ole chap, but today wasn't the time to mention that.

"Even terrible things are sometimes a blessing," the impeccably dressed lawyer said. "Maybe such was the case with Shelton."

"I want to know what his will says."

Rutherford didn't appear the least bit disconcerted by Caden's abrupt approach. He took his time and poured the steeped tea into a small china cup. He extended a cup to Caden, but he didn't take it. "That's right. I forgot. You don't drink tea. I should have remembered." Rutherford sipped the liquid as he looked at Caden over the rim of the cup.

"Should I have coffee brought in for you?"

Caden didn't want to be coddled. "I'm fine. I want to know who gets the farm."

"You and several other people want to know." Rutherford walked behind his desk and took his chair, relaxing against the heavily padded cushion. "Do sit down, Caden, you're making me nervous."

"I'm not here for tea or polite conversation, Rutherford." Caden placed the heel of his palms on the desk and leaned forward. "I want to know if Shelton left me the farm."

"I'm bound by Shelton's wishes not to reveal any contents of the will until a formal reading can be set up with all the primary beneficiaries. I've notified Pauline. I believe she and her son Stewart are enroute as we speak and should arrive in the next day or two. And Jake, of course, is always at the farm."

Caden tensed. Jake was in the will or he wouldn't be at the reading. What if Shelton had an attack of conscience and decided to divide the farm among the four of them. Dammit! He might have enough money saved up to buy out Pauline and Stewart. He really couldn't see them wanting to worry with land in Virginia with their home in Georgia. The real problem was Jake. Jake would never sell his share of Maxwell Farms.

"When I left for Alabama I know Shelton wanted me to have Maxwell Farms. Did anything happen to change that while I was away?"

Rutherford set his cup down on his desk. "I'll discuss many things with you, Cade. I've always liked you. But I'll not cross the line and discuss the will or any of its contents. I'm bound by law."

"Then what in the hell did I ride all the way over here for? I need some answers."

Rutherford remained calm. "Naturally, I assumed you were here to talk about your divorce." Rutherford laced his fingers together and laid his hands on the desk in front of him. His steady gaze left Caden no doubt he was comfortable with his authority in this matter.

The divorce. Caden had forgotten about it since hearing of Shelton's death. His mind raced. Did his uncle's death mean he didn't have to get the damn divorce now? He looked at Rutherford and thought he saw a smile in his eyes. No, dammit. Rutherford mentioned the divorce for a reason. And Caden had a feeling he knew what it meant.

"I don't know why in the hell Shelton approved of you as his lawyer."

"He was a bastard, wasn't he?" Rutherford chuckled amusingly. "I'm sure you're aware that I've been cut by his caustic tongue more than once. But he could always count on me to be honest. I was and I am. Keep that in mind should you ever need my assistance."

"You know what the will states?"

"Of course. Shelton called me to his bedside when he was wheezing so badly he could hardly breathe let alone talk, but he was of sound mind. I'm sure of that. I questioned him at length. I wouldn't have changed the will if I'd thought otherwise."

Caden felt as if his stomach turned over. "He changed the will?" This bothered Caden even though he'd never really known what Shelton's original will had stated.

Rutherford pushed his chair back and stood up. "Look at me, saying more than I intended. You're a sly one." He pointed a fleshy white finger at Caden. "I'll come out to the house as soon as Pauline and Stewart have arrived. Just send word."

Realizing he wasn't going to get any more information Caden said, "All right. What about the divorce?"

"It's a slow process. I've filed the necessary papers with the court, and now it will only be a matter of waiting for the initial hearing date. Any chance your wife will contest it?"

"No," he said firmly, but realized he had no guarantees Flair would sign.

"In that case we shouldn't have any problems with having you divorced in a matter of months. Since you can prove you haven't lived with her within the last ten years that should work to speed things up a bit."

"I brought her back with me. She's at the farm."

Rutherford pursed his lips. "It's not a good idea to have her living there. She could get very comfortable."

"Will it keep me from getting the divorce?"

"In the end? No. But it may take a little longer should she decide to protest."

Caden nodded, then picked up his hat and walked out. If what he suspected about Shelton dividing Maxwell Farms four different ways was true, how long the divorce took, or whether he got one wouldn't be an important issue.

* * *

Caden arrived back at the house with just enough time to change before dinner and make it to the parlor before Flair and Rich. He was in a foul mood and hoping a drink and dinner would help him feel better. He'd actually enjoyed the time he'd spent with Flair and her son at their home in south Alabama. Now he could very well be fighting for his home.

What would he do if Shelton had willed the place to Pauline and her insipid son, or to Jake and left him with nothing? He knew Shelton had never been happy about his marriage. Why had he waited so long to do anything about it? He should have done it years ago when Shelton had been so vocal about it, but back then it was his way of getting back at Shelton for his harsh words and demanding ways. Now he may have waited too long.

As Caden thought about those things he knew he missed the comfort he discovered in Flair's home. He hadn't been under any pressure to perform for Shelton or the men who worked the farm. He'd felt free to be himself, to relax for the first time in his life.

After pouring his drink, he automatically took the top off the whiskey decanter, then remembered that Shelton wasn't there to have his drink. There were some things about the old man he was going to miss. That made him laugh. How could he miss the hard-nosed bastard? He'd ridden his back every day for the past fifteen years. Caden was never tough enough, never mean enough, never man enough to please Shelton—so why was he sorry he was gone? But Caden knew what it was. It was the same thing that Shelton had tried to beat out of him when he'd heard him crying over his parents death one night. That soft spot in him that had made him weep for his parents when they were killed, and marry a beautiful young woman in trouble. That soft spot that made him want to comfort Flair and do whatever it took to take away her tears. For years he'd tried to shake it, but still it plagued him. Even now in death Shelton would hate to know that Caden was sorry he was gone.

"Caden."

He snapped around so fast he spilled the drink in his glass onto his hand. "I didn't hear you come in." He set the drink down on the sideboard and rubbed his hands together to dry them. His chest tightened as he looked at her. She was lovely in a dark blue dress with white lace at the collar and sleeves. That soft spot he'd just reprimanded himself for reared its head as soon as he looked at her. He didn't want to like her, or want to touch her, but he did. He was drawn to her. Dammit, he liked the way she took care of her son, the way she smiled, the way she handled adversity and made something positive from it. He liked the fact that she was strong and fought for what she believed in and what she thought was right.

"I hope I didn't startle you?"

"No," he lied. "What can I get you to drink? How about a light sherry."

She'd never had a sherry, but realizing things were done differently in this house she nodded her consent, adapting to his household as easily as he had to hers.

"Where's Rich?" he asked with his back to her, fighting the desire to simply go over and put his arms around her and hold her. He wanted to touch her, conquer whatever it was that had drawn him to her years ago and still held him captivated today.

"Already asleep." She sat down on the small settee. "He was so tired from the journey and playing that he ate early and went to bed. He'll probably be up at dawn ready to go back outside and watch the horses."

"He likes them, does he?"

"Oh, yes." She took the drink he held out for her. The glass was beautiful with a small tulip-shaped cup and short slender stem. After he sat down in the chair opposite her, she sipped the liquid. The drink was strong and sweet, with a bit of a sting. It was definitely something she'd have to get used to.

Caden was handsomely dressed in a black suit, waistcoat and tie. The only thing white was his shirt. He was obviously in mourning for his uncle. He'd seemed preoccupied when she'd come in. She decided to ask. "I understand you lost your uncle while you were away. I'm sorry to hear that. I'm sorry I kept you from him while he was so ill."

He sipped his drink, then wiped the corner of his mouth with his fingertips. "No need to be. He was a bastard of the highest quality. Most of the people around here won't miss him."

The harsh words offended her until she saw in his eyes that he was sorry for his uncle's death. She didn't know why he wanted to sound so tough.

"However, he is dead," he continued. "My aunt Pauline and her son Stewart are on their way here for the reading of the will. That should be interesting."

"Maybe this isn't a good time for me to be here. With your aunt coming and you in mourning."

He chuckled. "I think I made my feelings for Shelton clear. His death means nothing to me." Caden sipped his drink again. "Surely you can see I'm not in mourning. That's the last thing Shelton would have wanted me to do. I'm sure Pauline will stay no longer than it takes to read the will. There was no love between Shelton and his sister. She appears to be quite happy with her life in Georgia. And as for you being here, I thought we settled that before we left Alabama. I don't intend to change my plans. It's important to me that you be here."

As she looked in his eyes she couldn't decide if his last statement was a demand or a plea. She sipped her drink again and realized it didn't matter. She'd stay as long as he wanted her.

There was something about him she hadn't figured out yet. One moment he was smiling at her showing a gentle, caring side. The next he was doing things like shooting Douglas and dismissing his uncle's death as nothing to be troubled about. Which man was the real Caden Maxwell? And what was she going to do about her growing attraction to him?

Nine

The next day Flair sat in the parlor working on her green dress. All morning she'd alternated between pondering her romantic feelings for Caden and trying to get used to the different lifestyle at his house. Benny, the first young man they'd met after arriving at Maxwell Farms yesterday had taken Rich under his wing for the day and was letting him help care for the horses and clean the stables.

Flair couldn't remember a time she hadn't cooked her own breakfast—and everyone else's, too. Even when her mother was alive she'd helped with the cooking. She supposed it was natural for her to feel a little uneasy, and surprised to come downstairs and find a white linen draped buffet table filled with eggs, ham, biscuits, fried potatoes, and golden brown apple tarts warming above lighted candles.

Bernie had told her that Caden had eaten early and gone out for the day. Caden, she mused. He was a difficult one to figure out.

She didn't understand her attachment to him unless it was somehow tied to her appreciation for what he did for her. But would gratitude make her feel warm inside whenever he entered the room? Would appreciation make her stomach tighten and her breath grow short when their fingers touched by chance?

"Well look who we have here. Mrs. Caden Maxwell, I presume?"

Startled from her reverie Flair looked up from her stitching and saw a ruggedly handsome man leaning against the arched doorway. She glanced down the length of him. He wore clean clothes, not as expensive as Caden's, but nice. His shirt and trousers were black and his matching leather vest had three large silver buttons running down the front. In his hand he held a black hat banded with a ring of silver medallions. His smile wasn't friendly—it was leering, and that made her uncomfortable.

Laying her sewing aside, Flair rose from the sofa and faced him. "Yes. May I help you?" she questioned.

He arched his thick eyebrows and seemed to beckon her with his eyes. "Maybe. I'll certainly keep in mind that you offered."

Flair didn't like the way he answered her question but wondered if she was being overly suspicious of the man who'd appeared in the doorway. She wondered where Bernie and Silas had gotten off to.

He walked farther into the room and stood before her. "I heard Cade brought you back with him, and I had to come see for myself what you looked like."

She supposed a wife of ten years showing up for the first time would be cause for a lot of speculation and gossip, but she didn't like this man's brazen manner. She didn't like the way his gaze kept sweeping up and down her body and over her face. Having no comment for his statement she remained quiet, still, and let him look at her.

"Very nice," he mumbled. "You've caused quite a stir around here. But, I'm sure you know that. I'm surprised it took Cade so long to go after you. If I'd been married to you I would have said to hell with Shelton and gone after you."

Trying to be polite, but wanting him to know he was out of line, she stepped away from him and said, "I'm sorry. I don't believe we've met. You obviously know me, but I'm not enlightened as to your name."

His generous grin lifted only one corner of his mouth as he said, "Jake."

She didn't recognize his name, but it was clear he expected her to know him. He was obviously well known in the house for he'd entered without knocking.

"Jake—" She paused waiting for him to supply his last name so she could address him properly.

"Allen. Jake Allen." His eyes narrowed, his forehead furrowed. "Don't tell me Cade hasn't mentioned me."

"I'm sorry, Mr. Allen, he hasn't. However, I'm pleased to meet you. Are you looking for Bernie or Caden?"

He grinned again, some of his earlier frown relaxing in his strong features. "I just wanted to meet the woman who would end up being Cade Maxwell's downfall."

Stunned by his alarming statement, her eyes rounded in surprise. "How—What are you talking about, Mr. Allen? I don't know what you mean."

His lips spread into a thin smile. "He didn't tell you, did he?"

"Tell me what?" she said exasperated. His evasive comments were annoying her.

Jake chuckled. "Last I heard, Caden couldn't inherit this farm until he divorces you."

Smothering a gasp of surprise Flair said, "I don't understand."

"I'd be happy to *enlighten* you. It's not surprising Cade never mentioned it. I wouldn't either if I were married to a beautiful woman like you. Shelton never liked the idea that Cade came back from the army married. He tried to get Cade to divorce you back then, but Cade held his ground. A couple of months ago Shelton told him if he didn't divorce you and marry a woman of—social standing he would will the farm to me. So Cade went looking for you."

This time she was able to hide her surprise. Flair walked to the other side of the room before turning back to Jake. Her hand slowly crept up to the neck of her blouse. She felt undressed beneath his leering stare. The news that Caden would lose his inheritance if he didn't get a divorce shocked her. All this time she'd thought it was a woman who prompted Caden's decision. No wonder he was adamant when she tried to put him off. But she didn't like the fact that Jake had told her this. It should have been Caden's news to tell in his own time.

"And who are you, Mr. Allen? What part do you play in this?"

"Depends on who you ask. To Caden I'm nothing but a hired hand. I'd like to think that Shelton thought of me as a son. I've worked for Shelton close to thirty years. Been foreman for more than fifteen."

Something in the way he spoke, and the way he looked at her told her he was quite proud of this accomplishment, even though it appeared Caden wasn't.

The sound of horses approaching caught both of them by surprise. Jake walked over and, pushing a drapery panel aside, looked out the window. His grin of amusement returned. "Well, well the story continues. Shelton's sister has just arrived." He replaced his hat on his head, fitting it down on the crease in his hair. "I'll leave you to welcome the old biddy into the house. It was a pleasure meeting you, Flair. And I'll look forward to seeing you again."

As soon as he disappeared out the doorway in one direction, Bernie came bustling in from the other. "It's Miss Pauline and her son, Stewart," she said, wiping her chubby hands on her apron. "Best take your sewing upstairs to your room. She won't like seeing it all over the sofa. She's a queer sort. I'll stall her outside by the carriage and give you time to get it put away."

Flair's stomach turned and rolled in a nervous jerk. She didn't want to do anything to upset anyone in the house, especially Caden's relatives. She quickly gathered her skirt, needles, thread, and binding tape in her arms and hurried up the stairs to hide it all in her room. She took time to look in the mirror and retuck loose strands of hair into her chignon, and pinched her cheeks to add a blush. She wasn't sure what was going on about the divorce, but she planned to find out as soon as Caden returned.

A few moments later as she was coming down the stairs, a medium-height woman in a black traveling suit and a tall, husky young man walked into the foyer. Flair realized that whether she wanted it or not, and whether or not Caden liked it, for the time being, she was the lady of the house. And in being thus, it was her job to welcome everyone who came through the door, be it the unsettling foreman or the intimidating aunt from Georgia.

Flair put a smile on her face, ran a hand down her skirt and smoothed it as she reached the bottom of the stairs. "You must be Aunt Pauline, and Stewart. So nice to meet you and welcome you here. Come into the parlor and rest. Bernie, bring some cookies and tea. Maybe Stewart would like something stronger a little later."

"Who are *you,* a stranger, to welcome *me* into my own brother's home?" Pauline's teeth were clinched, her voice rumbled dangerously like lurking thunder on a cloudy afternoon.

Flair was aghast that the woman took her to task over her friendliness, but realized she had to continue now that she'd started. Clearly,

Pauline felt Flair was the one who was the interloper.

Quickly regaining her composure, Flair smiled again and said, "I'm Caden's wife, Flair Bowen—Maxwell."

"Oh my God, Stewart, did you hear that?" She placed an open palm against her chest and turned a pale face to her son. "Cade married and never invited us to the wedding. What did we do to deserve this?"

Stewart looked down at his over-dramatizing mother and patted her shoulder. Obviously at a loss for the right words for Pauline he turned to Flair and asked, "When did this happen? Why weren't we notified?"

Flair hesitated while she studied the best way to handle this situation. Honesty was the only way to go. She took a deep breath and softly said, "We married ten years ago."

Pauline's mouth fell open, softening the brittle lines of her pale lips. She set her dark gaze on Flair and pulled a handkerchief from her fringe-tipped reticule. "Don't give me that poppycock. Ten years ago? I don't believe a word of it."

"I was here not more than three years ago and you weren't here," Stewart spoke up, moving between Flair and his mother. Where Pauline blanched, Stewart's cheeks reddened. "We went into town together and—and—" His cheeks flushed a dusty pink as he realized what he was about to say. "Er—take my word for it, he didn't act like a man who was married." He turned to his mother. "I'd swear to it."

Feeling set upon by the two, Flair tried to regain her aplomb by leading them in to the parlor. She supposed it was natural Caden hadn't told his relatives he had married, considering the circumstances, but how was she to know?

"Caden and I married when he was in the army. He was in town only a short time. Afterward, I stayed at my father's home in Alabama while Caden went on to Texas with his troop."

Stewart and Pauline followed her into the parlor like she'd hoped. She motioned for them to take a seat on the settee. "For personal reasons I'd rather not go into, we've been apart all these years."

Pauline's gaze didn't waver from Flair's face. The older woman remained standing with her hands clasped together tightly at her waistline, her fringed purse dangling from her wrist. "Did Shelton know about this outrage?"

As Flair opened her mouth to answer the woman's rude question the front door opened and crashed against the wall, jarring everyone. The sound of small running feet reverberated on the tiled floor of the foyer.

"Mama! Mama!" Rich called, rushing into the parlor. He skidded to a stop in front of Flair. "Benny wants to let me ride one of the horses, can I? Can I?" he asked, pulling on her dress.

Flair cringed at Rich's manners. She'd taught him better. She tried not to be angry because she knew he was excited. Pushing aside her need to reprimand him, she calmly said, "It's *may* I. And have you forgotten your manners, young man? We have guests in the house."

He looked up at her contritely. "I'm sorry," he told her. He immediately turned a serious face to the company. "How do you do? I'm pleased to meet you," he said in a very grown-up voice.

A smile of pride and pleasure beamed across Flair's face. Seeing Rich behave so gentlemanly made her feel she could handle anything. Her shoulders eased back, her spine straightened, and she lifted her chin ever so slightly. "Aunt Pauline, cousin Stewart, this is my son Rich Maxwell. Caden's son."

Dinner was a strained affair. Caden did his best to keep Pauline from being openly hostile. He couldn't let her know he was worried about the contents of Shelton's will.

He looked down the candlelit table and realized he liked seeing Flair sitting at the other end. She had a wholesome blush to her cheeks that he found very attractive. He liked the way the candlelight played off her hair. Her neck was slim, white, and beautiful. If they were alone right now he'd get up and kiss her.

Caden watched her lean over and speak to Rich who sat quietly at the table eating his dinner like a little man. The thought that they belonged in his home occurred to him, but then he remembered that very possibly without the divorce he'd have no home. Flair noticed him watching her and smiled at him.

Caden felt a fluttering in his chest. She was beautiful and she was his wife. Maybe there was some way—

"I still find it almost impossible to believe," Pauline said, breaking into Caden's thoughts. "That the two of you have been married all these years. Something's not right about that."

"It's highly inappropriate for you to speculate on my marriage," Caden remarked in a less than friendly tone.

Pauline placed her hands in her lap and set her lips in a grim line, making it clear she didn't like being reprimanded by Caden. The clank of silverware ceased and every eye turned to Pauline. "And I find it highly suspicious that you show up with a wife no one has ever heard of two weeks after Shelton died."

"Shelton knew about Flair," he stated calmly.

"Hurrumph," Pauline muttered under her breath. "Well, I've no doubt you were aware of Shelton's ailing health and assumed if you could produce a *family* he would be more generous to you in his will."

Her accusation made Caden chuckle. If only she knew how Shelton had felt about his marriage. He sipped his claret wine.

His aunt didn't take kindly to his laughter. "Just because your father was a wastrel and left you no inheritance and Shelton took you in, is no reason for you to assume you should inherit all of Shelton's estate."

The smile left Caden's lips. He wouldn't have her speaking ill of his father. "Leave my father out of this. He has nothing to do with it."

"No, you're wrong. He has everything to do with this. If Pearson hadn't given everything he had to the church you wouldn't have been left to the mercy of a man who never wanted you, a man who despised you for what *you* represented."

Abruptly pushing his chair back, Caden rose. His gaze met every pair of eyes in the room, before he returned his attention to Flair. Pauline could say whatever she wanted to him, he didn't care, but not in front of Flair or Rich. No one knew more than he did that Shelton had never approved of him or his father. Shelton considered his father a weakling because he preached brotherly love from the Good Book.

For the first time Caden wondered if there was more to why Shelton disliked his father than the fact that he wanted to be a preacher, but Caden had never understood how teaching from the Bible made a man weak.

"Why don't you take Rich upstairs and get him dressed for bed."

"I think that's a good idea," Flair said. "Rich say good night—"

"No, I think your wife should hear all of it," Pauline interrupted. "Shelton is dead now. The will is written. I don't have to be afraid of him any longer. Both Shelton and Pearson were in love with your mother, Caden. Did you know that?" She smiled. "I didn't think so. Shelton never forgave your father or your mother because she chose the thoughtful, gentle man over the gruff and tough man. Shelton always considered himself superior to Pearson."

Caden didn't doubt her story for a moment. He should have guessed. His cold gaze swept from Pauline to Flair. "Take Rich upstairs."

Flair gave him an understanding smile as she took Rich's hand. Caden watched Flair as she walked gracefully from the room, the skirts of her blue dress swirling behind her. That smile from Flair did more to calm him than anything else could have. Some unusual feelings bubbled up inside him. He had an overpowering urge to chase after Flair and tell her how much that smile meant to him, but instead he reluctantly turned his attention back to Pauline. Her lips pursed into a tight bud. Her shoulders and back were erect. She'd probably wanted to tell him that bit of damning information for years. Now he understood why Shelton was always so hard on him. Shelton obviously wanted to make sure he turned out like him and not Pearson. If Pauline thought the information would upset him she was wrong. In a way it freed him. And as much as he disliked Pauline he couldn't ask her to leave the house. After the will was read tomorrow she could very well own it.

Scraping his chair against the floor as he stood up Stewart said, "I think I'll go into town and see if I can find a card game. I don't suppose you'd care to join me, Cade."

Caden shook his head. "Rutherford will be here at nine o'clock in the morning. I'll meet both of you in the library. Good night."

As soon as his nightshirt was buttoned Rich jumped up on the four-poster bed, bouncing up and down a couple of times before settling onto the mattress. Flair started to pull up the sheet, but he stopped her. "I'll pull it up later if I need it."

"All right. It is rather warm tonight." She was trying not to rush her time with Rich but she desperately wanted to get back downstairs. If Caden needed her she wanted to be there for him. Surely it was only natural for her to want to help him after all he'd done for her.

Rich folded his small hands in his lap. "Mama, I wonder why Aunt Pauline doesn't like Cade? I think he's all right. Don't you?"

She smiled and reached down and kissed Rich's forehead. "Yes, I do. And I don't think you have to worry about him. He's a strong, capable man who can handle Aunt Pauline."

Rich pursed his lips and nodded, then folded his hands behind his head and leaned back against his pillow. "Mama, do you think I should call Cade Papa?"

Flair had wondered when he'd get around to asking that question. Caden had told her they'd discussed it. From the first day Caden had returned she'd known that he was only in their life temporarily. Flair knew she hadn't spent enough time thinking about how the decisions she'd made would affect Rich and his future, but getting him away from Douglas had been more important at the time.

"Mama?" he questioned. "Did you hear me?"

"Yes. I was thinking about it." She cleared her throat and looked into her son's beautiful brown eyes. She wished it were true that he was Caden's son. "What do *you* want to call him? That is what's important."

Rich wrinkled his nose and twisted his lips as he thought. "I think I'll call him Cade awhile longer. Do you think that will be all right?"

Flair ruffled his hair and laughed lightly, but inside she wasn't so calm. "I think that will be fine. Now, lie down and close your eyes, or you'll be too sleepy to get up in the morning."

"Good night, Mama." Rich reached up and gave her a hug and wet kiss on her cheek.

Flair held him tightly for a moment and closed her eyes, savoring her son's small arms around her neck.

Flair turned out the lamp and went back downstairs to the dining room. It was empty. She checked the parlor and Caden's office. She started to go back upstairs, thinking he must have gone to his room when she thought about checking the front porch. She remembered that he liked sitting outside in the coolness of evening. Putting aside all the reasons why she shouldn't, Flair opened the door and stepped onto the porch. At first she didn't see Caden, but after her eyes adjusted to the semi-darkness she saw that he sat on the side of the front steps. He hadn't turned around to look at her when she opened the door, and she thought for a moment that he probably wanted to be alone, but she had a strong desire to talk to him, to be with him. Picking up the hem of her skirts, she walked down the first three steps and sat down beside him.

He still didn't acknowledge her. She knew that was his way of telling her she should go away and leave him to his thoughts, but something deep inside made her hesitate. Caden had comforted her when she needed it, and she had to be there for him, too.

She stayed.

"I'm not in the best frame of mind tonight, Flair," he finally said.

"I know."

"I'm in a mood to growl and bite and right now you are the closest person to me."

"I don't mind," she answered softly, knowing that what Pauline had told him bothered him. "Have Aunt Pauline and Stewart gone to bed?"

He looked over his shoulder at her. Starlight fell across his worried face. She was glad she'd stayed. He might not know it, but he needed her beside him.

"Stewart rode into town. I left Pauline sitting in the dining room."

"She must have gone upstairs. She's not there now."

"Thank God," he whispered under his breath. "I don't think I could take another encounter with her tonight."

Flair had an overpowering desire to pull him into her arms and hold him. She had felt so much better after she'd received a hug from Rich. Should she comfort Caden that way? Could she? Unsure of herself, she remained where she was and said, "You know, all this time I thought the reason you wanted a divorce was because you wanted to marry another woman."

Caden remained quiet for a few moments,

but finally asked, "Has something happened to make you change your mind?"

"Yes, Jake told me you couldn't inherit the farm—"

"Jake!" He turned all the way around and faced her. "When in the hell did you talk to him?"

Startled by his explosion she quickly answered, "He came to the house this afternoon just before your aunt arrived. He told me if you didn't get the divorce you wouldn't inherit this farm."

"That may or may not be true. In any case, it wasn't his place to say anything. What exactly did he tell you?"

His voice was calmer, although his eyes were still lit with fire. Moonlight danced on his face and in his dark brown hair. Over his shoulder she saw the midnight sky and for a brief moment she wished things could be different between them.

She looked into his eyes. "Just that you couldn't inherit the farm unless you divorced me and married someone else." She could have added that he said a woman of social standing, but didn't want him to know she knew that.

Caden breathed in deeply. "That's what Shelton told me before I left, but Rutherford said he changed his will while I was gone. I have no idea what it says now. He could have given the entire farm to Aunt Pauline or Stewart, or Jake while I was away."

Flair was intensely aware of him beside her. She tried to deny what she felt but she couldn't. In a move that was innocent and caring, she laid a comforting hand on his shoulder and said, "I don't think your uncle would do that to you."

"You didn't know Shelton." He looked at her hand resting on his shoulder, then lifted his gaze to her eyes.

Her stomach muscles tightened. "No, but I know family. We might not have had a loving relationship, but we had a good one. I think my father finally got over me marrying you so quickly." With a tentative movement she rubbed her palm across the top of his shoulder and down his back. Through his clothes she felt his muscles relax and knew she had done the right thing in touching him.

"You heard what Pauline said. I should have guessed there was something more to the reason Shelton hated my father, something more to his unrelenting hardness. I won't be surprised if Shelton carried through with his threat and willed the entire farm to Jake."

"I'm certain he didn't do that," she encouraged him again, letting her fingers snake underneath his collar length hair to knead the tense muscles in the back of his neck.

"You can't be certain. You're just trying to make me feel better." This time he gave her a smile. "And you're succeeding." He rotated his shoulders. "Mmm—that feels wonderful."

Caden scrunched his shoulders a couple more times, then reached up, took her hand and held it in his. Their eyes met again and held as he softly kissed the back of her palm.

The pressure of his hand upon her skin was warm, his lips cool and moist. She felt that tightening sense of arousal in the pit of her abdomen. She wanted to be held and kissed, something she hadn't felt in years. Just as quickly a little voice inside her screamed, "No!" Men were not to be trusted. Kisses led to caresses and caresses led to—

"Did you ever tell your father about Douglas?" Caden asked.

Flair gave herself a little shake. The night must be getting to her. "No. You saved me from all those questions. Besides, there was no reason to tell anyone about Douglas. I was in the wrong that night. I shouldn't have agreed to meet him down by the pond. I should have known he wanted more than kisses. But I was young and foolish enough to think he loved me."

Caden shifted and his knees brushed up

against hers. "Are you telling me you and Douglas weren't lovers?"

She opened her mouth to speak, but hesitated before she asked, "Is that what you've thought all these years? That Douglas and I were lovers?"

His eyes narrowed as if he were studying her intently. He nodded. "If not lovers, what?"

She lowered her lashes over her eyes. Did she want to tell him the truth about that night? Did she want him to know that Rich wasn't conceived in love? Should she tell him? *Rich carries his name,* a little voice told her.

Gently, he placed his fingertips under her chin and lifted her head. "Open your eyes and look at me, Flair."

His voice so soft and comforting eased her pain. She had no choice but to respond. She looked into his eyes.

Holding her hand tightly he asked, "How did you get pregnant with Rich?"

She moistened dry lips and gazed into understanding eyes. Briefly, she told herself, tell him only the major points. "I met Douglas at a party his father had given. Douglas danced with me, showed me a lot of attention that night. He came over to see me a few times when Papa was out working. We kissed a little. When he asked me to slip out of the house and meet him by the pond, I knew he'd kiss me—I wanted him to, but I didn't know he had other things in mind." She stopped, not sure she could say more about what happened when she tried to stop Douglas's kisses.

"Douglas forced himself on you?" he asked, a dark frown clouding his features.

She nodded again. "He wouldn't take no for an answer. One moment we were just kissing, and the next he had me on the ground, pulling at my clothes. Thank God it was over quickly." She slid her hand from his and turned away. "It was my fault. I shouldn't have agreed to meet him." All the old feelings washed over her. She remembered groping hands, the body pounding against her lower abdomen. Suddenly she wanted to run away from it all. She tried to rise, but Caden gently took hold of her wrist and held her down.

"No, Flair, it's all right. Don't run away. Look at me. You have nothing to be ashamed of. Come on, lift your head and look at me."

With effort she faced him, afraid of what she'd see in his eyes. Instead of the disapproving look she expected she saw tenderness, understanding. Her heart softened toward him even more.

"You don't have to say anything else. I can imagine the rest." He mumbled a curse under his breath. "I should have killed Douglas when I had the chance."

"Don't say that, Caden, I should have known better than to meet him," she said. "It was my fault. I—"

"Hell no! It wasn't," he exclaimed in a soft but firm tone. He turned her loose and pointed a finger at her. "You listen to me about this. It wasn't your fault and I don't want to hear you say that again. There's nothing wrong with a few stolen kisses in the dark. Douglas went too far. You didn't do anything wrong."

She didn't realize how shallow her breathing had become until she looked into his eyes. He didn't blame her. That made her feel so good she felt light-headed.

"Are you sure?" she asked in a whispered voice.

Caden smiled. "Yes. Flair, I'm saying these things because they're true. Kisses don't have to go any farther than *you* want them to. It's your right to say no, and the man's responsibility to accept that. Let me show you."

Very slowly, as if not to frighten her, Caden lowered his face toward hers. He was going to kiss her. She knew she shouldn't let him, but she felt powerless to move away from him. She didn't know why, but she wanted him to kiss her. Maybe she hoped Caden's kiss could wash away the memories of the past.

When his lips touched hers they parted slightly. She felt his breath, his palm against her jaw, his fingertips against her cheek, his thumb brushing the side of her nose. An excitement of awareness grew inside her and the strain of the past eased away. She welcomed Caden's warmth. The kiss was so soft, so unhurried, she softly sighed. She slowly savored his lips upon hers. She placed her hands against his chest to steady herself and felt a slight tremble in him. Their lips began to move together. He kissed her gently, softly as if he had all the time in the world.

Desire grew inside her.

Flair arched toward him, wanting to feel his arms around her. She wanted to press her breasts against his chest and feel the hardness, the breadth of the man who kissed her. As if reading her movements, his arms encircled her waist and he pulled her to him. She relaxed against him.

It had been a long time since Flair had been kissed, but she would have remembered if it had been this wonderful, if it had caused that tightening feeling in the pit of her abdomen, if it had made her want more than the soft kisses he gave. She wondered if her kisses to him felt as wonderful as his to her.

He spoke her name softly against her lips without breaking the kiss. His lips offered desire. They didn't selfishly demand fulfillment. He ran his hands up and down her arms, over her shoulders and back and down her face. He touched her with slow deliberate movements. His breath was like a soft but quick wind. His touch offered her a promise, but she wasn't sure she was ready to know what it was. She wasn't sure she was ready to believe she could trust this man with her heart.

But what her mind thought wasn't in tune with what her body desired. She didn't understand her feelings for this man. After what had happened with Douglas how could she want a man to kiss her and touch her so intimately? Was it that she'd pushed her feminine feelings aside for too long? Or was it that she remembered a nice young man of ten years ago who saved her when she thought her world was coming to an end?

"Mmm. You smell good. You feel good," he whispered as his kisses moved to her cheek and down over her jawline. "I don't want to stop touching you."

His hand slipped from her shoulder down her chest to gently cup her breast. She inhaled unevenly. Blood rushed to her ears. His kiss deepened, his tongue parted her lips and probed her mouth. Flair tensed. What was he doing? Where were the soft kisses, the gentle caresses? All of a sudden she was reminded of groping hands, bruising lips, and pressing weight. A small cry of alarm escaped her lips, and she pushed away from Caden and moved to the other end of the step. He let her go without question.

His breathing was ragged, hers shallow. For a few moments she'd forgotten how easily kisses could turn into more than she wanted.

"I don't think we should have done that," she managed to say to him as she rose and looked down at him. "I—I think there must be some kind of magic to the midnight sky."

"It's not magic, Flair. It's fire. It's been burning between us for a long time. There's an attraction between us that I've felt from the beginning. Tonight proves we can't deny it."

She couldn't argue with that. "We don't have to give in to it."

"Why not? I'm nothing like Douglas."

"I know, but—"

"There's nothing wrong with us exchanging a few kisses?"

"I understand that."

"You are my wife."

"But not for long," she answered, feeling a little miffed, and not sure why. He had never offered her more than his name. "I'm here to get a divorce and things like kisses can only complicate matters between us. Just stay away from me."

He rose and looked down at her, a frown on his handsome face. "Maybe you were right. It must be the night air. I guess I was just looking for a little comfort."

"I wanted to give it, but—"

"Don't try to explain, Flair. I know how difficult it must be for you to put your trust in a man." He turned and walked away.

Flair was angry with herself as she watched him disappear into the darkness. How could she have allowed herself to be so free with him? She couldn't start accepting his kisses even though they made her feel so wonderful. Even though she dreamed of being held in his arms. Even though she wanted to trust him. When she accepted Douglas's kisses she believed she had a future with him. Caden had made it clear she didn't have a future with him.

Caden had to have the divorce to inherit what was rightfully his. She couldn't let the feelings she was developing for him continue. She had to think about Rich and what was best for him. He was settling in very nicely to Maxwell Farms. Was it fair to let him believe this might one day be his home? She didn't know any more. She only knew that Rich was beginning to care for Caden—and so was she.

Ten

With only a few more minutes to wait, Caden was afraid he wasn't going to get it. All because of the damn marriage he wasn't going to get the farm. A marriage he could have easily terminated years ago, but didn't because he knew it was a thorn in Shelton's side. And the hell of it was that now he was getting to know his wife, now that he'd kissed her, he was beginning to believe that maybe he didn't want to divorce her. But, he reminded himself sternly, there was no use worrying about any of that until the will was read.

Caden had deliberately called them all into Shelton's office, and he deliberately took the seat of honor behind the desk. That's what Shelton would have done had he been present at the reading of his will. Caden couldn't help but smile as he looked at his tight-lipped aunt, spoiled cousin, and the aggressive foreman. Shelton would have been pleased that

they'd all dressed in black for him and that
they all hated every minute of this little gath-
ering of the relatives. The old man was probably laughing. Even Rutherford looked as if
he was sporting a new suit of clothes for this
special meeting.

Even though Caden remained cool and
calm on the outside his hands were sweaty,
his stomach roiled, and his chest felt as if his
ribs had been bound with iron bindings.

Bernie set the coffee tray on the side table,
then quietly closed the door on her way out.
Silence filled the room. It was time to begin.

Pauline and Stewart sat in the two arm
chairs in front of the highly polished oak
desk. Even though there were other chairs in
the office Jake elected to remain standing
close to the door, holding his hat in his hand,
his feet and legs spread defiantly. Caden
knew the foreman had less reason to inherit
than anyone present, however, Jake wouldn't
be in the room if Shelton hadn't mentioned
him in the will.

Without a shred of doubt Caden knew he
deserved the farm. Not because he was Shelton's nephew. Stewart was his nephew, too,
but the Georgia relative hadn't worked for
Shelton for seventeen years.

Caden looked over at Rutherford who stood
at the side of the desk. A muscle worked in

the lawyer's jaw causing his goatee to quiver. Caden had expected Rutherford to speak first, but after a few moments of silence Caden decided they were waiting for him to start the proceedings.

He straightened in the chair. "We all know why we're here, Rutherford. You can begin any time you're ready."

The lawyer nodded to Caden. He opened his leather folder and took out an envelope and made quite a production of breaking the red ribboned seal. He removed three sheets of stiff paper and laid them down on the desk beside him.

He clasped his hands together in front of him and looked around the room, catching everyone's eye. "Before I read the will I'd like to state that I have known Shelton and have been his lawyer for fifteen years. At all times during our relationship Shelton knew he could count on me to do what he asked. He paid me for my work on this will before he died. And I'm entitled to no other compensation. He asked that I pay any and all of his outstanding debts. To the best of my knowledge all of them have been settled. If anyone in this room knows of outstanding debts in Shelton's name would you speak at this time. I'll see that they are taken care of promptly."

No one spoke.

"Very well." He picked up the pages and read. "I, Shelton Adam Maxwell, am of sound mind and steady hand and do make this my last will and testament. Other than my trusted servant Rutherford there should be four people present in this room. My sister, Pauline. Her son, Stewart. My foreman, Jake. And my dead brother's son, Caden. If that is not the case, no further reading should take place." Rutherford stopped and looked around the room before continuing. "Assuming everyone is accounted for, I have a few things I want to say before I go about distributing my life's work to this ungrateful assemblage. First, before anyone present in this room can inherit what I've provided for them in this document they must remain present in the room for the entire reading of this will.

"Pauline, I always liked your show of strength, your determination to get what you wanted. You did very well for yourself by marrying that wealthy widower over in Georgia. For that and that alone I have remembered you. However, I never liked the fact you and your husband made a simpering ninny out of your son."

Pauline gasped and reached over and whispered something to her son. Stewart shifted uncomfortably in his chair, but Rutherford kept reading.

"I feel obligated to give you a token from my estate even though you don't need it. I have set aside five thousand dollars for you. I know it's not what you wanted, but more than you deserve."

Again Pauline murmured something under her breath. Caden didn't hear what she said, but her expression told him it was a nasty comment. For once, he didn't blame her. Shelton hadn't been kind to her.

Rutherford continued reading. "Stewart, it's a shame you never had a chance of becoming a real man. Had you been left in my care the way Caden was, I could have done more for you. As it is, you'll inherit your parents' holdings some day and I know that's considerable. However, you are lucky your mother married for money. I hope she's taught you enough so you'll know how to take care of it when she dies. I doubt she'll let you control one penny before that happens."

Pauline jumped to her feet and glared at Rutherford. Outrage showed in her expression. Her hands held the strings of her reticule so tightly her knuckles whitened. "Hah! I didn't come all this way to be insulted or have my son insulted by an unforgiving dead man. It isn't necessary that you read all the words of that pathetic old man. Just get on with the reading of what he left us."

"I'm sorry, Mrs. Fendly," Rutherford said in an unemotional voice. "I have to read everything he wrote, the way he wrote it. You are free to leave the room anytime you wish, but I must remind you that you give up rights to your inheritance if you choose to do so."

Stewart reached up and took hold of his mother's wrist. "Settle down, Mother so he can continue. You never let anything Uncle Shelton had to say bother you before. No reason to start now. We've always known how he felt about us. Besides, I'd like to know if he left me anything or if he simply wanted to criticize me like always."

Pauline retook her seat. She patted Stewart's hand and smiled at him. "You're right, of course. Shelton found fault with everyone but himself. Nothing he says is true, so I shouldn't let it bother me."

Rutherford looked around the room again, then continued. "For having to put up with your mother for these twenty-three years, Stewart, I leave you the sum of ten thousand dollars."

Caden saw Stewart's eyes light with happiness and a satisfied smile graced his thin lips. Apparently he hadn't expected to fare so well.

Truth was, the large amount surprised Caden too.

"Along with this bequest, Stewart, I want to give you a piece of advice."

"Naturally," Pauline chimed in ungraciously. "And no doubt we have to hear it before we're allowed to leave this place."

Rutherford gave her a firm look. "Take the money and run like hell."

Caden smiled. Jake chuckled. Pauline gasped again, and Stewart looked as if he was considering the advice. But when Jake's light chuckle turned into full blown laughter Stewart turned a murderous look upon him.

"I wouldn't be laughing if I were you, cow hand. You don't know what he said about you, yet."

The lawyer gave an exasperated sigh, his gaze darting between Stewart and Pauline. "I must ask that the two of you discontinue your constant interruptions. I'll be happy to listen to you or answer any questions you might have once the reading is finished."

"Please carry on," Stewart said in an overly polite tone. "I'm dying to know what comes next."

"Very well." Rutherford stuck a finger down his collar and pulled on it. "I'll continue."

"This part of the will gave me great pain as I studied over what to do. It's especially difficult since Caden hasn't made it back from Alabama and I grow weaker. Over these years I've tried to treat Caden as a son. Sometimes he made it difficult. Other times he made it impossible. I did my best."

How like Shelton to make it sound like he might have liked him.

Damn, his stomach hurt, thought Caden.

Caden's gaze strayed to Jake. Jake was watching him. It had always been this way. They had never been friends. They'd always been rivals.

"I'll have to simply trust my judgment on this one. I usually make the right decision when I do that. In order to ease my brother's dying breath, I promised Pearson I'd look after his boy. I knew he meant he wanted me to teach him about horses and the farm. He wanted me to teach him how to be a man, something he would never have been able to do. It was Pearson's hope that I'd leave the farm to Caden.

"Being a traveling preacher, Pearson had nothing to leave the boy except a tattered Bible filled with worthless sermons. I threw that away years ago. A boy can't learn how to be a man reading such nonsense as written in that book. It never did anything for Pearson."

Undiluted anger welled up in Caden and cramped his insides tighter. Sweat broke out on his forehead. Dammit! His father had left him his Bible, and Shelton hadn't given it to him. He had no right to throw it away.

"Caden's unexpected marriage has bothered me for years. Marrying that girl was a foolish thing for him to do, the kind of thing his father would have done. I've told him so many times. But I believe he's finally decided to make things right, so I'm leaving my will written thusly. In order for Caden to inherit the full of Maxwell Farms save what is otherwise bequeathed, he must divorce his current wife and marry a woman of social standing in the county. The day Caden remarries, he's to be granted full rights to Maxwell Farms, and Jake is to be given ten thousand dollars and five horses of his choosing so that he can start his own farm or ranch in the West he has so often talked about. Caden is to be given sufficient time to obtain his divorce. During that time he is to act as sole owner of Maxwell Farms, and Jake is to keep his position as foreman."

Jake didn't twitch a muscle. Neither did Caden.

"If Caden returns and refuses to divorce his wife, Maxwell Farms in its entirety is to be turned over to my trusted foreman Jake Allen for his many years of unquestionable loyalty and dedication to the prosperity of

Maxwell Farms. Although he's not a relative, I've always approved of how Jake handles himself.

"If for any reason Caden does not return from his journey, or should he die before he remarries and produces an heir, Jake is to be given twenty acres and five horses of his choosing. The rest of the farm is to be sold and the money given to the state-operated widows' pension for the wives of those brave men who died in the war.

"I have charged Rutherford to see that these my last wishes are carried out. I don't expect any of you to appreciate these bequests. I fully expect all of you to enjoy what I have so generously given."

Rutherford laid the last sheet of paper on the desk. "That concludes the reading of Shelton's will. Are there any questions?"

Pauline rose with an audible sigh and started pulling on her gloves. "How soon can we get our money? I have a house to manage in Georgia, and I've tarried too long here as it is."

Caden was still trying to take it all in while Rutherford pulled another folder from his leather case. "I have two bank drafts here. One made out to you and one for Stewart."

"Thank you for handling this so promptly," she said without any gratitude in her voice.

"Stewart, let's get our luggage and go on into town today. We can catch the first train out of here tomorrow morning. I can't get away from here fast enough to suit me."

She looked over at Caden, and he stood up. "No wonder we never heard of your bride. You had the audacity to marry without Shelton's blessings." She laughed huskily. "But it didn't do you any good, did it? All these years you haven't had a wife. And now that you have, you must divorce her. What a shame." She laughed again. "I'll be waiting for the invitation to your *next* wedding." Without giving anyone else a glance she walked out of the room.

Stewart looked at Caden and said, "You know, I'm not the weakling he always thought I was."

Caden nodded agreement, but knew if Stewart thought he had to tell him that, Shelton was probably right.

Jake walked over to Caden after Stewart and Rutherford left the room. The foreman's satisfied smile bothered Caden. He was glad Shelton put that clause in the will about what should happen if he died. Obviously Shelton knew Jake well.

"That wife of yours is a mighty pretty woman, Cade. With all that golden hair and those big blue eyes. She's woman enough to make a man lose his head. It's going to be damn tough divorcing her."

Caden reached out and grabbed Jake by the collar of his shirt and dragged him over the desk, knocking over the inkwell, a small clock, and scattering papers everywhere. He brought Jake's face up close to his. "Stay away from my wife or you won't live to see if we divorce."

Jake grinned lazily. "Shelton taught you well."

Caden kept his gaze on Jake's face a moment longer, then shoved him away. "The reading of the will is over. You have work to do. As soon as my divorce is final I'll give you your money and horses. Then I want you off my land."

Jake straightened his shirt, placed his hat on his head, and turned and walked out.

Eleven

Flair stood outside the corral watching Rich ride the gentle mare named Muffin, but her thoughts were on what was going on inside the large white house. She couldn't shake the feeling that whatever happened it wouldn't be good for Rich and her.

She thought back over the kiss she and Caden shared last night. She couldn't get it off her mind. Why after all these years of denying those warm feelings of desire had they returned? Was it a simple case of appreciation she felt for Caden for having helped her, or was it more than that?

It was foolish, she knew, maybe even crazy, but somewhere deep inside she hoped Caden wouldn't have to divorce her. She'd sworn to never trust another man and for ten years it had been easy, but now that Caden had come back into her life she was wondering if that had changed.

Last night as she lay in bed and remembered Caden's tender kisses, his soft caresses, and how they made her feel she knew she could be falling in love with him. She didn't know why or how it was happening. She didn't want those feelings. She tried chastising herself about such silly notions, but as much as she hated to admit it to herself, she knew it to be true.

Even now while she stood out in the warm sunshine her fate was being decided for her. If things turned out as she expected they would, she might have to leave Caden and Maxwell Farms before the divorce was final. She had to agree to come here. Getting Rich away from Douglas had been uppermost in her mind, but she never thought about what it would be like when it was time for her and Rich to leave.

"What do you think, Mrs. Maxwell?" Benny called to her. "Isn't he doing a fine job?"

Flair waved and said, "He's doing great. He'll be able to ride by himself soon—as long as he's on a gentle horse like this one." She looked at her son in his old and crumpled felt hat sitting atop the large horse. If they ended up staying here through the summer she would have to get him some riding boots.

As she watched Rich, she remembered him holding the shotgun on Douglas and laughed to herself. Since her father died, he'd always done his best to be the man of the house. He was eager to help Booker and Samp in the fields and seldom grumbled about doing his chores. Booker had been good for him and had done a good job of filling the void her father's death had left in his life, but Rich needed a father, a strong yet caring man. A man like Caden. Caden could teach him so many things.

Rich smiled and waved to her as he bounced up and down in the saddle. She returned both as he trotted around the corral, learning how to post, how to get the horse going, how to stop him, and how to ride with the horse rather than just sit on top of him.

Watching Rich caused a catch in her throat. She swallowed hard. She wished she could have done better for her son. It pained her to know Rich actually had two fathers, but he couldn't grow up with either of them. When Douglas remarried and she could let her divorce be known in town maybe she should do something about trying to find Rich a father.

She heard a noise behind her and turned to see Stewart striding her way. She tensed. The reading of the will must be over. Stewart appeared to be in a hurry. She wondered what that meant. Had Caden lost the farm? Was Stewart coming to throw them off his land, she worried in a wild panic?

"Benny!" he yelled before he reached her. "Hitch a carriage immediately. We're leaving." He continued walking until he came up beside her.

"Morning, Flair." He tipped his gray hat, then rested it low on his forehead.

His voice was friendly and he smiled, but Flair knew by his facial expression he wasn't happy. His nose was red and a muscle in his jaw twitched. Things obviously hadn't gone the way Stewart wanted them to.

"Hello, Stewart. Is it over?" she asked.

He nodded as he threw the sides of his jacket behind him and rested his hands on the wide belt that rode high on his waist. "Yes. Mama and I are going to ride into town today so we can be ready to leave on the first train tomorrow. No use in hanging around here. I can't say I have any fond memories of this place."

If they were leaving, maybe that meant Caden was staying. Her mind reeled with possibilities. She tried to hide the glee that rushed through her as she said, "We didn't have time to get well acquainted, but I wish you Godspeed on your journey."

"It's a long one all right, but the trip over here was worth it. I did all right. The old coot left me more than I thought he would, but I had hoped he'd leave me half of this place. Guess it was old age that made him soften and leave me anything. He gave Mama a few dollars even though he never liked her—and he made a point of reminding her in the will."

Flair wondered what kind of man would do that, but remembered Caden didn't have any kind words for his uncle either.

"Caden?" she asked.

Stewart looked into her eyes, his nostrils flaring as he smiled. "Caden did all right, too. I'd say you are the big loser of the day, apparently Shelton didn't like you any better than he liked me or Mama."

She was unable to hide her sudden intake of breath. She expected it. No, she knew it, but his callous choice of words still pained her.

"But I'll let Caden tell you the bad news," he said.

Not knowing what else to say or do she smiled softly at him and said, "If you're referring to the divorce, I know about it, and that's the reason I'm here."

"Don't take it too hard, cousin Flair," he said. "That bastard Shelton never liked anyone. God, what a wretched man he was. You heard last night that he and Pearson were in love with the same woman and he never forgave her for choosing Caden's father over him. Guess that's what turned him into the miserable man he was. Well he's dead now and I'm happy." He looked around the corral. Spotting Rich, he nodded in his direction. "It's too bad I can't stay longer. You and the boy are the only two members of this family I can tolerate."

While she appreciated Stewart's kind words, Flair was always offended when men refused to use Rich's name. She lifted her gaze to his and said, "My son's name is Rich."

He looked back at her. "Interesting name that. I wonder if it will bring him any luck." He tipped his hat again. "If you ever find yourself in Georgia, dear cousin by marriage, stop in to see us."

He turned and walked toward the house.

Flair felt like crying, but knew better than to give in to such a foolish emotion. As soon as she had a few moments alone she'd be all right. She'd be able to cope with whatever was to take place when she saw Caden.

Benny came running over to her. "I'll probably have to drive Mr. Stewart and his mother into town. When you get ready to go inside just have Rich unsaddle the horse and lead him over to his stall in the barn the way I showed him. He knows what to do."

"Then I'll see he does it," she told the stable hand.

While Rich rode around the corral Flair divided her time between watching him and the house. After Stewart went back inside Jake came out, mounted his horse, and rode away. A short time later the expensively dressed lawyer climbed in his carriage and left, too. Only minutes later Stewart's and Pauline's luggage was hoisted onto the back of the carriage and Benny drove them away.

Flair knew Rich had been riding too long as it was. He'd be so sore he couldn't walk tomorrow if he didn't take a break. She lingered because she didn't want to go back inside. It was silly, but she didn't want to hear that the divorce had to continue. And she didn't want to have to tell Caden that she needed to leave so she wouldn't fall in love with him, so Rich wouldn't come to depend on him as a father.

"Mama, look at me," Rich called to her.

Flair turned away from the house and gave her attention back to her son. "You're doing very well, Rich, but I think you've been riding long enough for one day," she said. "Now it's time to show me how well you can take care of the horse. It's time to put him away."

"Just a few more minutes please, Mama? *Pleeease?* I won't be sore. I promise."

Reluctantly, Flair nodded. She hated to stop his fun. Even though she needed to be work-

ing on her green dress she would stay out by
the corral until she saw Caden leave for the
day. Then she would go inside.

Thank God the house was quiet once again,
Caden thought as he looked across the front
lawn and saw Flair standing by the corral. He
didn't know which he thought about more last
night, the reading of the will, or Flair. He
couldn't forget the way he'd felt when he held
her in his arms and kissed her. Not only did
he feel the need to protect her, he wanted to
possess her, to love her. He'd wanted to lie
with her and show her how it could be between
a man and a woman. She brought out feelings
in him that he'd never felt with any other
woman.

He should have done more to Douglas than
wound him in the arm when he saw him
shaking Flair. If he'd known then the bastard
had forced himself on her ten years ago he
would have.

There were so many things to like about
Flair. How could he not be impressed by a
woman who'd been through as much as she
had and managed to hold up her head and
make a good life for her son? Not only was
she a beautiful, capable woman, she seemed
to touch his heart and soul. Over the years

he'd been with women, but none of them had ever affected him the way she had. He'd come to believe women were only good for one thing, as Shelton had told him. But as he'd talked with Flair last night, as he'd held her and kissed her, he saw her as a woman he would enjoy spending more time with, a woman he wouldn't mind having around all the time.

Douglas had showed Flair how a man abuses a woman. He wanted to show her how a man loves a woman.

Bernie had told him how she handled Pauline and Stewart when they arrived yesterday. How she'd welcomed them into the house and treated them like honored guests. He was certain she wouldn't have any trouble being the mistress of his house. And Rich. He could raise him as his own son—but for the damn will. Shelton. His hatred must have run deep. The divorce had to go on or Caden would be left with nothing to offer any woman.

He looked over Flair's petite figure as he hurried down the front steps toward her. The truth was he didn't want to marry anyone else. Why should he want another when he was already married to this beautiful woman? *But this one you can't have,* an inner voice reminded him. Maybe that was why he was so drawn to her. Could it be that was the reason

MORE PASSION AND ADVENTURE AWAIT... YOUR TRIP TO A BIG ADVENTUROUS WORLD BEGINS WHEN YOU ACCEPT YOUR FIRST 4 NOVELS ABSOLUTELY *FREE* (AN $18.00 VALUE)

Accept your Free gift and start to experience more of the passion and adventure you like in a historical romance novel. Each Zebra novel is filled with proud men, spirited women and tempestuous love that you'll remember long after you turn the last page.

Zebra Historical Romances are the finest novels of their kind. They are written by authors who really know how to weave tales of romance and adventure in the historical settings you love. You'll feel like you've actually gone back in time with the thrilling stories that each Zebra novel offers.

GET YOUR FREE GIFT WITH THE START OF YOUR HOME SUBSCRIPTION

Our readers tell us that these books sell out very fast in book stores and often they miss the newest titles. So Zebra has made arrangements for you to receive the four newest novels published each month.

You'll be guaranteed that you'll never miss a title, and home delivery is so convenient. And to show you just how easy it is to get Zebra Historical Romances, we'll send you your first 4 books absolutely FREE! Our gift to you just for trying our home subscription service.

BIG SAVINGS AND CONVENIENT HOME DELIVERY

Each month, you'll receive the four newest titles as soon as they are published. You'll probably receive them even before the bookstores do. What's more, you may preview these exciting novels free for 10 days. If you like them as much as we think you will, just pay the low preferred subscriber's price of $3.75 each. *You'll save $3.00 each month off the publisher's price.* (A postage and handling charge of $1.50 is added to each shipment.) Of course you can return any shipment within 10 days for full credit, no questions asked. There is no minimum number of books you must buy.

4 FREE BOOKS

TO GET YOUR 4 FREE BOOKS WORTH $18.00 — MAIL IN THE FREE BOOK CERTIFICATE T O D A Y

Fill in the Free Book Certificate below, and we'll send your FREE BOOKS to you as soon as we receive it.

If the certificate is missing below, write to: Zebra Home Subscription Service, Inc., P.O. Box 5214, 120 Brighton Road, Clifton, New Jersey 07015-5214.

FREE BOOK CERTIFICATE

4 FREE BOOKS

ZEBRA HOME SUBSCRIPTION SERVICE, INC.

YES! Please start my subscription to Zebra Historical Romances and send me my first 4 books absolutely FREE. I understand that each month I may preview four new Zebra Historical Romances free for 10 days. If I'm not satisfied with them, I may return the four books within 10 days and owe nothing. Otherwise, I will pay the low preferred subscriber's price of just $3.75 each; a total of $15.00, *a savings off the publisher's price of $3.00.* I may return any shipment and I may cancel this subscription at any time. There is no obligation to buy any shipment. (A postage and handling charge of $1.50 is added to each shipment.) Regardless of what I decide, the four free books are mine to keep.

NAME

ADDRESS _____ APT

CITY _____ STATE _____ ZIP

TELEPHONE
( )

SIGNATURE _____ (if under 18, parent or guardian must sign)

Terms, offer and prices subject to change without notice. Subscription subject to acceptance by Zebra Books. Zebra Books reserves the right to reject any order or cancel any subscription.

ZB1894

he wanted to scoop her up in his arms, cover her with kisses, and carry her to his bed.

Shelton was controlling him from the grave. It was damnable that a man who'd never married was so concerned about who Caden married. Even in death Shelton couldn't give up control of his life. Shelton must have truly hated Caden's parents.

Flair turned and looked at him when she heard his boots crunching on the ground. The wind had blown fine strands of her hair away from her bonnet. The sun sprinkled her cheeks and nose with a hint of sunshine, giving her a beautiful wholesome look he found very appealing. He wanted to pull her into his arms and just hold her. In a way Shelton had known something he didn't know until this very moment. He was ready to have a woman in his life. Something else struck him. The woman who stood before him was the one he wanted.

She moistened her lips and he ached to feel her lips beneath his once more, but he knew the folly in allowing himself to become too involved with her. That she was his wife was no matter. He had to divorce her or lose the farm to Jake. As he looked into her beautiful blue eyes he knew he didn't have to say a word. She sensed the outcome of the reading.

"Cade, look at me. I'm riding by myself!" Rich called to him as he approached the corral.

"You're doing good, Rich," he answered. "Shorten up on the reins and keep your seat low in the saddle. Try not to bounce," he told him before giving his attention to Flair. He looked into her eyes. "You've been out here a long time. I was watching you from the porch."

As if she were afraid to look at him too long, she let her gaze stray to the landscape over his shoulder. "Benny had to take Stewart and Aunt Pauline into town. I told Rich I'd let him ride a little longer before he had to put the horse away. I don't mind. I like being out here. It's so nice out today. Maxwell Farms has some of the most beautiful countryside I've seen."

He nodded. "Land doesn't get much better than this. The grass is good for pasture."

"I watched everyone leave. Were you pleased with your uncle's will?" she asked.

"No. But it said exactly what I expected it to say. Shelton simply put in the will what he told me I had to do before I left to go find you."

"So nothing's changed?"

"No. Remember when I told you Shelton's death meant nothing to me?"

Flair remained quiet and nodded.

"I was wrong. It means I have the chance to inherit Maxwell Farms."

"But you won't inherit unless we divorce."

"That's right." He saw that she swallowed hard, so he took hold of her arm and moved her away from the corral and closer to the doorway of the barn. He didn't want to think about her leaving, but what could he promise her? He hurried to say, "This doesn't change any of our plans. I want you to stay here until the divorce is final, then you can go back to your farm. If Douglas doesn't find out we're divorced, he shouldn't bother you again."

"I find that it's not Douglas I worry so much about now that we're here. I don't think he'll try to take Rich away from me again. I think you made that clear the day you shot him in the arm. I'm hoping he'll be married by the time we return because he was eager to have a son before he got too much older. It's Rich I worry about. Look at him, Caden. He loves it here already and it's only been two days. And just last night he asked me if he should call you Papa. I worry what it will do to him after he's spent the summer here and he has to go back to our home. Our lives are vastly different from yours, you know. I'm beginning to think we should go back before he becomes attached here."

"I've thought about that, too. Rich thinks I'm his father, and I want it to stay that way. I don't want him to ever know that Douglas Eagerton is his real father. And Flair, Rich will always be welcome here. When he's older and doesn't need to be watched he can spend his summers here if he wants to." He looked into her eyes and knew he wasn't arresting her fears, but what was he to do?

She looked away from him. "I don't want Rich to ever find out Douglas is his real father either. You'll marry one day, Caden. I'm not so sure your new wife will like the idea of my son staying here at the farm."

He didn't like the sound of what she said. "You let me worry about any wife I might have. I've told Rich I was his father. I'll always treat him like a son. He'll be an heir to Maxwell Farms—with any other children I might have. I don't want him told anything different." But even as he said the words he knew they sounded like a hollow promise.

The bushes growing beside the wall of the barn shook as Jake eased away from Flair and Cade talking so quietly. He silently walked toward the back of the barn where he'd tied his horse. When he was a safe distance from them he chuckled. He stopped beside his horse and took the makings of a cigarette out of his shirt pocket. He carefully shook a smidgen of strong scented tobacco from a small tin into the thin paper and rolled it, sealing it together with his spittle. He put the cigarette in his mouth and held it between his lips while he struck a match on the bottom of his boot.

Shelton was the only man who'd known Cade better than Jake. And both of them knew him better than he knew himself. He chuckled again as he drew in heavily on the handmade cheroot. He'd just learned a valuable piece of information. So Rich wasn't Cade's son after all. He walked to the other end of the barn, but stayed far enough away that no one could see him and watched the boy still riding the old mare. He inhaled smoke from the cigarette.

Even though Caden had always pretended to be hard-assed and uncaring like his uncle, Jake knew Caden to be a man of honor and integrity with a soft heart underneath all that hard muscle. He'd bet the five horses Shelton left him Caden would call off the divorce before he'd leave Flair to the mercy of this man named Douglas. He'd married her one time to help her, and Jake had a feeling he'd stay married to her to save her. By the expression in his eyes he hadn't gotten the woman out of his system. He'd be in her bed before the week was out if he hadn't already been there. Jake was sure of that.

A thought suddenly struck him and he grinned. He knew what to do. What would these two do if Douglas showed up wanting to take the little wife and son home with him?

Well, they'd just have to see because Jake was going into town tomorrow to find someone who wanted to earn a couple of dollars taking a letter to Douglas Eagerton in south Alabama. Why should he settle for five horses and a few thousand dollars when he could have it all by creating a little mischief for Caden and his wife?

He laughed again as he threw the cigarette down and mashed it into the dirt. A small pebble caught his eyes and he had another idea. He'd scare the hell out of the little bastard. He picked up the rock and mounted his horse. He waited for the boy to ride down his way. When Rich turned the horse Jake let the pebble fly. The horse reared up on his hind legs and the boy toppled from the saddle.

"Damn!" Jake whispered.

* * *

Booker led the team of horses out of the barn and over to the wagon where Samp stood with a basket of food in his hand. His father had heard that everyone brought what food they could afford, then the church group spread it on a long table and shared. Booker hoped that was true. He was tired of trying to eat his papa's food. They hadn't had a decent meal since Miss Flair left more than a week ago.

"How do I look in my new clothes?"

"You a fine looking man, son." Samp's faced beamed with a smile to match his words.

"You think I can find a woman who'll give me the eye?" he asked when he saw how pleased Samp was with the way he was dressed in his dark brown trousers, white shirt, and dark gray jacket.

"Sure you can. Any woman will be proud to be your wife, all dressed up the way you are. But listen son, don't plan on marrying any one of them today."

Booker chuckled. "I know that. I want to do some courting. You think they gone welcome us over at that church, Pa?" he asked as he picked up the wagon rod and started hitching it to the harnesses on the mares.

Samp set the basket in the wagon bed.

"Sure they will. Church is open to anyone. I 'spect they'll be plumb happy to see us."

"You reckon the preacher will know we're there because I want to find me a wife?" Booker asked as he patted the horse on the rump and shoved the mare forward out of his way.

Samp laughed. "Ain't nobody knows what's in your mind, son, 'less you tell 'em." He brushed a bit of dust off the sleeve of his new coat. "There's nothing wrong with wanting a woman to hitch up with. You got a good job. We can make room for her in our house. Miss Flair might be pleased when she gets back and finds we got us a woman to look after us, and she won't have to cook and sew for us no more. She might be so happy she lets us add a room to the house so's you can have your private times."

Booker grunted his approval. He'd already thought of the second room. Sleeping in the same room with his father was fine for now. Booker had become used to his father's snoring a long time ago. But when he got himself a wife he didn't want his father sleeping in the same room.

The sound of a horse approaching made both of them look up. "It's that Mr. Eagerton," Booker said. "Wonder what he's doing riding over here for?"

"I don't have any idy but I 'spect you better let me do the talking. We don't want no trouble from him with Miss Flair gone."

Booker finished hitching the wagon and walked over to the wheel to stand by his father. It was a warm day for May and he wasn't used to wearing his shirt buttoned so tight. A trickle of sweat rolled down the side of his cheek and he brushed it off with his fingertips.

"What can we do for you?" his father asked looking up at the white man who stopped his horse in front of them.

"I've heard talk in town. I came out to see if it's true."

"What did ye hear?" Samp asked.

He squinted his eyes. "That Flair and her husband left town and took Rich with them."

"That's true enough." Samp nodded slowly and scratched the back of his head.

Booker remained quiet, but didn't take his eyes off Mr. Eagerton. If Miss Flair didn't like the man, then he didn't like him either. Besides, he'd never trust a man who wore his hat so low you couldn't see his eyes.

"Do you know where they went?" Eagerton asked, propping one arm on the saddle horn and holding the other close to his chest.

"I know it's Virginny but not exactly where.

Said she'd be write'n me if'n she wasn't going to be back by the end of summer."

"Do you know why they left?"

"I'm not rightly sure 'bout that." He shook his head again. "She didn't tell me nothing 'cept to look after the place."

The white man looked around the barnyard and the back of the house. His gaze drifted over to the left field. "What are you going to do with all those tomatoes you have in the field and the rest of the summer crop?"

"Mr. Cade took us into Mobile before they left and fixed us up with some customers. Miss Flair tole us what to do 'bout everything else before she left. We'll take care of this place. Don't you worry 'bout that. We won't let her down."

"What about you, boy?" he said, turning his attention to Booker. "You've been quiet. Maybe Flair told you why she was going to Virginia."

"Miss Flair ain't told me nothing," Booker lied. He knew they were going to a place called Maxwell Farms near Richmond—the city Rich was named after—but he wouldn't tell this man.

Eagerton pulled a gold coin from his jacket pocket. Samp's and Booker's eyes widened at the sight of the twenty dollar gold piece.

"You see this?"

They both nodded eagerly. "One of you ride over to my place and let me know when she comes back and this is yours. Understand?"

Booker remained quiet, his gaze fixed on the white man. He could use that money, but he wouldn't tell on Miss Flair.

"I 'spect she'll be bringing her husband back with her. You still wants me to come over?" Samp asked, surprising his son.

"Yes." He reached up and rubbed the arm he held to his chest. "I have unfinished business with her husband, too."

"Yes, sir, I'll come right away," Samp told him.

Eagerton nodded once. "Where you boys going all gussied up in new clothes? You didn't steal them, did you?"

"Oh, no sir. We ain't stole no clothes. Miss Flair fixed these up for us before she left. We're going to the church meeting over by Holmes Creek."

"Yes, I've heard of it. Some of my coloreds go over there on Sunday. It does them good to be with their own kind once a week. You boys don't do any drinking over there, do you?"

"Oh, no sir. We don't mess with that stuff. No sir."

Mr. Eagerton flipped the coin in the air and caught it in his hand. "You boys remember what I said." He turned his horse around and rode away.

Booker tapped angrily on his father's chest with his forefinger. "Why did you want to kiss his ass that way. He's a troublemaker, and Miss Flair don't like him. Mr. Caden done shot him once for messing around with her."

"I know. I know," he said, brushing Booker's hands away from his chest. "But he's gone hear from some one when Miss Flair returns. We might as well get that gold piece as someone else. I figure we'll be the first to know. Besides, I plan to tell Miss Flair about it. She won't mind me taking his money. She has her husband now, and he'll take care of her."

"All right. But I think we should get her permission before we go telling him she's home."

"We will son, we will. Now help me up in the wagon before we're late for our first service."

Twelve

Flair heard the horse whinny and Rich yell. She whipped her head around in time to see the horse rear up on his hind legs and Rich fly backward through the air. She screamed. In horror, she watched as her son landed with a gruesome thud. The horse kicked and bucked a couple of times before moving away from Rich's still body. Fear grabbed hold of Flair's heart.

"Rich!" she screamed again, and started running. Her feet didn't seem to be taking her any closer to her fallen son.

Caden rushed past her, quickly jumping over the fence. Her heart hammering wildly in her chest, Flair ran to the gate, knowing she couldn't get over the fence in her long skirts, already tangled about her legs keeping her from running faster to Rich.

With cold numb fingers she worked frantically at the latch of the gate until it finally opened. "How is he?" she called to Caden over the fence when she saw him slide into the dirt on his knees beside Rich. She could hardly breathe. Her heart pounded loudly. She ran so fast she tripped herself, caught her balance, and rushed on to the other side of the corral where Rich lay. With a cry on her lips she fell to the ground beside Caden.

"Rich!" she whispered desperately, looking down at her son. For a moment she lost her breath. Rich wasn't moving. There was a bleeding gash on his face. He lay so still she thought he'd died. A scream bubbled up in her chest but only a strangled groan passed her lips.

Caden laid his hand on Rich's chest over his heart. "He's alive," Caden told her.

Those words gave her so much relief she almost crumpled. "H-he's not moving," she answered, trying to calm her breathing, trying to slow her racing heartbeat as she looked at him. A jagged cut started an inch above his eye and ran down to just below the eye. Blood dripped and pooled beside him. Already his face and lips paled.

"Rich," she whispered again and reached to take him into her arms. She needed to hold him and tell him everything was going to be all right.

"No, Flair." Caden held her back. "Don't touch him."

"Why?" She gasped, trying to pull away from his grip. "I want to hold him."

"I know you do. But we don't know how badly he's hurt."

Pushing his hands away from her arms she insisted, "No, let me go. I want him to know I'm here." She struggled to get away from him, panic mounting inside her as she looked at her son lying so still, blood trickling down the side of his head. "Let me go. I need to—"

Strong fingers firmly closed around her arms. Caden's face appeared right in front of hers. "Listen to me, Flair. Don't think about what you want right now. Think about what's best for Rich."

Flair blinked rapidly. Of course he was right. She nodded, afraid if she tried to speak again only a scream of terror would emerge.

"I want to check him before we move him. I need to make sure nothing is broken. We could do more damage if we don't know how badly he's hurt."

She looked into Caden's greenish-brown eyes and saw fear. A chill shook her. He was worried about Rich, too. Consumed with raw fear she managed to ask, "Broken?"

Suddenly her mind was blank. It was as if she couldn't think. She couldn't feel. She trembled so badly her teeth chattered, and her chest felt as if it were caving in on her heart.

"I think the horse must have kicked him here on the side of his face and knocked him out. But he could have broken a bone when he fell."

Her hands clenched tightly. She tried to retain control of her shaking, of herself. She watched as Caden gently placed both his hands to either side of Rich's head. Slowly his fingers slid through the dusty brown hair. He felt all around Rich's head, carefully touching the area surrounding the open wound. He gently pressed all the exposed area of his neck before unbuttoning his shirt and checking his shoulders and upper chest.

"I don't think his neck is hurt," he said in a husky sounding voice. Caden checked each arm, over his ribcage and down each leg before he looked back to her and said, "I can't find anything broken, but we need to be careful. There may be internal injuries from the fall."

"Oh, my God, no!" She clasped her hands to her chest, her control slipping. "I shouldn't have taken my eyes off him. I shouldn't have walked away from the fence where I couldn't see him."

Caden covered her hands with his. "Flair, get hold of yourself and listen to me. That wouldn't have helped. Something spooked the horse. He might have seen a snake. You couldn't have done anything to stop the fall or the horse from kicking him, even if you'd been standing right beside him."

She looked into his eyes, realizing he was right, desperately wanting an answer. "What can I do?" she pleaded. "I've got to do something to help him." She freed her hands, reached over, and picked up Rich's small hand and held it in hers. "He's warm." She looked up at Caden, hope filled her. "That's a good sign, isn't it?"

He brushed a strand of hair away from her face and gave her a brief smile. "He's going to be all right, Flair. He's alive and right now that's the most important thing."

The concern she saw in Caden's expression brought fresh tears to her eyes. "Oh God, please don't let him die," she whispered earnestly.

"Flair, listen to me and do what I say. Rich needs your help not your tears. Do you understand me?"

She sniffled and nodded.

"Find Benny and tell him to ride into town and get the doctor."

Her dry, tight throat hurt as she said, "He's gone to take Aunt Pauline and Stewart into town."

"Damn, that's right." He looked toward

the house. "Run ahead of me to the house. Tell Bernie to find Porter, Rodman, or one of the other hands and send them into town for the doctor. Tell them to take my horse. He's the fastest."

Panic erupted inside her again. He wanted her to leave Rich. She shook her head furiously and carried his hand to her breast. "No, I don't want to leave him. I can't leave Rich!"

"Go, Flair! I'll be right behind you. You can't carry him. You're wasting time. He needs a doctor. You and Bernie have to find one of the workers and get them into town. Fast."

The urgency of his words hit her and she comprehended them. "Yes, yes." She stumbled on the hem of her dress in her haste to stand, but she quickly righted herself. She turned back to look at Caden. He was carefully lifting Rich into his arms.

"Don't wait for me. Go now, Flair. Hurry!"

She picked up her skirts and took off. She ran as fast as she could, pumping her arms, stretching her legs, putting her whole body into the effort of getting to the house as quickly as possible.

"Bernie! Bernie!," she called, nearing the front steps. "Bernie!" Flair took the steps two at a time and rushed inside the house.

The housekeeper came bounding down the stairs, carrying a load of clothes.

Breathless, Flair said, "Send someone for the doctor right away. Rich fell off the horse and he's unconscious."

"For heaven's sake!" The broad shouldered woman threw the clothes aside and pushed past Flair at the bottom of the stairs. "Silas is just outside the back door in the vegetable garden. I'll send him."

"Tell him to take Caden's horse. It's faster. Hurry! Caden's bringing Rich inside. Meet us in his room with some fresh water and what medical supplies you have."

Bernie flew down the hallway to the back of the house. Flair heard Caden on the front porch and held the door open for him, then rushed up the stairs ahead of him. In one brisk sweep she pushed the covers aside. Caden came up behind her and laid Rich on the bed.

Flair fell to her knees by the bed and took hold of his hand again. Rich looked so calm. So peaceful. He looked more than asleep. His pale face, colorless lips made him appear lifeless. There wasn't even a twitch in his eyes. She held his hand to her lips and kissed it long and hard before looking up at her husband. "Oh, God, Caden, what will I do if he doesn't make it?"

He placed a comforting hand on her shoulder. "I told you not to talk like that. His breathing is good. He'll come around in a few minutes."

She looked at the dried matted blood in his hair and the trickle of fresh blood that circled his ear. Caden was wrong and she knew it. She swallowed down a tormented sob and rose. How was she going to live through this? Her eyes darted around the room. If she got angry maybe she could handle this without going crazy. Her gaze darted to the door.

"Where's Bernie? I told her to bring up fresh water as soon as she sent Silas for the doctor. What could be keeping her?"

"Don't worry, Flair."

"No. I need to wash his face. I have to get the blood off."

Caden remained calm and spoke softly. "She'll be right up. Come on and help me take his clothes off so we can make sure he's not hurt anywhere else. You get his boots and I'll get his shirt and trousers."

She obeyed. Moving as if something was locking her joints, Flair picked up one foot and untied his boot and slipped it off. His feet and legs were limber, his skin warm. *He's just sleeping,* she told herself.

Within a few moments Bernie arrived with

the water and box of medical supplies. Caden and Flair set to work.

Bernie mumbled the Lord's Prayer over and over while Flair and Caden washed Rich's wound and dressed him in his nightshirt. They placed a cool wet cloth on his forehead. There was nothing more to do but wait for the doctor to arrive. Flair sat on the edge of the bed holding Rich's hand, talking to him, asking, begging, praying he'd wake up. Her stomach was in a continuous jumping state and her heart felt as if it might beat out of her chest, but outwardly she maintained control.

Time had never progressed so slowly. She was stiff from sitting on the bed so long. Noonday passed and the sun slowly etched a brilliant trace of sunshine across the western sky. Still the doctor hadn't come.

Late in the afternoon Silas returned and told them Doctor Wilkerson was on his way. He'd been at another house on the other side of town, and Silas had to ride over to get him. Over the course of the afternoon Bernie and Caden had tried to get Flair to eat something, but all she managed to get down was a few sips of tea. How could she eat when her son lay so close to death upon the white sheets? Caden and Bernie didn't know it but she knew she'd never forgive herself for bringing Rich to Maxwell Farms if he didn't wake up. *What would she do if he died!* she thought.

The doctor arrived an hour after Silas. The heavy-set middle-aged man insisted on seeing Rich alone. Flair protested but Caden finally talked her into letting the doctor do his job by himself. She resigned herself to pacing outside Rich's bedroom door. Bright daylight sky faded into twilight. Bernie lit the gas jets that were mounted to the hallway walls. Caden tried to talk to her, to get her to drink something, but Flair brushed aside all his attempts to get her mind off her son.

At last the door opened.

"He has a concussion," Dr. Wilkerson said, stepping out into the hallway and joining them.

"We know that," Flair said desperately, turning expectant eyes upon him. "How can we wake him up?"

The doctor's gaze swept past Flair to Caden who stood behind her, his chest to her back, his hands on her shoulders. He closed his black bag. "We can't."

"No," she whispered, begging his words not to be true. Her hands made fists so tight her knuckles whitened and her fingernails bit into her tender flesh.

"I'm sorry, Mrs. Maxwell. Medically there's

nothing we can do but keep him comfortable until he wakes up or—"

"How long can he stay asleep like this?" Caden asked cutting off the doctor's sentence.

He shook his head once and pursed his lips making his full mustache wiggle. "There's no telling. Never known of any two people staying unconscious for the same length of time. As best I can tell the fall or the blow from the horse bruised his brain and caused swelling. This deep sleep is nature's way of giving the brain time to heal. The pain would be too great for him to bear if he woke up."

"And when the injury heals he'll wake?" Caden asked, squeezing her shoulders gently.

Doctor Wilkerson nodded. "The sooner he wakes up the better chance he has of making it."

"And if the injury doesn't heal, he won't wake up?"

"Flair."

"No, Caden," she pulled away from him and turned on him angrily. "I need an answer. I want the truth."

"What you said is true, Mrs. Maxwell. Right now there's nothing to do but wait."

"I don't want to hear there's nothing I can do to save my son." She bit back a strangled sob. "There must be something I can do. I can't stand around and watch him die. I won't."

An expression of intense anger flew to Caden's face. "Dammit! Will you stop saying he's going to die. He's just asleep. He'll wake up."

Flair jerked back as if he'd slapped her. Of course he was right. Why was she talking like this? Rich was going to be all right. She couldn't lose control again.

Caden paused and his voice grew softer as he said, "You've got to believe that."

Unbidden tears rolled down her cheeks. "Yes. I do. I do believe it." Numbly she turned and walked back into Rich's room.

Caden stood on the front porch sipping his Scotch, his foot propped against the railing, wondering how in the world he was going to get Flair out of Rich's room for a while. How could he ask her to leave when he wanted to be there all the time, too? Like Flair, he felt somehow responsible even though he knew there was no way either of them could have prevented the accident.

He'd stayed in the room with Rich and Flair for an hour or two after the doctor left. He finally had to force himself to leave. He couldn't stand seeing Rich so still and pale.

He wanted to see the defiant little boy who met him at the door with a shotgun. The one who threw rocks into the pond. He wanted to see the laughing, smiling young man who rode atop the horse.

But—he left the room because of Flair, too. He hated seeing her drawn face, worried eyes and trembling lips, knowing he could do nothing to make her feel better, nothing to ease her pain. He'd thought about taking her in his arms and holding her, but fearing she'd take his action as aggressive rather than comforting, he'd refrained. He would feel better if he could hold her close, but would she? Did she need him at all?

The sound of boots crunching on the ground came to his attention and he looked up. Slowly he was able to make out Jake's dark figure walking toward him. He wondered if the reason the man always dressed in black was so he'd be hard to spot in the dark.

He stopped at the bottom of the steps and looked up at Caden. Moonlight shimmered off the silver medallions that circled his hat and adorned his vest.

"I heard about the boy. I came to check on him."

Caden straightened, surprised the combative foreman would care enough to stop by and ask about Flair's son. Bernie had told him that Rodman, Porter, and some of the other hands had stopped by and inquired. Silas had spent the entire evening in the house wanting to help in any way, but Caden never expected consideration from Jake.

"There's no change in his condition."

Jake placed a booted foot on the bottom step and pulled the makings for a cheroot out of his breast pocket. "Did you find out what happened?"

Caden sat his glass on the top of the railing. "No. I went down to the corral and looked around. I didn't see signs of a snake but that had to be what spooked the horse."

"I'd agree. Muffin is the gentlest horse on the farm. She hasn't reared back on her legs in years. I thought she was too old to do it."

Something about the way Jake readily agreed with him made Caden uneasy. That same feeling he had the day Jake let the rope slip when he was bringing the calf up the cliff passed over him again. But what could Jake have done to Muffin? How could he have had anything to do with the horse's behavior when he and Flair were standing so close to the corral? They would have seen or heard something.

"I don't guess a horse gets too old to be spooked," he finally answered.

"Damn shame. I saw the boy on the horse when I rode out today. Looked like he was doing a fairly good job of handling the mare to me. Damn shame."

It wasn't like Jake to be so concerned over anyone and that made Caden feel even more uneasy about the incident and Jake's possible involvement.

"He'll be all right."

"Good." Jake shrugged. "Look, Cade. I just wanted to say I have no hard feelings about the will. If you get the farm fine. I never expected to have a chance at it. But, I'll be happy to take it from you if you decide you don't want the divorce."

The glint in Jake's eyes outshone the glimmer of moonlight on his silver medallions. Caden grunted decisively. "Don't worry." He paused. "I'll get the divorce, and I'll give you the money and horses Shelton promised you."

They stared at each other, neither man backing down from his position.

"I'll give you the horses and money now if you're ready," Caden offered.

Jake shook his head and chuckled low in his throat. "No. Can't say I ever expected to own this place one day, but I'm not going to give up my one chance that easily. That's a mighty pretty woman you're married to. If you do get a divorce I'll pick up my due from you at that time. But until then, I'm your shadow." He turned and walked away.

Caden watched Jake fade into the night before picking up his drink. He and Jake had always been rivals. Shelton had seen to it that hadn't changed. He finished off his drink and walked back inside the quiet house.

He found Bernie in the kitchen shaking her head as she looked at the untouched tray of potatoes, chicken, beets, and bread.

The toil of the day's events showed in her eyes as she looked up at him and said, "I couldn't get Mrs. Maxwell to touch the food. Drank her tea, though."

"That's enough for tonight. I'll see she eats tomorrow. You go on to bed, Bernie. I'll turn out all the lights on my way upstairs."

She gave him a worried look. "You won't leave her alone tonight, will you?"

A protective feeling struck him. "No. I'll stay with her and Rich. They won't be alone."

Bernie smiled.

Upstairs Caden walked into the dimly lit bedroom and saw Flair exactly where he'd left her—sitting on the bed, holding Rich's hand. She wouldn't be able to move tomorrow if she stayed there all night. Sensing what needed to be done, he walked down to his room and picked up the velvet-covered wing back chair and carried it to Rich's bedside.

Flair didn't seem to notice he'd entered the room. His heart ached to comfort her.

"Any change," he asked over her shoulder.

"No. I keep dropping small amounts of sugared water past his lips like the doctor suggested, but I'm not sure he swallows any of it."

"I think he does. He's just resting, like you need to do. Flair," he said, placing his hand on her warm shoulder. "You can't sit on the bed all night."

"I'm not going to leave him," she whispered, without looking at him.

"You don't have to. I've brought a comfortable chair in." He gently pulled on her arm as he seated himself in the cozy chair. "Come sit here on my lap and let me hold you."

"No, I—" she protested but not with any show of strength.

"Come here, Flair," he said softly and for the first time since he walked in the room she looked over at him. His heartbeat quickened. He needed her. "Let me hold you tonight and help you through this."

Her eyes searched his for a moment, then, without hesitating she slid off the bed and into his arms. She laid her head against his shoulder and snuggled her nose into the crook of his neck, her legs drawn up tight to rest against the arm of the chair.

Caden breathed easier as he encircled her with his arms. He laid his cheek against her forehead. For the first time that day he felt like he could handle whatever happened with Jake and the will, whatever happened to Rich.

Thirteen

Time stood still.

On the afternoon of the third day the doctor returned. In her grief Flair refused to talk to him. If he couldn't make Rich well she had no use for him. She blamed him for not being able to heal Rich—awaken him and bring him back to her.

She refused to leave her son's bedside for longer than it took her to visit her room to use the chamber pot or take a sponge bath from the basin. She ate and drank only enough to sustain herself. Knowing her state of mind Bernie and Caden had stopped trying to get her to rest during the day. Nothing gave her pleasure, but each night she was able to sleep when Caden came into the room, pulled her into his arms, and laid her head on his shoulder.

Late into the night of the fourth day Flair rested in Caden's arms. Something awakened her. What, she wasn't sure. She looked over at Rich. He hadn't moved. She looked up at Caden and in the soft yellow light she saw that he slept peacefully, his hair tousled about his forehead. She'd been so concerned about Rich she'd failed to thank Caden for standing by her, staying with her when she knew he had important things to do. She didn't know how to thank him for being there for her. She only knew she would have gone crazy without his guidance, his comfort, and his encouragement. She wanted to reach up and give him a kiss, but thinking it might awaken him she contented herself to merely watch him sleep.

As she stared at him she realized she loved him. She had to. What else could it be that gave her that quickening in her stomach, that desire to be with him, to enjoy his kisses and caresses. She'd had a youthful experience with sexual desire but that had turned ugly because of Douglas. With Caden it was different. It was stronger, yet softer—deeper than the surface feelings she'd had for Douglas ten years ago.

But Caden had to divorce her to keep the farm. They could never have a life together. He must never know how she felt about him.

After a few minutes of sleeplessness Flair needed to stretch out of the curled position she'd slept in. Careful not to wake Caden she eased away from him and knelt beside the bed. She bowed her head and offered up another prayer of petition. She felt something pull her hair, and thinking she lay on it she tried to raise her head. There was a definite tug on her hair. She reached up and felt a hand on her head. Alarmed, she twisted around and found Rich's fingers tangled in her hair. She looked down at him. He stirred fitfully in his sleep. She gasped in joy. It was the first time he'd moved since the accident.

"Caden!" she whispered loudly. "Caden, turn up the light."

Caden jerked to his feet and turned up the wick on the lamp. "What's wrong?"

"Look, he's moving! Caden, thank God, he's waking up."

With the brighter light she could see Rich's face contort as though he was in pain. He didn't open his eyes or speak. His legs jerked and quivered and his hands worked, opening and closing.

Caden wrapped her in his arms, picking her up off the floor as he hugged her tightly. They laughed, they kissed, they rejoiced.

A mumbling cry broke them apart and Flair wiggled out of Caden's embrace and knelt down to her son. "Rich, can you hear me? Can you hear me, darling?"

"Rich, son, you're going to be all right,"

Caden said, brushing back the little boy's hair.

All of a sudden Rich reared his head back against the pillow and let out an ear-piercing scream. He jerked his hands to each side of his head and continued to scream.

Terror filled Flair's heart as she tried to soothe him with soft words. "Rich, tell me what's wrong? I want to help you," she cried.

Caden placed his hands over Rich's hands. "His head is probably hurting."

The door burst open and Bernie rushed in, her long gray hair flying about her broad shoulders.

"His head is hurting him, Bernie, get the laudanum," Caden said excitedly.

Flair's gaze darted over to his. "No!"

Anger flew across his face. "No? What the hell do you mean? Flair, the pain is killing him."

Fear rooted itself too deeply inside her to think rationally. "No, the laudanum will put him back to sleep. I don't want him to go back to sleep," she repeated, trying to hold Rich still.

Caden let go of Rich who continued to scream and thrash in the bed and grabbed Flair by the shoulders, pulling her to her feet. His eyes were wild. "Are you crazy? He's in pain. He needs the goddamn medication."

"No, Caden," she whispered, afraid to give in. "I'm terrified he won't wake up again. Please, we have to find another way to stop the pain."

His eyes softened. "There is no other way. Laudanum is all we have." He turned her loose. "Pour the medicine, Bernie."

Flair hiccuped and glanced over at Bernie who stood on the other side of the bed, robe and nightgown disarrayed, holding the bottle and spoon in midair. Caden was right. Rich was screaming with pain. Pushing her fear aside, she nodded to Bernie.

For the next forty-eight hours Rich either cried and screamed or slept as the painful headaches continued. The doctor was called back to the house and he assured them the headaches would get less severe each day. On the third day when Rich awoke he was able to sit up in bed and talk for a while without the piercing pain. By nightfall he was eating soup and drinking warm milk.

Shortly after Rich fell asleep for the evening Caden came into his room and said, "Bernie's on her way up to stay the night with Rich."

"That's not—"

"Necessary," he interrupted. He touched

her lips with his fingertips. "I think it is. No argument this time, Flair. You've been in this room for almost a week. You need a long soak in a tub of warm water and a night's sleep on the bed. Silas is preparing you a bath in my room."

"Your room?" she questioned, knowing she hadn't minded sleeping in the large chair comfortably curled in Caden's strong arms.

"I've installed a large tub. The bathroom is quite modern. I think you'll enjoy it." He smiled. "Don't worry. I'll give you privacy."

She looked down at her son sleeping peacefully. She was so thankful the bad headaches were subsiding. "The bath sounds wonderful but I couldn't possibly leave Rich for the whole night."

"Yes, you can. Remember, I said no argument. Bernie is more than capable of awakening you should Rich need you in the middle of the night. You need the rest, Flair."

The ache in her shoulders and back told her to listen to Caden. Her hand went to her hair and she smoothed back some wayward strands. She hadn't taken care of herself. She'd been too worried about Rich. "You're right," she agreed finally. "I do need the rest."

"I'm going out for a while. Take your time. I won't be back until late."

Flair watched Caden walk out of Rich's room and sighed heavily, wondering where he was going.

As soon as Bernie arrived Flair went to her room and gathered her rose scented soap and nightgown and walked down the hallway to Caden's room. She'd heard about the new indoor bathrooms that were gaining popularity, but she hadn't seen one. She felt odd at first, stepping into Caden's room alone. Gas jets had been installed on each eggshell-white wall and all of them burned low, giving the room a wonderfully cozy feel. Handsome Queen Anne cherrywood furniture with beautiful brass fittings on it graced the room. Gold and claret-colored striped drapes hung at each window and over the fireplace was a mirror that extended all the way up to the high ceiling.

She walked across the large room and into another room that appeared to be an extension of the spacious bathroom. Flair saw the claw-footed bathtub sitting in the far corner, steam rising from the water. The commode and basin were boxed in a rich oak. The room looked so inviting she immediately undressed and stepped into the tub.

While she soaked in the warm water, scrubbed her face, and washed her hair, Flair found her thoughts on Caden instead of Rich. She had to think of some way to repay Caden for standing by her and helping her through the crisis with Rich. She had to let him know how grateful she was. But what could she give him that he didn't already have? What could she do for him that he didn't have workers to do? The one thing he wanted from her, the divorce, she'd already agreed to give. Still there must be something.

The longer she stayed in the water, the sleepier she became. Reluctantly she emerged and dried her body before slipping on her white sleeveless nightgown. While she towel dried her long hair she walked back into the bedroom and looked around again. The bed, plush and plump with pillows and a coverlet of claret red with gold stripes looked irresistible. She'd sit on it just for a moment to see if it was as soft and comfortable as it looked.

It was. She let the towel drop to the floor and ran her hands over the heavy brocaded material. One pillow, beige moire trimmed in a gold braid looked especially soft. Maybe it wouldn't hurt if she lay upon it for just a minute or two. She pulled the length of her damp hair over to one shoulder so she wouldn't water mark the beautiful material and lay her cheek against its softness. It felt wonderful. She brought up her legs and curled them under the skirt of her nightgown. Within moments her eyes became heavy with sleep. Surely Caden wouldn't care if she lay back against the soft pillows and closed her eyes for just a moment.

Something disturbed her sleep. Hands gently touched her, rolling her, picking up her legs, scooting her aside. She felt a snuggling warmth heat her back. A light covering slid up her legs, over her hip, past her waist and stopped at her shoulders. An arm slid under her neck, another dropped lightly around her waist. She felt secure, protected. She sighed peacefully and wiggled her backside farther into the firmness and warmth behind her.

"Be still, Flair," came a huskily soft voice. Her eyes popped open. She wasn't in her bed. She twisted her head around and her nose bumped Caden's. Moonlight filtered in through the window. She stared into his brownish-green eyes and felt the length of his body next to hers.

"Oh," she gasped and tried to move out of his embrace, but he held her fast.

"Don't move. I didn't mean to wake you," he whispered. "I only wanted to get you under the sheet. Shhh—go back to sleep."

"No, I didn't mean to fall asleep in your bed. I only meant to rest my eyes."

"It's all right. I didn't mind coming in and finding you here."

"Caden, this isn't a good idea," she offered, realizing her thin nightgown was the only barrier between them.

"I know, but I want you here. I'm not going to force you to stay in my bed." His voice was husky. "I'd never force you, Flair."

Looking into his eyes she believed him. In that moment Flair realized this was her chance to thank Caden for what he'd done for her and Rich. It gave her the opportunity to explore the wonderful feelings he stirred inside her. This was her chance to be with the man she loved. Douglas had forced her. Tonight it was her choice. Did she want to miss this opportunity to know what loving between a man and a woman was all about? Did she dare lose this chance and spend the rest of her life wondering what it would have been like to lie in Caden's arms and make love? She was hurt once. Did she dare trust a man again? Could she forget the pain of the past? As she looked at Caden she thought back over all the things he'd done for her, and knew if she was ever going to trust another man it had to be this one.

"Do you want me to stay?" she asked fully aware of what she was asking, frightened but courageous.

"Yes," he answered with emotion. "But you have to want it, too."

I do.

Her heartbeat quickened, her stomach tightened. It was truly up to her. The flame of desire had been lit and only Caden's loving would put it out. Filled with tenderness, she reached over and caressed his cheek. His stubble of beard tickled her palm. She swallowed hard and smiled. "Yes, I want to stay."

His intake of surprised breath pleased her. Caden scooted closer to her, slipping his arm back under her head. He moved his face closer to hers until his lips were directly in front of hers. She felt the warmth of his breath on her skin. A thrill of excitement, expectancy rushed through her. As her breaths grew shorter he gently placed his lips upon hers. They were soft, supple. To her surprise he didn't hurry, instead he slowly savored the kiss, causing a fever of longing to grow inside her.

Flair sighed contentedly, enjoying the slowly building desire the kiss prompted. His tongue came out and teased the inner edge of her lips. She responded by parting them. His tongue entered sending shudders of wonderfully sensuous feelings spiraling through her.

"You're tired," he whispered against her mouth.

"Not too tired for this," she answered and pressed her lips harder against his. Tonight wasn't the time to be shy, coy, or reluctant. Tonight was hers to enjoy. She wouldn't deny either of them whatever they wanted, and she wouldn't hurry it.

Caden eagerly answered her pressure by snaking his tongue into her mouth again. He pulled her closer to his body, flattening her breasts against his chest. Again she felt the length of his body, the hardness that rubbed against her womanly parts and a soaring hunger filled her.

One hand played in the thickness of his hair. With the other she slid her open palm over his shoulder, across his chest, loving the feel, the texture of his bare skin. Her fingers rippled over firm muscles, glided down damp skin. Her hands slid past his waist over his hip where she discovered he wore nothing.

His tongue sought the secrets of her mouth and she opened wider, giving him all the access he wanted. Impatient for more, she returned his hard demanding kisses to show him how desperately she wanted him.

His hand slid down her neck and cupped her gown-covered breast. Suddenly fear spurted inside her, erasing the sensuous heat between them. She grabbed hold of his hand and tried to pull it away.

"No, Flair," he whispered against her protests. He looked into her eyes. "It's me. I'm not going to hurt you. This is part of making love. Let me show you what it's like. I promise it won't hurt."

The tender expression on his face told her she could trust him with anything, including her body. He wasn't going to hurt her. She nodded.

Carefully he replaced his hand over her breast and gently caressed it, massaged it. He was right. It didn't hurt. In fact, it felt wonderful. She loosened her grip.

He looked into her eyes. "I'm going to love you, Flair. Relax and enjoy what is going to happen between us. Nothing I'm going to do will hurt you. I promise. When I kiss your breasts, or when I touch you here—"

His hand slid down to her most private part and she gasped, but not from shock, from the thrill that shot through her.

"Don't be alarmed." He soothed her. "Everything I'm going to do will give us both pleasure, but I'll stop if you ask me to. Do you trust me to do that?"

Flair didn't know if she was breathing. He held her spellbound with his promise, his sexual talk. "Yes," she managed in a hoarse whisper.

"If at any time I hurt you or you're frightened, just tell me."

She felt herself relaxing. She wanted this. It

was her choice, and she decided to let her desire for this man outweigh all other feelings.

Her hand let go of his wrist and slid up his arm to his shoulder, the hair on his lower arm feeling seductively ticklish. Beneath the nightgown he lifted, stroked, and molded her breast with his hand. Her abdomen grew taut with expectation. She liked the way his stroking made her feel and she found herself arching her breasts against his hand. She liked the way it tightened her insides. When he rubbed her nipple between his thumb and forefinger she gasped in delight from the flagrant desire that rushed through her. Her gaze flew to his. He gave her a comforting little smile that answered her question. *It was supposed to feel this wonderful.*

For long minutes they touched, stroked, kissed, and moved.

With slow gentle movements Caden pulled her gown up and over her head, tossing it aside. She shivered and crossed her hands over her breasts.

Caden rose up on his knees and reaching over her turned up the wick on the bedside lamp. He lowered himself back to her and said, "Don't hide yourself from me. I want to look at you."

Flair relaxed further, denying all her inhibitions. She felt as if she'd been waiting all her life for this night, for this man. Looking up into his face, she slowly pushed her arms and hands to her side, leaving the length of her body exposed to his view. She watched as his gaze raked down her body quickly, then soared back up to her breasts to linger, to savor. He reached out and touched, caressed each one before his eyes and hands followed the same route down her ribcage, over her indented waistline, past her flat stomach to linger, to feast at her most womanly part.

"You are a beautiful woman." His gaze darted back up to her face. "Oh, god yes, Flair let me love you. Let me show you how much I want you, how wonderful you make me feel, how good it can be between us."

His words were so hoarse she barely recognized them. She smiled and reached her arms toward him, welcoming him into her heart.

Hard with desire, Caden pushed the rest of the covers to the foot of the bed with his feet. He hungered for the taste of her.

He'd only meant to hold her close and sleep with her when he'd come into his room and found her curled so innocently upon his bed. He'd thought about carrying her to her own room, but wanting to disturb her as little as possible he'd decided it best to leave her and try to get her under the cover rather than on top of it. He'd almost made it without waking her. Now as his eyes admired her naked beauty he was glad he hadn't.

One man had hurt her. He would see to it she was never hurt again. Pulsating with ardor he looked into her trusting eyes again. His desire for her grew. How could he not want this woman? She had the beauty to attract him and make him want to bury himself deeply within her softness, but what he was feeling for her was so much more than desire for a beautiful woman. He didn't need or want just any woman. Flair was the one he craved. Only this woman could put out the fire burning within him.

Slowly, his gaze swept to her breasts, pale, flesh-colored mounds with pinkish-brown circles that looked up at him and enticed him to cover them with his mouth, with wet kisses. They were small, but beautifully rounded with just the right amount of pucker from the nipple. They teased him, they beckoned him with their pertness, their firmness, their softness. He lowered his head and pulled one of the tempting nipples into his mouth and sucked the sweetness from it. It hardened beneath his flickering tongue. He savored the way she felt in his closed mouth. His manhood grew painfully harder. A fiery heat drove his ministrations. He slid his hand up and cupped her other breast running his

palm over it time and time again. The rose-
bud tip tickled his palm. He touched her
with sweeping caresses, trying to feel all of
her at once. His fingers, his hands had never
worshiped a woman before this one. Reluctantly he let his tongue lead the path from
one to the other, not wanting to miss the ti-
niest bit of her skin.

God, she was so good, sweet, clean tasting.
All the other women he had been with over
the years had smelled and tasted heavily of
perfume but Flair had clean, delicious tasting
skin.

He buried his face in the warmth of her
breasts a few more moments, then snuggled
farther down and kissed her belly, her navel,
lower and then back up to her lips again.
Never had he taken so much time with a
woman. Never had he wanted to. He threw a
leg over her and wrapped his foot around her
ankle as if to hold her to him.

"I know this is going to sound crazy," he
whispered as he held the sides of her face in
his hands and kissed her, "but I've wanted
you since that first night I saw you. I don't
know why. I only know I have."

"I'm yours," she murmured softly.

He answered her with a moan of passion
and slid on top of her body. *She was his.* How
could he be gentle when he'd wanted her so

badly for so long? Did she know how desperately he wanted her? Not just any woman, but her.

His body was telling him he needed release, but he also needed to make it good for her. She trusted him, and he wouldn't break that trust for a throbbing need that pained him. She needed to know how a man is supposed to treat a woman when they make love. He needed to kiss softly but he kissed her hungrily. He needed to be patient, draw out their love-making, but his body told him to go quickly.

He loved the taste of her, the smell of her, the feel of her beneath him. She was small but not lacking. She was tight but not stiff. The little sounds of pleasure she made increased his own pleasure in loving her. How could he not love her, enjoy her when she gave herself so freely to him?

Gradually he let his hand slip lower, finding that intimate part between her legs. She stiffened, but he soothed her with soft words.

"I won't hurt you. I promise I'll go easy until you're used to the size of me. It may be uncomfortable, love, but it won't hurt."

She was hot, wet, ready for him. He wanted her as he had no other woman. He covered her with his body. Easing her thighs apart he entered her. Bravely she stifled a little moan,

but within seconds her moistness eased the
tightness and made it easier for him to move.
When she relaxed, desire grew and she rose
up to meet him. They moved together. He
wrapped his arms around her, pressing deeper,
trying to reach her soul and claim it for his
own. He couldn't get enough of her. He
wanted never to leave the warmth of her body.
Never again would he be satisfied with a
woman he'd paid for her pleasures.

He watched and listened as her desire grew
stronger and stronger until she cried out, bit-
ing into his shoulder before relaxing against
him. Caden closed his eyes and released his
seed into her. He shuddered above her as delicious shivers of relief shot through him.
Panting, he calmed from the love-making.

He caressed her cheek, kissed the tip of
her nose. He smiled at her. Just looking at
her made him happy.

"Did I hurt you?" he asked.

"There was a moment of discomfort but
no pain." She returned his smile. "It was so
much more wonderful than I expected it to
be. I felt as if—" She paused. "As if even my
skin was singing. Does that sound stupid?"

He laughed. "No. I felt the same way." He
bent his head and kissed her. It was good.
He kissed her harder.

They needed to talk, but that could be

done tomorrow. Already he grew hard again. He wanted her. How could he not want to kiss those tempting lips, lave those beautiful breasts, and dip his manhood once again into her hot tightness?

God yes he wanted her.

Fourteen

He didn't know when she left his bed—only that she was gone when he awoke. A strange sense of disappointment filled him when he realized Flair no longer lay beside him. He wanted to touch her one more time. He longed to feel her beneath him again. He dreamed of burying his nose in that soft skin behind her ear and breathing deeply, inhaling her essence and filling himself with Flair.

Lying in the bed he stretched his arms up and over his head and stared at the ceiling. He wanted to forget the work day that was ahead of him and remember last night. All of it. He didn't want to forget about one kiss, one caress, or one soft sigh that purred past her lips.

Flair was a beautiful woman. She had soft skin, a shapely figure, and enticing moves that even now had him hot for her. She was an alluring lover, learning quickly how and where to touch him to bring him to climax long after his body should have been spent. During the midnight hours she'd set his body and soul on fire for her. He had to have her again and again.

Thoughts of their bodies entwined caused Caden to ache with need for Flair. He rolled over and buried his face in the pillow where she'd lain her head, where her golden hair had fanned out. He breathed in deeply and was rewarded with her scent. The sheet tickled his palms as he rubbed it. He moistened his lips and found the taste of her still in his mouth. He settled his body onto the bed. For a moment he imagined her beneath him and his manhood grew hard. He wanted her. He needed her.

Chuckling he turned over and chided himself. He was acting like a lovesick kid who'd had his first woman. But he couldn't get the smell of her out of his mind, the feel of her off his hands, or the taste of her out of his mouth. As he lay on the bed and looked up at the ceiling in the light of early morning thoughts of Flair relaxed him, pleased him, captivated him.

He had been with many women over the years, but he'd never loved any of them. He wanted her as he had no other woman. Last night he realized he'd always wanted her.

And now, after spending a night loving her, Caden knew he'd never give up Flair.

There had to be a reason he felt this consuming need to have Flair with him. Surely he could have gotten the divorce without bringing Flair to Virginia. But he'd wanted her with him. Now he knew he wanted her with him as his wife. But how would she feel about that? Had last night meant as much to her as it had to him?

His gaze drifted out the window to the rolling hills behind the house. He saw horses grazing on the open field. How could Shelton had ever doubted his love for Maxwell Farms? Maybe he hadn't. Maybe he just hadn't known how to give up control.

Caden's gaze strayed back to inside the room, his thoughts back to Flair and his night with her. He'd lain with soft skinned, beautiful women before, but none of them had touched his heart. Flair had. He jerked as it dawned on him that he was in love with Flair. That had to be it. What else could it be? He had always loved her. That was why he had wanted to go back for her when he came out of the army. That was why he had defied Shelton and hadn't divorced her years ago when Shelton tried to force him.

Caden rubbed his eyes. He loved her? Was that true? Couldn't it be something else? But what? What else would cause him to want to have a second look at the will and see if anything had been overlooked? What else but love could make him feel as if he couldn't live without Flair in his life? Dammit! He loved Flair. He didn't want to divorce her.

He rose from the bed, not bothering to put on his robe, and padded barefoot over to his shaving mirror. He needed to talk to Flair. How was she taking what happened between them last night, this morning? He would probably find her in Rich's room, he thought as he rubbed his scruffy face with his fingertips and looked at his beard in the mirror. If she thought she could hide in there all day she was mistaken. He needed to see that she was all right, then he was going to Rutherford to find out what could be done to break that damn will.

Flair may not love him, he thought with some reluctance as he lathered his shaving soap, but he knew she cared for him. She would never have let him make love to her if that hadn't been the case.

Dammit, he hoped it had been as good for her as it was for him. She was coming from a different place than he was. She had to overcome her experience with Douglas. It appeared she had. After their first time together she'd seemed relaxed, comfortable, even eager to continue. She'd murmured softly at times and cried out with passion a couple of times during the night, but still he worried. What did she feel this morning?

He hoped he'd been able to erase from her mind the damnable incident with Douglas. Douglas. He wished he'd done more than shoot him in the arm when he had the chance.

And there was Rich to consider, Caden pondered as he painted a white beard of lather on his face. He picked up the razor. He liked Flair's son. He wouldn't mind having Rich call him Pa. Caden chuckled to himself again and whistled cheerfully as he puckered to shave over his chin. Now that he thought about it, his and Flair's children would probably like having an older brother around the house.

But within moments the contents of the will overshadowed his merry feeling. What could he do about that damn will? Surely somehow he could find a way around it. Caden couldn't stand the thought of the farm going to Jake any more than he could the thought of divorcing Flair. He resolved not to let Shelton win. He'd find a way to keep Maxwell Farms and his wife.

A few minutes later, dressed in a collarless white shirt and black trousers Caden walked down the hallway and stuck his head in Rich's room. As he suspected Flair sat on her son's bed talking gently to him. Rich was sitting up in bed and spied him almost immediately.

"Cade," he called. "Mama won't let me get out of bed. Will you talk to her for me?"

"I can try," he answered.

Flair stood up and faced him as he walked into the room. His pulse raced at the sight of her. She looked lovely in her white blouse and copper-colored skirt, her hair pulled back into the neat chignon she wore each day. An attractive blush stained her cheeks.

He smiled at her and said, "Good morning, Flair."

She returned his greeting and the smile, but it wasn't the warm, loving acknowledgment he expected. Her smile appeared forced and she looked a bit nervous. His stomach contracted. Something was wrong. Could it be that she didn't know how he felt this morning? Maybe she was worried about how he felt about last night? No, his smile was warm, sincere, encouraging. Flair stood straight and stiff beside the bed. Where was the loving woman he held in his arms last night?

Feeling uneasy he walked past Flair and placed his hand on Rich's shoulder.

"Mama won't let me get out of bed, Cade,"

Rich said again. "Can you tell her I'm all right?"

Caden looked over at Flair as he asked, "Did she tell you why you couldn't get up?"

Flair kept her gaze on Rich. Why wouldn't she look him in the eyes? Did she worry that their time together last night was only a one night stand?

"She thinks I'm still sick. I told her I don't have a headache anymore, but she won't let me get up." He folded his arms across his chest and huffed loudly as he looked up at Caden.

He had to be careful. He didn't want to come between Flair and her son. "I think that's because she's afraid you'll get a headache if you get up and start moving around before you're completely well. You were a very sick little boy for a while. She just wants to take care of you."

"I'm not sick anymore, Cade. I feel fine." Rich remained adamant.

"You do look better," he hedged, wondering how he was going to get out of this without Flair or Rich being angry with him. "But I have a feeling you're not as strong as you think you are. Why don't you go ahead and mind your mama today and stay in bed? If you don't have a bad headache today, I think it should be all right for you to get up for a little while tomorrow. How about it? Does that sound like a good deal to you?"

His lashes came down and covered his big brown eyes. "I guess so." Rich's tone and expression left no doubt he wasn't happy about the compromise.

"It will be better this way, Rich. Does that sound like a good plan to you, Flair?"

She glanced at him but again didn't meet his eyes. "I think so. I'll agree that Rich can get up for a few minutes tomorrow, *if* he doesn't have a headache at all today."

"Why don't we leave it at a *bad* headache." He smiled at Rich. "I don't think we should count a little one, do you Rich?"

"Right, Cade. Anybody can have a little headache." A smile lifted the corners of his mouth, and he relaxed in the bed.

Flair turned angry eyes upon Caden. "Wait a minute. I didn't agree to—"

"Excuse me, Flair. Could I see you outside for a moment?" Caden asked. "I'll see you later, Rich," he told the boy and nudged Flair out the door.

Caden took hold of her arm and walked her down the hallway. When they were away from Rich's door Flair yanked her arm away from him and said, "I'm not happy about what you just did," she told him.

Her anger baffled him, surprised him. "I

had to say that, Flair, and if you'll think for
a moment you'll know why."

"I know I don't need you taking care of
Rich for me. I'm perfectly capable."

"Of course you are, but it doesn't mean
you always look objectively at things. Rich
could very well have a minor headache and
be afraid to tell you for fear he won't be able
to get out of bed tomorrow. You don't want
him to do that, do you?"

She rubbed her forehead. "No, of course
not. You're right, I wasn't thinking straight."

He softened, remembering how she'd worried about Rich and how he'd kept her from
getting any rest last night. No wonder she
was ill tempered.

"You're tired, and—" He hesitated, wondering if he should mention what had to be on
her mind, too. But knew he had to. He had
to tell her how special she was. He wanted
her to know just how much what they shared
meant to him. "Because of me you didn't get
much sleep last night."

Flair felt her blush deepen. She'd been a
ball of nerves since she'd awakened to find
herself lying naked beside Caden. What she
had to say would be difficult but it had to
be said for her own peace of mind, for Rich's
future. She clasped her hands together and
said, "I'm glad you mentioned that." She

looked down the hallway, trying to find strength for what she was about to say. "This isn't easy. Once again I find myself deeply indebted to you. I want you to know that I'm very grateful and appreciative to you for the comfort you gave while Rich was so ill."

His eyes narrowed. A frown creased his brow and he took a step toward her, forcing her to back up against the wall. "What the hell are you trying to say?" His voice was low and angry.

She moistened her lips and lifted her chin. She wanted to ask him to hold her, to kiss her, and to love her just one more time, but she couldn't. She couldn't ask him to do more for her than he already had. If only she could tell him what was in her heart. If only she could tell him she loved him and wanted to be with him. But what good would that do? He couldn't stay married to her, he'd made that very clear.

"I'd been so worried about Rich I was beside myself. You've been so understanding and helpful. I needed the—comfort you gave me last night. Thank you for allowing me—"

"Comfort! Damn it, Flair, don't do this to me." Caden placed both his hands on the wall beside her head and looked down into her eyes, his expression furious, his chest heaving with anger.

His words sounded more like a low growl, but she understood them. How could she tell him that what had happened between them was so wonderful that she'd never be able to describe to him what she felt? How could she tell him that she wanted to live with him and be his wife in every way possible.

"My motives weren't entirely selfish," she hurried to say. "I wanted to thank you for standing by me while Rich was so sick and for all that you've done for me. I've done nothing but cause you trouble and it was time I did something nice for you."

His face came closer. His eyes were cold, his expression turned darkly chilling. "Nice for me? You made love to me last night because you wanted to thank me and be nice to me?" He almost spat the words.

Flair's heartbeat was so loud she couldn't hear her own breathing. Perspiration dampened the back of her neck. Her stomach churned. "Yes. I wanted to do something to repay you for giving Rich your name, for helping me through his accident, and for all your kindness and support to us. You seemed receptive to—ah—to a night with me. I thought it was something you wanted so I hope you'll accept last night as payment." There, she'd said it.

A low chuckle rumbled in his chest and his expression remained black.

It seemed the more she tried to explain, the angrier he became. She thought he'd rather hear she accepted him as a lover because she wanted to thank him than for undying love which he couldn't return. Trying to soothe him she said, "Last night was all my doing. It happened because I wanted it to. I planned it and you have no reason to feel any obligation to me whatsoever."

Fire lit in his eyes. "Obligation? Thank you for telling me that, but responsible isn't what I'm feeling, Flair."

From the corner of her eye she could see a muscle working in his arm from the pressure he applied to the wall. His fingers twitched and for a moment she wondered if he wished his hands were around her throat.

"Good," she said, wishing her voice had been stronger, wishing she didn't have to lie like this, wishing she'd known this was going to tear her heart out. But how could she tell him she was falling in love with him and wanted to be his wife. He'd laugh at her. He had to divorce her in order to get the farm. She had to make that as easy for him as possible. She took a shallow breath and continued. "I'm glad. You helped me, and I thanked you. That makes us even."

A look of pain crossed his face but it was quickly replaced by a smug look of contempt. "Is that what happened between you and Douglas? Were you merely thanking him for a favor, too?"

Flair gasped and bit her lip to hold back a cry of pain. She turned her face away from him. How could he suggest such a thing? How could he even bring up that horrible man's name? What she'd shared with him was nothing like what Douglas did to her. Caden's words hurt her so badly tears stung her eyes and made them water. She fought to hold them back. No matter how badly she wanted to absolve him of any blame for their night together she couldn't let him think that what happened between them was anything like what happened between her and Douglas. What she'd shared with Caden had been too special.

"No!" Her voice was a husky whisper.

Holding in the tears she managed to look into his hard unyielding stare. Her hands were tight fists. "What Douglas did was an act of violence. What happened between us was loving and by mutual agreement." Her voice broke on the last word. She had to get away from him before he saw how badly he'd hurt her. With all her strength she pushed past his outstretched arms and hurried down the hallway toward Rich's room.

"Flair! Flair!"

She heard him call her name, but she fled into the safety of Rich's room. There she had no choice but to get hold of herself. She had never let her son see her cry, and the first time wouldn't be today.

Darkness had been replaced by early morning light. Caden stood outside Rich's door. He wanted to be there when Flair came out of her son's room to go to her room to freshen up for the day. She'd spent the last three days in his room, refusing to come down for dinner or to do more than briefly speak to him when he'd go in to check on Rich or when she took him for a walk outside.

Dammit! He knew he hurt her the other day when he mentioned Douglas. What an idiot he'd been! She'd hurt him with her talk of gratitude, but he should have held his temper and not lashed out at her about that. He was wrong to do it, and he needed to apologize. He believed her when she said Douglas had forced himself on her. And she was right that what happened between them was the way love should be between a man and a woman. But damn, it tore him apart when she told him she only let him make love to her to thank him and be nice to him.

He huffed silently. She felt gratitude when he'd felt the earth move. Caden leaned against the wall. No. No, she'd felt more than gratitude. He'd bet his life on it. And what she felt went deeper than the physical act of making love. His kisses, touches, and caresses had made her feel good, but she never would have allowed them if she didn't care for him. He had a feeling she lied to him about it because of the divorce. He should have understood what she was doing and not taken it so hard.

The door handle turned. He stepped back.

Flair gasped and put her hand to her chest. "Oh, goodness, Caden, you frightened me."

Even rumpled from sleeping in the big chair in Rich's room she looked beautiful. Strands of hair fell from her bun and framed her face. Her eyes were dreamy with sleep. Her lips looked full and tempting. How could he have hurt her? "We need to talk Flair."

She cleared her throat and lifted her shoulders. "No. We've said all there is to say to each other." She turned to walk away but he grabbed hold of her arm and held her.

"You can't hide in Rich's room any longer."

Looking up into his eyes she said, "I have to be in this house to sign the divorce papers when they are ready. As soon as they are signed I will be on my way back home, and it can't be too soon for me. Where and how I spend my time while I'm forced to live here is of no concern to you." With one swift jerk she freed her arm, but didn't hurry away.

He blamed himself for her coldness. His words had been unforgivable, but he had to apologize. "Flair, I'm sorry for what I said the other day. I was angry and I wanted to hurt you. I shouldn't have made that remark about you and Douglas. I was wrong."

She nodded.

"I know it hurt you."

Flair lowered her head and looked down the hallway. "Yes, it did. Thank you for apologizing." She nodded again. "Now if you don't mind, I'd really like to forget the whole incident."

His anger was renewed. Now that she'd properly thanked him by sleeping with him, she wanted to forget about it. A knot formed in his stomach. "All right, but something's come to mind since the other night." His voice changed from soft to abrasive. "You could be pregnant from our time together the other night."

"Well, rest assured I won't take anything

from you or make any demands on you, if that be the case." As if taking her cue from him her cool tone returned. "I have raised one son by myself, and I can surely take care of another. In fact, it should be much easier the second time around."

"Dammit, Flair, that's not what I meant. If you are pregnant I'll take care of *my child.*"

She took a deep breath, her chest rising and falling with the effort. "Well, there's no use in arguing about that at this time. I'll surely be here another month or two and we'll know by then if what we speak of is true. We'll discuss that *if* it happens."

"Cade, I thought I heard you talking." Rich appeared in the doorway, rubbing his eyes, his nightshirt tucked between his legs, his hair rumpled about his head. "Are you and Mama arguing?"

"I guess we were talking a little too loud. How are you feeling? I'm glad to see you feel like getting out of bed and walking around."

Rich's eyes brightened. "I haven't had a bad headache in two days. Mama said I could get dressed today and go outside for a little while if I promise not to run and get hot."

"That's good. I can tell you're better." He bent down on one knee and reached into his pocket. "I have something for you." He pulled out his hand and opened it. Lying in his palm were six colorful marbles.

Happiness, excitement danced in Rich's eyes. He looked at Caden. "For me?"

"I don't have any other son to give them to."

Rich started to reach for them but pulled his hand back and glanced up at his mother. "Can I?"

A trembly smile spread across her lips. "It's may I, and of course you may have them."

Caden opened Rich's hand and laid the sparkling toys in the little palm and folded his fingers over them. "Now you go get dressed and later today you can play with them."

"All right!" he exclaimed and ran back in his room.

"Don't run," Flair called to him.

Flair looked back to Caden. "Thank you for that."

That was the first sincere smile he'd received from her since their night together. He wanted to hold her and love her but instead he said, "There's something else we need to talk about."

"What?" she asked.

"Rich has to get back on a horse."

"No." She gasped and grabbed hold of the tail of her skirts. "How dare you suggest such a thing. I'll never allow him on a horse again."

Caden remained calm and firm. "Flair, he got hurt, but he's better now. And the rule is when you fall off a horse, you get right back on."

"No. Not for my son. I won't let him."

He was trying to be patient. He knew she'd put up a fuss at first but he thought she'd give in easily enough when she realized Rich couldn't spend all his life being afraid of horses. "Flair, you don't want him to be afraid of horses. The longer he waits the harder it will be for him to get back on one."

"I don't care if he's afraid of them. One almost killed him. He has good reason to be afraid."

"Of course you care," he said, his voice rising. "You don't want him to be considered a weakling."

"Maybe he'll get back on the beasts when he's a man and can handle them, but not while he's still a boy, and certainly not tomorrow. In the meantime he can always go by carriage or one of those bicycle things."

"He has to get back on, Flair," he snapped sharply. "For God's sake if he's afraid of a damn horse he'll never be a man."

She blinked as if he'd struck him. Suddenly Caden realized he sounded just like Shelton.

He was berating, scolding her like a child for not seeing this the way he saw it. Damn, he didn't want to sound like that man. He didn't want to be like him.

Caden abruptly turned away and walked down the hallway. He hurried down the stairs, through the kitchen to stand on the back porch and look out over the vast, rich land of Maxwell Farms.

How could he have allowed himself to act like Shelton? He'd hated the man. He'd hated the way Shelton always made him feel like less than a man when he didn't agree with him. Would it make Rich less a man if he never learned to ride a horse? Hell no!

His breathing calmed. He didn't have to be like Shelton. His uncle was gone and he didn't owe him anything. Caden closed his eyes and remembered his father gently comforting and reassuring his mother. That was the kind of man he wanted to be. He pushed aside Shelton's training and remembered how his father had handled situations when he was a little boy. Pearson's voice had been gentle as he took the time to explain things. He didn't bellow like a bull and demand that everything be done his way.

Caden thought back to the time his father had wanted him to go out into the eerie darkness of early morning and milk the cow and feed the chickens. He'd heard a strange noise he couldn't identify and hadn't wanted to go back out into the dawn alone the next day.

His father had been patient and talked softly to him. He'd taken him outside and stayed with him to show him there was nothing to hurt him but fear. Caden took a deep breath. That's what he had to do for Rich. He had to show him that being on the horse wasn't going to hurt him.

Peace settled over Caden. He'd take it slow and ride with Rich the first few times. He'd show him how the animal could be his friend. He'd teach him how to stay in the saddle whenever the horse reared up again, for surely it would happen again.

A smile slowly grew across Caden's face. His hand made a fist and he shook it at the sky. "I'm not going to let you win, Shelton Maxwell. I won't let you turn me into the cold, hard bastard you were. And I won't let you take my wife away from me."

Booker sat in the straight-back chair and rocked on the hind legs, his favorite way to sit, while he sipped his morning coffee and watched the day break. He rubbed his stomach. He was hungry. His father didn't know how to cook anything but beans and boiled potatoes. He hadn't had any fried meat since Miss Flair left. He missed her cornbread and syrup and the occasional sweet bread she baked, too.

He'd been quiet on the way home from the church meeting last night. But even now as he thought about it his heart started to pound. He'd found the woman of his dreams, the woman he'd seen in town a few months ago. Parthina. What a beautiful name. She looked like an angel to him.

She hadn't been there the first meeting he and his father attended. He'd dreamed of her since the day he'd seen her. It had taken him more than an hour to work up the courage to go and speak to her after the services. He didn't get to talk to her long because a man named Wilson came up bringing her a dinner plate heaped with food. Next Sunday he'd be the first one at the table. He'd prepare her a plate of food and take it to her before Wilson had the chance.

"That coffee ready yet?"

Startled, Booker let his chair down on all four legs. He'd been so deep in thought he hadn't heard his father rise. "It's ready, Pa," he answered, looking over to the far corner of the room. He could barely make out his father's form sitting on the edge of his bed, tying the strings of his work boots.

"What did you think of the woman named Parthina?" he asked in what he hoped was a level tone of voice while he walked over to the fireplace and picked the pot up off the bed of hot coals.

"My my. She's a pretty one all right."

Booker filled the tin cup and replaced the pot. "Did you see her talking to me."

"I did. But looks to me like she already has that older feller eye-balling her. What was his name? Wilson?"

"Yeah. That's his name."

Samp walked over to the table, pulling up his suspenders. "Better not get your heart set on that one. I think Wilson's already courting her. Best you look for another one, son."

Setting the coffee on the table in front of his father, Booker shook his head. "That man don't bother me none."

"Well he should." Samp picked up the coffee and blew into the cup, but didn't sip from it. "You don't go messing around with another man's woman." His words were spoken with conviction. "Now, I saw Saralee looking your way a few times. She ain't taken."

Booker rubbed his nose. "Parthina ain't either as far as I know. She smiled at me, and come next Sunday I'm gone ask her if I can come calling."

Samp blew in his coffee again and ran a hand over his head. "Wilson may have a thing or two to say about that. He don't seem like the kind who's going to let you just move in on his woman."

Remaining firm Booker said, "Nothing he can say, if she say it's all right. I aim to court her, Pa."

Shaking his head Samp walked over to the open doorway and looked out on the morning. "Don't get in no trouble over a woman, son. They ain't worth it."

He walked up behind his father. "This one is."

Booker looked out at the dark blue skies of morning breaking clear. He wished Miss Flair was back. She'd be able to advise him. He didn't like what his father was saying. There were plenty of men at the church who didn't have as good a life as he and his pa and Wilson was one of them. He and his pa had good jobs with responsibilities and a home. Booker was already saving up to buy the lumber to add another room to their house. The only thing he needed to make his life complete was a woman to hold at night.

Parthina was just the woman he wanted.

Fifteen

Jake stood well away from the door of the barroom as he surveyed the clientele within. It'd been a couple of weeks since he'd been to town. Most of the time he had his evening drink alone in his office at the bunk house before he had supper with the rest of the hands. But today he'd finally received the message he'd been waiting for.

Lively piano music, loud talking, and scattered laughter filled the room with a roaring sound that made Jake's skin crawl. He would have preferred that this meeting take place in the expanse of wide open skies and rolling hills, but decided Eagerton might be more comfortable meeting in town the first time. Dim lighting and crowded barrooms made him feel closed in.

He casually looked over the occupants and spotted the man who had to be Douglas Eagerton sitting at a table in the far corner. The stranger was the only man dressed in a fancy suit of clothes. On the small table in front of him sat a whiskey bottle, two shot glasses, and his hat.

Jake pushed his hat back farther on his forehead and walked over to the table. "Douglas Eagerton?" he asked.

Dark brown eyes looked up at him. "Depends on who's asking?"

Jake didn't like his reply or the snobbish expression on his face. But he knew he didn't have to like the man to work with him. Their relationship would be strictly business. Besides, he hadn't been expecting a hell of a nice guy.

"Name's Jake," he finally answered.

"Sit down."

With the toe of his boot, Douglas pushed the chair opposite him away from the table. Jake grabbed it, turned it around, and straddled it as if he were sitting on a horse. With so many years in the saddle no other way felt comfortable.

Eagerton filled a shot glass with whiskey and pushed it toward Jake, sloshing some of the fiery liquid on the table in front of him. Jake smiled to himself. The man could act tough if it made him feel better, bigger, or meaner. He didn't give a damn as long as Douglas went along with his plan.

Keeping his gaze on the dandified man he

picked up the glass and downed the whiskey in one gulp. He wiped the corner of his mouth with the back of his hand and winced loudly. He hadn't expected it to be so strong.

"That's good stuff."

He gave Jake a curt nod. "Only a foolish man or a poor man drinks bad whiskey."

Oh god! A man who's inflated his self-worth, Jake thought.

Douglas pushed his chair back and crossed one leg over the other as he hooked his thumbs in the small pockets of his waistcoat. His eyes were set in an uninterested glare. "I hope I didn't come all this way for nothing."

Jake returned his glare with a cold stare. He wondered how much of this man he could stand for the chance of getting Maxwell Farms. *A lot,* he answered himself. He'd let the man feel big if that was what was needed to get the job done.

There had been enough cat and mouse play. It was time to get down to business. "I'll tell you what I know and you decide."

"Talk."

God! it was no wonder Flair didn't want that boy to know this man was his father. He was a real bastard.

"I'm assuming you know Flair Maxwell and her son Rich or you wouldn't be here."

"I know them." Douglas picked up his glass

and took a small sip of his drink. He extended his little finger showing off the gold ring that circled it.

"I overheard a conversation I thought would be of extreme interest to you."

"I'm listening but you're not saying anything. I grow weary."

Jake almost smiled but caught himself in time. He looked around the room and acknowledged a couple of men with a slight nod of his head. The piano player decided to take a break for which he was grateful. The noise level of the room seemed to have lessened.

He turned back to the prig sitting across the table from him. "Apparently you are the boy's father." Eagerton's expression told him it was true. "And apparently you have tried in the past, unsuccessfully, to take Flair's son away from her."

Picking up the whiskey bottle Douglas poured Jake another drink. "Go on. So far you haven't told me anything I don't already know. Rich is my son."

Jake hoped his guilty conscience didn't show. Dammit, he hadn't intended to hurt the kid. He only meant to scare him a little. How could he have known the boy would fall off and almost get killed. Benny should have shown him how to hug the horse with his knees and feet to stay on. Jake downed half the shot before he continued. Maybe his next bit of news would shake the hell out of Douglas.

"Flair and Cade Maxwell are getting a divorce."

Eagerton's poker face crumpled into a look of shock. "You lie," he insisted.

Slowly Jake shook his head. "No. It's true. I can give you the name of the lawyer who will confirm it. Besides, why would I bring you all this way to tell something that could be so easily disproved."

Douglas's eagerness showed in his body movements. Suddenly it was as if he couldn't sit still. "How do you know this?"

Eagerton's interest was keen and Jake couldn't help but enjoy his squirming. "I'm the foreman at the farm where she's staying. I overheard her say she didn't want you to know they were getting a divorce."

"What else do you know?"

"She's afraid you'll try to take her son away from her. She plans to go back to her own farm as soon as the papers are signed and let everyone, including you, think she's still married."

"That bitch!" He spit the words between clenched teeth. "If what you say is true, I'll see you're well paid for this information."

"That's what I'm hoping." Jake laughed. "Don't worry. It's true. I'll give you the name of the lawyer who'll confirm what I say."

"What's your price?"

"Five hundred now and another five after you're satisfied what I've said is the truth."

Eagerton slid his hand round the whiskey bottle and topped off his glass before taking a sip of his drink. He swished the liquor around in his mouth as he thought on what Jake told him. "That's a lot of money."

"Information doesn't come cheap. If I hadn't squealed on her the little lady would have never said a word."

"I'll have to go to the bank. I don't have that much on me."

Jake took his pocket watch out and looked at it. "You have five minutes to get to the bank. It's right down the street. I'll wait here for you."

Rising from his chair, Douglas said, "Pour yourself another drink." He pushed the bottle over to Jake. "I'll be right back."

"I'll be waiting. Oh, and by the way, you might want to ride out to the farm later. Rich had a little accident a few days ago."

Douglas's eyes narrowed. "What happened?"

"Nothing serious. A horse threw him. He's fine now."

As soon as Eagerton cleared the doorway

Jake laughed, quite pleased with himself. The dandified man fell for his scheme. Right down to offering him money. If everything went according to his plan, Eagerton would ride over to the farm and let Flair know he knew about the divorce. That should cause Cade's protective instincts to rush to the surface. Jake knew Cade was honorable enough to drop the divorce proceedings and give up his right to the farm if he thought Douglas intended to get his son as soon as the divorce was final.

Jake poured himself another drink and smiled. Yes, he was certain Douglas Eagerton would cause trouble and Cade would rise to the occasion, and the hell of it was that Eagerton thought he was doing this for the money. Jake laughed again. Integrity. It was a fine thing for some people to have.

While sitting with Rich through his recuperation Flair had been able to finish her forest green dinner dress. Since she was short on material after having made the full skirt to go with her white blouse, she'd had to go with short puffy sleeves instead of the long ones she would have preferred. She was unhappy about the neckline, too, she decided as she looked at herself in the mirror. She was definitely showing too much of her bosom. How had she gotten it so low? She moaned and went back to pinning her hair into a neat chignon. No use worrying about it now. The next time she went in to town she would buy some lace to tack around the facing.

Even though she tried to stay calm, she was excited. This would be her first dinner with Caden since their argument about Rich getting back on a horse three days ago. After she'd calmed down and thought about what he was trying to do, she realized he was right. Her fear didn't matter. It was important for Rich not to go through life being afraid of horses.

She intended to apologize to Caden tonight. Earlier in the day she'd asked Bernie to send word to him that she would be joining him for dinner. She'd promised to stay until the divorce was final and she couldn't live with this polite coolness between them. But, she had to be careful not to fool herself into thinking anything else between them would change. It couldn't. The divorce had to go on no matter how much she'd like for that to be different.

As she finished with her hair a knock sounded on her door. That had to be Bernie. She must have tarried over the dress longer than she thought. Caden had probably sent the housekeeper after her. "Coming," she called and hurried to the door.

Bernie gave her a big smile. "You look stunning in that dress, Mrs. Maxwell. Turn around. Let me take a closer look at you."

Flair laughed and twirled for her. "I didn't think I'd ever finish it."

"You did a wonderful job. Mr. Ca—Maxwell's eyes are going to pop out of his head."

If only that were true, Flair thought as she walked out of her room. "It's not too low is it?"

"No, course not. A married woman is supposed to wear low-cut dresses like that," Bernie encouraged her.

"I guess Caden's wondering what happened to me. I didn't mean to be late for our first dinner together since Rich's accident. I must have been daydreaming."

"Oh, you were so pretty I forgot to tell you. That's the reason I came up here. Caden sent word by one of the hands that he'd be about an hour late, but he'd like for you to wait for him if you don't mind."

Flair picked up her skirts and started down the stairs. "No, of course I don't." In fact she was glad for the reprieve. It would give her time to get her thoughts together. "How's Rich?"

"He and Benny left about fifteen minutes

ago. Don't you worry about him. He's going to be fine. Benny will take good care of him."

"I don't know. I'm still worried. It's only been a few days since he stopped having headaches."

"But you can't make a baby out of him. It doesn't take young ones long to get over things like falling from a horse. They bounce right back."

"I guess you're right. Why do boys want to do things like spend the night in the bunk house?"

Bernie laughed heartily. "Because men like their independence. They're born full of it."

Flair laughed, too. Letting Rich grow up wasn't going to be easy. As they reached the bottom of the stairs there was a knock on the door. "You go on into the parlor and have your sherry. I'll see who it is. If it's someone for you, I'll send them in and go on out to the cook house to see about keeping dinner warm until Mr. Maxwell gets here."

Still chuckling Flair walked into the parlor. She hoped Caden wouldn't take too long. She wanted to apologize and start over with him. She cared too much for him to be at odds with him, especially when he was right and she was wrong.

Flair walked over to the sideboard and took

the top off the decanter. She closed her hand around the weighty piece of crystal and remembered her night with Caden. She wanted never to forget it. How could she? No other experience had ever come close, not even the first time she held Rich in her arms. Caden had touched her soul. She'd always felt a deep gratitude to him, but that's not what made her stay in his bed that night. It was the overpowering love she felt for him. And that love is what would keep her here in his house until the divorce was final. Flair cringed. Even the word divorce sounded so—

"Hello, Flair."

She spun around so fast she dropped the top of the crystal decanter onto the sideboard. "Douglas!" How had he found her? "What are you doing here?"

He grinned arrogantly. "I'd follow you anywhere, Flair. You should know that. You look beautiful tonight."

His dusty brown hair was neatly combed away from his forehead, and his dark brown eyes seemed to undress her with a leering stare.

She moved away from the table, farther away from Douglas. "I asked you what you're doing here."

"I heard Rich has been deathly ill. I came to see about him. How is he?"

How had he known? "Better." Her voice was too husky. She didn't want to show her fear. Could he have had her followed?

"I want to see him."

"No," she answered, overcoming her shock at his presence and regaining her aplomb. She needed to get angry, not frightened. Douglas couldn't hurt her anymore and she wouldn't let him get close enough to Rich to hurt him. "You must be mad to come here to Caden's house after what he did to you in Alabama."

He chuckled. "Guess this lets you know just how serious I am. Where is your trigger-happy husband anyway? I thought dinner time would be the perfect time to catch him home."

"He's on his way. But I really don't think it would be a good idea for you to be here when Caden arrives."

"I do. I want him to know just how serious I am about making you my wife and having my son live with me."

A chill of fear swept over her and she took a step back. His self-confidence worried her. "You know that's not possible. Why do you insist on saying such things?"

That arrogant grin stayed on his lips. "I intend to have you and Rich."

"How many times do I have to tell you I'm

married and very happy to be so." She realized as she said it that it wasn't a lie. She was happy to be married to Caden. And Douglas didn't have to know that it would end in divorce.

"Happy? I don't think so, Flair. I've been doing some checking. You didn't think I was going to let you walk out of my life without a fight, did you?"

She stood her ground. "Yes. I want you to go away and leave me alone. I'm quite happy with my husband. We have a wonderful life together." She hoped that little lie didn't show on her face.

"Is that so?"

"Yes," she lied again.

Douglas walked over to the tray of liquors and poured himself a drink. "I hope you don't tell such lies to my son. It's really not a good way to bring up the boy."

She cringed at Douglas's reference. "What are you talking about?"

"You're getting divorced. Isn't that true, Flair."

"No," she lied without hesitation, without thinking, without conscience. She had to keep Douglas away from her son. She'd do anything to protect Rich. "It's not true."

He sipped his drink. "For shame, Flair. What has happened to you? I've spoken with a man named Rutherford. Ring a bell? He confirmed that he had filed the necessary papers with the court for your divorce. It's public record. Naturally I was happy to hear it."

"No," she whispered desperately. How could he have found out? He must have spied on them. Inside she cried from the unfairness of it. "How did you find out about this? How did you know to go to Rutherford?" she demanded.

"Now you know I can't tell you that." He set the drink down and walked over to her. "Flair, this proves how important you are to me, how much I want my son. I intend to have him. I told you, I'm forty years old. By the time I can marry and have another son, I'll be too old to enjoy him and teach him the things I want him to know. Rich is just the right age. And you are a beautiful woman. Why shouldn't I want you?"

"No! No!" She gasped.

"Look what I have here," he said, reaching into his pocket. "I bought this for you. As soon as your divorce is final I want you to put it on."

He opened a black velvet box and showed her a sparkling diamond and blue sapphire ring.

How could she even consider marrying Douglas after the way he'd treated her? Now that she knew how beautiful and loving a re-

lationship could be between a man and a
woman? There was no comparison to the way
Douglas had used her and the way Caden
had loved her.

"No, Douglas. I'll never marry you because
of what you did to me ten years ago."

He smiled cunningly. "I was a young man
trying to obey my father. I know now I should
have defied him and married you, but it's
worked out all right for you, hasn't it?"

Anger coiled around her neck like a snake,
sapping her breath. "It's not just the fact you
wouldn't marry me. You raped me. You held
me down on the ground and forced yourself
on me. I'll never forgive you for that."

"Why do you continue to use that offensive
word? It's not true and you know it. You met
me by the pond. You allowed me to kiss you.
If you hadn't wanted it, why did you meet
me?"

"Yes I met you, but kisses were all I wanted,
I begged you not to do what you did," she
defended.

"Why are you harping, Flair? If what I did
to you was so terrible, why did you come to
me two months later and demand I marry
you?"

"Because I was frightened." Why did she
have to justify herself to this man? Because
she wanted to be vindicated. She wanted him

to believe that what happened wasn't her fault. "I didn't know what else to do. I didn't want my father to know what you had done. I didn't want to have the baby alone." Her voice grew softer. "Back then I believed you cared about me."

"I did care for you. I do now. I intend to have you and our son."

"It's too late," she said on a final note.

His eyes probed hers. "You have two choices, Flair. After your divorce you can marry me and come live as my wife with our son, or I'll tell Rich I'm his real father. If I can't have him, you won't either."

Her breath left her. She felt light-headed and dizzy. Rage settled inside her. "You wouldn't do that to him. He's just a little boy."

"Of course I'll do it. He's my son. You'd be foolish to doubt me on this."

"H-he won't believe you. He thinks Caden is his father. Even if you tried to explain he wouldn't understand. He's not old enough."

"How old is he? Almost ten? Maybe not today or tomorrow but next year, he'll know what goes on between a man and a woman, Flair and I'll find him alone one day, and I'll tell him."

"No!" she whispered earnestly. "You can't."

"Yes. I'll make sure he knows all the sordid details of our little love affair."

"You brute! How dare you suggest it was a love affair, how dare you threaten telling him? Get out! Silas!" she called, running to the doorway of the parlor.

"I want my son, Flair. I dare anything. And don't think your husband will shoot me this time. If he's divorcing you he obviously doesn't care what happens to you or the boy."

"Yes, Mrs. Maxwell?" Silas asked, appearing in the doorway.

"Show Mr. Eagerton to the door. He's leaving."

"Yes, ma'am."

"No need. I'm leaving, but I'll be back. There's nowhere you can hide from me."

Douglas turned and walked out. Flair covered her face with her hands. What was she going to do? She jerked her hands down. She couldn't panic, but she couldn't stay here either. Douglas was mean enough to seek Rich out and tell him. Flair ran out of the parlor and bumped into Bernie.

"What's wrong with you? You look like you've seen a ghost."

"No, I have a headache. Please tell Caden I won't be able to dine with him after all."

She didn't wait for questions from Bernie. She was too upset to talk so she hurried up the stairs. She had to think and plan. Her green skirts swirled about her legs, almost tripping her. She couldn't stay here, that much was clear. She would take Rich and they would run away together. No, they couldn't run away— she didn't have enough money without selling the farm and she'd promised Caden she'd give him the divorce.

Her mind was so troubled she realized she was panicking. But what else could she do? Her heart beat so fast she trembled. She tried to clear her confused mind. She had enough money to get them back to Alabama. They would go back home and sell the farm while she waited for the divorce papers. Yes, she couldn't disappear until she signed those papers for Caden. He'd been too good to her. She loved him too much to run out on him and make him lose the farm.

The thought of leaving him tugged at her heart as she reached under the bed and pulled out her luggage and laid it on the bed. She wouldn't try to take everything. Only enough to get by. She could buy more clothes later.

She'd pack tonight, and tomorrow while Caden was at work she and Rich would leave. She opened the small satchel and started filling it with clothes from the lowboy.

Someday she would have to tell Rich that

Douglas was his father. She'd tell him the entire ugly story. But not now. He was too young. He wouldn't understand.

"What the hell are you doing?"

She spun and faced Caden.

Sixteen

Anger burned in his eyes—with good reason, she knew. Flair took a deep breath. Once before she'd faced a crossroads and had to make some hard decisions. Things were supposed to get easier with time, she thought. This proved they didn't. Leaving Caden would break her heart. The scowl on his face intimidated her, making her want to retreat inside herself and not open up to him.

"I'm leaving," she said.

"Just like that. You're leaving." He shook his head. "Why? Because I'm fifteen minutes late for dinner?" His words sounded hoarse and brittle.

"No, not because of that," she defended, her chest heaving with the rush of fear that Douglas had caused. A shudder passed through her.

"Then why in the hell are you leaving?"

Suddenly tired, Flair dropped her arms to her sides and moved away from the bed. She was tired of hiding her feelings from Caden. Tired of running from Douglas. Tired of all the lies. She looked over at Caden standing in the open doorway. His bewildered expression tore at her heart. She'd rather see him angry. Sadness overwhelmed her. He was so handsome. His broad shoulders, firmly muscled arms, and slim hips seemed to beckon her to let him help, but could she?

Taking control of her warring emotions she moistened her lips and said, "Douglas found us. He's threatened to tell Rich he's his real father. I can't let him do that."

"What?" He shut the door and walked farther into her room. Light from the lamp cast his large and powerful looking shadow across the wall.

"It's true. Somehow Douglas found me, and he found out about the divorce. He must have had me followed. He was here just a few minutes ago."

"God dammit! I'll kill the bastard." Caden turned and headed for the door.

"Caden, no!" Flair rushed to the door and stopped him as he put his hand on the door handle. She forced her way between him and the door. "Don't go after him," she pleaded, afraid this time he might actually kill Douglas.

He looked down into her eyes with the

steadiness of an iron weight. "I'll kill him if he's touched you again."

She believed him. "He didn't touch me. He didn't come near me. But even if he had, do you think I want you to kill him? I just want to keep him away from my son. I don't want Rich to ever find out about what happened ten years ago, and certainly not from Douglas."

"I'll take care of him, Flair."

She breathed a heavy sigh of relief. His words were more of an appeal than a demand. Her hands tightened on his upper arms. "No. I've upset your life too many times in too many different ways as it is. I won't let you add murder to the long list of things you've done for me. I just feel like running away with Rich where Douglas can't find us."

Caden's features softened. "Running isn't the answer any more than killing is."

He brushed her cheek with the back of his hand. Love for him overwhelmed her. How could she leave him when she desperately wanted to stay forever? *Forever.* She longed for it when she looked into his eyes, but even if she stayed the night, her days with him were numbered. As soon as the divorce was final she'd have to leave. Wouldn't it be easier to leave now? No, her heart answered, wanting to take every day, every moment with him that he'd allow.

"I don't know the answer."

He slid his hands round her neck and laced his fingers together at her nape, drawing her closer to him. "Let me tell you some things you may not know. You didn't force me to marry you ten years ago, and I haven't been forced to stay married to you."

The atmosphere around them changed as he talked, as his eyes searched hers. His hands were warm, comforting. She felt his breath on her face and welcomed it. Concern mixed with the anger in his eyes. She still held his arms. She tried to keep her mind on the conversation and not on the way he touched her or the way she felt when she looked into those beautiful greenish-brown eyes. Her breath quickened as his expression relaxed into a look of loving desire. She wondered if he knew what she'd been thinking. Did he know she wanted to be the woman he needed, the woman he desired, the woman who shared his bed and life? Did he know she wanted to belong to him heart and soul? Did he know she didn't want to leave him now or forever?

"That's true," she said, forcing her thoughts back to the matter at hand. "You weren't forced into anything. It's also true that you'd have full rights to this farm right now if you hadn't married me."

His hands slid down her back and pulled her close to his chest. "The farm be damned, Flair."

"No," she whispered earnestly. "I can't let you give it up."

"It's not your choice to make," he whispered. "It's mine."

Looking into his eyes, she realized she wanted him to know how she felt. If she could do nothing else for him, she wanted him to know that he was loved. "I can't take advantage of you any more. I love you too much to let you ruin your life over a man like Douglas. I love you too much to let you throw away your inheritance."

He blinked rapidly. His arms tightened around her waist. "Did you say you love me, Flair?"

"Yes," she answered softly, a smile lifting the corners of her lips. Her hands held his arms gently but with no pressure. Her expression and voice were earnest when she said again, "Yes, I love you. I know I said all those things about gratitude and wanting to thank you. And I am grateful to you, but I stayed in your bed and in your arms that night because I love you, and I desperately wanted to be with you."

Caden swooped down and picked her up in his arms. He swung her around as he squeezed her tightly to his chest. "Oh, Flair, my darling, I love you, too. It took me a long time to realize it, but I finally figured out why I married you, and why I never divorced you when Shelton kept insisting. I always thought I did it just to defy him. Now I know I fell in love with you that first time I saw you crying in that alley. You were so beautiful, so young and vulnerable, yet so strong that I knew I'd do anything I could for you."

Flair felt as if her heart might beat out of her chest with happiness. He loved her. Thank God! She slid her hands up his arms and around his neck and hugged him generously, passionately, giddy with gladness.

"Caden, I find it hard to believe you feel the same way I do. I—I don't know what to say."

"That you love me is enough. What more could I want?" He bent his head and gave her a warm, lingering kiss, before lifting his head and saying, "You've had me so tied up in knots these past few days that I've been a bear to everyone, including myself. I love you, Flair." He laughed and hugged her again before setting her back on her feet. "Now that I've admitted it I want to say it over and over again."

Flair laughed, too. "I want to hear it again and again. I love you with all my heart," she whispered, knowing it sounded childlike, but wanting him to know how deep her love for him went.

"You know, loving you had to be the reason I insisted you come here with me. I wasn't ready to say good-bye to you, but I knew I had to get back here."

His head swooped down and his lips claimed hers in a long, deeply sensuous kiss. He backed her against the door as his hands roamed over her body, touching her neck, her arms, her shoulders, her breasts and back up to remove the pins from her hair.

Flair sighed softly and relaxed, letting her body melt against him. One hand played in the back of his hair while the other ran across the width of his shoulders. His hair was soft, fine. The cotton material of his shirt felt good against her palm. Didn't love conquer all odds? Couldn't they defeat Douglas and Shelton's will with the weapon of love?

"What are we to do?" she asked when he broke the kiss and moved his lips over to her cheek and down her neck.

"Make love," he whispered huskily, warmly against her skin.

She smiled and held him tighter, enjoying

the feel of his lips on her heated skin. "I mean about Douglas and Shelton's will."

Caden cupped each side of her face with his hands and peered down into her eyes. His lips were wet from their kisses, making her want him to reach up and kiss her again. "We do need to talk about that, but not right now. Not tonight." He gave her a short kiss. "Tomorrow is soon enough. Right now we're going to do what we want. We're going to think about us."

"What about your dinner? Bernie's keeping the food warm for you."

He chuckled softly. "I think Bernie will know that a closed door means dinner is over. If we get hungry for food in the middle of the night I'm sure we can find something to nibble on."

She nodded, deliriously happy that the whole night belonged to them. Caden was right. Tomorrow was soon enough to think about Douglas's threat and the problems the will caused.

"I want you to love me," he said. "Everything else can be worked out later. Do you want me to make love to you, Flair?" he asked softly.

Rich was safe with Benny for the night. Flair drew a deep breath. She was going to enjoy making love to her husband. "Yes," she answered clearing her mind of everything except Caden's touch.

He gently ran his hands up and down her arms. His gaze swept over her face and down her neck to where the swell of her breasts showed from beneath her dress. "You're my wife, Flair, a part of me. I won't let anyone take you from me."

His words gave her comfort, power, contentment.

Caden swung her up in his arms and carried her over to the bed. Gently, he laid her down and lowered his body over hers, claiming her for his own. She accepted the weight of his body, circling his neck with her arms. His lips came down on hers in a deep hungry kiss that made her stomach muscles contract with wanting. As if with a will of its own her pelvis rose up to meet the pressing movements of his lower body. He kissed her cheeks, her neck, and the swell of her breast. His stubble of beard stung her lips, so she moved to the soft skin at the base of his throat. She sucked it into her mouth and tasted him. His body quickened beneath her. Tremors of desire flooded her.

Freedom to touch him, kiss him, and love him consumed her. She wanted to cry out with joy.

Desire mounted between them as he pinned

her to the bed beneath him. They kissed, hugged, touched and whispered words of love. Pillows were shoved to the floor. The bed covers twisted and wrinkled beneath their wiggling.

With ragged breath Caden rose up on his elbows and simply looked at Flair for a moment. His palm scanned down her cheek, her neck to the rise and fall of her breast to tease the hidden nipple. "You're beautiful. I like your new dress." He smiled cunningly. "But I'm going to have to take it off."

She returned the smile. "Be my guest."

Caden moved to Flair's side and rolled her over on her stomach. He was straining the confines of his trousers, hurting from need for her. Would he ever get enough of her so that his body wouldn't pulsate demandingly and make him want to hurry his time with her. He was used to accepting the instant rush of gratification. With Flair, he couldn't let his body betray him and leave her unfulfilled.

He straddled her buttocks and moved her hair out of his way. Hastily, he unfastened the tiny buttons at the back of her dress. When the bodice was unfastened he spread it open, pushing it off her arms. She had a beautiful back and shoulders. Gently, he laid his hands palm down on her soft skin. Her skin was warm to his touch. He ran his hands liberally over every exposed inch of her back. He loved the feel of her firm buttocks pressing, arching against his manhood. The rise and fall of her gentle movements beneath him drove him wild with desire and he grew harder.

Damn, she felt good.

Bending over her, he lowered his head and pressed his lips to her upper back. His tongue moistened her soft skin. His manhood hardened. He kissed along the crest of her shoulders and down to her wider shoulder blades. A thrilling sensation rippled through him, making him shudder. He felt as if he was going to explode with desire for Flair. With hungry movements he kissed his way down her spine to the small of her back, exploring every little indentation along the way. He stuck out his tongue and licked her skin. Desire flared inside him.

Damn, she tasted good.

Caden moved up her back and buried his nose in the length of her hair. He rubbed his face against its softness and inhaled, filling his lungs. The fresh scent of her hair had been with him since the last time he made love to her. He moved his face over to that soft skin behind her ear lobe and breathed deeply, drinking her essence.

Damn, she smelled good.

When he could take the wonderful foreplay no longer, he groaned huskily and turned her over. He lowered his mouth to hers and kissed her as he struggled to push her dress farther down. Pausing in his ardent haste of love-making, he took time to wiggle out of his clothes and boots and to finish undressing Flair. With their clothes no longer a barrier between them, he lay beside her and gazed worshipfully at her lovely face, rounded shoulders, and firm breasts. He liked the way her waist nipped in at the sides, flattering her hips. Her stomach was flat, her navel a small indentation. His gaze lingered on her most womanly part before traveling down her beautiful thighs and shapely legs to her cute feet.

Damn, she looked good.

"I love you," he whispered as he rose over her and pressed his chest to hers. "I want to make our loving good to you."

"You will," she answered softly, looking dreamily into his eyes and sliding her arms around his neck.

Caden loved every inch of her. Thank God she was his.

"Caden, old chap, come in. It's been awhile since I've seen you." Rutherford rose from his expensively carved desk. "Do make yourself comfortable. I assume you're here to check on the divorce, but I'm afraid there's no news. These things take time."

"No, thank you, I'll stand. And actually, I'm not here about the divorce." Caden walked farther into the room, tightly gripping the sheets of paper he held in his hand. "I want to discuss the contents of Shelton's will. I've spent most of the morning studying this document and the way it's written."

Puzzled, Rutherford squinted. "I assure you it's written by standard guidelines for testaments, Caden."

"I'm not questioning that. What's bothering me is how Shelton put his words together and what you say they mean."

Rutherford leaned a slim hip against his desk and crossed his arms across his chest. He pointedly looked at the toe of his highly polished shoe. "What part don't you understand. I'll try to explain it to you."

The lawyer was bordering on condescension, but Caden decided to ignore it. Apparently he considered Shelton's will a closed matter that shouldn't be revisited. "This is the copy you left with me." He handed the papers to Rutherford. "Read the last sentence of the second paragraph on page three."

Rutherford didn't do a good job of hiding his annoyance when he took the papers and looked at them. He ran a hand down his chin and lightly pulled on his goatee.

"Read it out loud," Caden prompted.

"In order for Caden to inherit the full of Maxwell Farms save what is otherwise bequeathed, he must divorce his current wife and marry a woman of social standing in the county." Rutherford looked up at Caden with a weary expression. "That means you have to divorce your current wife and marry another woman."

The corners of Caden's lips lifted in a sly smile. "Does it? Read it again."

"Come, Caden, please. You can't make this say anything other than what it says," he said in an exasperated tone.

"Then why are you?"

"What?" He straightened.

Caden took the paper from him and read, "He must divorce his current wife and marry a woman of social standing in the county."

"Exactly!" Rutherford rested his case. He moved away from the desk and walked over to the sideboard and poured tea into a delicate china cup. He extended it to Caden.

Caden shook his head. "Would you consider Flair Maxwell a woman of social standing?" he asked.

"Your current wife. By all means. But the

will states you must divorce her and marry another woman."

He gave the paper back to Rutherford. "Where does it say that?"

Rutherford set the tea down quickly, rattling the cup in the saucer. "My god! Caden you'd try the patience of Job. Right here it states you must remarry a woman of social stand—a woman—" Stunned, he stopped and looked up at Caden.

"Does it say I must marry *another* woman?"

The lawyer's gaze darted around the room as if he expected to find the answer lurking somewhere within. "You may be on to something here," he said in a quiet voice.

"The will doesn't say another woman or a different woman, does it?"

"No, it says *a woman*. Damn it! You're right. I always read that into it because I knew it to be Shelton's intention that you marry someone else." Defensive eyes looked up at Caden. "I took the will down word for word as he spoke it. I didn't make a mistake. I'm sure of it. This isn't my fault, Caden."

Caden laughed. Did Rutherford really think he was going to blame him for this mistake? Hell, could it be considered a mistake if it was the answer to his problems? "Is there any reason I can't remarry Flair since she's a woman of social standing in the county?"

"Ah—Er—well, no I don't think so, but maybe I should look into this matter more thoroughly before I give you an affirmative answer."

"Do it."

Rutherford walked back to his desk. "I'll get right on it." He paused and looked up at Caden. "You know, I can agree to this, but it doesn't mean Jake will. He's a bit forceful and I don't think he'll let you get by with it. There's a good chance if you try this he'll take you to court over it."

"I expect it, but it won't make a difference. I intend to follow every step of this will. The divorce will go on. Jake doesn't have to know about this until the divorce is final. Then, I'll tell him I'm remarrying Flair. In the meantime, you can get a judge to go ahead and make a ruling."

He looked up at Caden. "You know full well that wasn't Shelton's intention."

"Shelton's intentions don't matter a damn to me. It's what he wrote that's important."

"I'll get right on it."

Caden started to walk out, but turned back to the well-groomed lawyer and said, "And Rutherford, my name is Caden, not old chap."

"Certainly."

Seventeen

Dressed for traveling, Flair looked out the window of her bedroom and stared at the gently sloping hills of the Virginia country-side. The sky was a hazy shade of blue and scattered with wisps of white clouds. Horses grazed on the crest of the largest hill and cattle dotted the rest of the vast landscape stretched before her eyes. Fields lush with greenery beckoned her to walk them and sup from their serenity.

Sometime late into the night she'd fallen asleep and slept soundly as a baby. Nestled in the crook of Caden's arm, her body completely relaxed, how could she sleep any other way? She hadn't awakened until well into the morning to find Caden gone from her bed and Bernie and Rich bringing her breakfast on a tray.

While she'd drunk her tea and eaten the buttered bread and cooked apples, Rich filled her in on his adventure of staying the night with the farm hands at the bunk house. Attentive to his stories, Flair laughed, smiled, and cringed in all the right places. It was a nice treat for him since he'd been so ill from the accident. She was pleased Benny took up so much time with Rich and she knew Rich appreciated him, too.

But at the back of her mind, Flair knew she had a difficult decision to make. As she'd watched Rich's face she'd realized he truly loved it here on Caden's farm. There were so many more things and people for him to be involved with than at their small farm. Samp and Booker had too much work to do to spend a lot of time teaching him all the things a young man should know. And as much as she hated to think about it, Rich was going to have to learn how to ride a horse.

"Just not at this ranch," she murmured to the silence of the empty room. Her stomach quaked from the thought of what she had to do. Even now she should have already been on her way, but still she tarried, hoping another idea would cross her mind. One that would give her Caden and give Caden his inheritance.

Weak with foreboding Flair turned away from the window and looked around the bedroom she'd thought of as her own. She'd miss the brightly decorated walls and fine furniture. Her gaze scanned the packed bags which sat on the floor by the door. All she had to do was get Silas to take them downstairs, then she and Rich could be on their way. Writing a note to Caden was the only thing holding her up. What could she say that would make him understand, make up for leaving him?

Rich and Benny were already in the barn. She'd told them to prepare the carriage for a ride. Her son wasn't going to be happy about leaving, she knew, but what else could she do? She'd caused Caden enough trouble. She must have been crazy last night to think she could let Caden give all this up for her. This morning she couldn't.

This farm was his inheritance. He'd worked and lived here for fifteen years. She had her land and it might keep Caden satisfied for a time, but over the months and years the small vegetable farm would prove too limiting when he was used to a large cattle and horse farm and grander lifestyle. It wasn't right for her to do that to him. She didn't doubt his love for her or hers for him, but the sacrifice he had to make for her would be too great. She couldn't ask it of him. She loved him too much for that.

On watery legs Flair walked over to the

small secretary and sat down. But instead of
picking up the pen, she cupped her hands in
her lap. She had to be very careful what she
wrote in her letter to him. She couldn't have
him following her. She'd never be able to resist him should he try to persuade her to stay
married to him. The only kind thing she
could do for Caden would be to remove herself from his life and give him the opportunity to make a new one here on the farm
that belonged to him. She would be abusing
the feelings he had for her if she allowed
him to give up this land for her. She'd ask
Rutherford to send the divorce papers to her
when they were ready.

Her only choice was to go back to her own
farm and live there. She still had the problem
of what to do about Douglas and his threat
to Rich. There, too, she didn't seem to have
but one choice. She didn't doubt for a moment that he meant every word he said about
telling Rich he was his real father. What she
had to do was make sure she told Rich about
her past with Douglas before he had the opportunity. But even thinking about that brought
questions about how much she should try to
explain to a nine-year-old boy. Should she try
to tell him the entire story? If she did it would
eliminate one of her problems—Douglas
wouldn't be able to blackmail her into mar-

riage with him, but would Rich hate her if he fully understood what happened between them? Would he want to spend time with Douglas? That thought chilled her.

Forcing down all those thoughts Flair picked up the pen. All that could be decided on the long trip home. Right now she had to write Caden and get into town before he returned home.

Taking a nerve steadying breath she dipped the pen into the ink well, then onto the paper. *Dear Caden,* she wrote.

Bernie stood on the front porch when Caden rode up to the house late that afternoon. He didn't pay her any mind until he saw her hurry down the steps toward him. Sensing trouble he kneed his horse to a canter.

"Mr. Maxwell," she called, her robust frame bounding down the steps to meet him.

Caden reined his horse to a stop at the hitching rail and Bernie met him. He didn't like the concerned look on her face and her eyes were red as if she'd been crying. Now that he was close enough it was easy to see she was upset. He stiffened.

"I thought you'd never get back. I've had Silas out looking for you most of the day. Nobody seemed to know where you were."

Something had happened. He remained calm while he dismounted and asked, "What's the problem, Bernie?"

After he'd seen Rutherford that morning, he'd gone to all the hotels in town looking for Douglas. He found where he'd been registered at one of them, but he had already checked out.

"Mrs. Maxwell. She had Benny take her and Rich into town to the train station."

Throwing the reins over the post he glared at her, "What did you say?" Surely Bernie was mistaken. Flair wouldn't have left. Not after last night.

Bernie rubbed her eyes and they teared again. Her whole body heaved with exertion. "She and Rich left. I tried to get her to wait until you got home. Even Rich was upset about going. He begged her to let him stay. Poor little thing didn't want to go."

Caden felt as if his chest was caving in on his heart it was so tight. His stomach seemed to be caving in on his backbone. He hadn't eaten supper last night nor had he eaten today. Why would Flair leave? What happened to make her go after all they'd shared last night? Why? He thought everything was settled between them. Maybe Douglas had been back.

"Did she have a visitor this morning? The man who visited her before, did he return?"

"No sir, no one. I'm sure of that. She came down with her bags packed shortly after Rich and I took her breakfast tray up to her."

God damn, he was shaky. He moistened his lips, then wiped them dry with the back of his hand. He didn't want Bernie to know how deeply Flair's leaving hurt him. "What time was that?"

"Late morning. I told Benny to hurry back so he could try to find you. He and Silas are still out riding the pastures hoping to find you."

Damn! She was in town leaving while he was in town trying to find Douglas. But why did she go?

"She asked me to give you this letter." Bernie reached in her apron pocket, brought out an envelope, and handed it to him. "She wouldn't tell me what we did wrong, only that it was best for you if she left. I told her you wouldn't be happy about her leaving, and certainly not before you returned to talk to her, but she said she and Rich would walk to town if I wouldn't let Benny drive them. I could tell by the set of her mouth that she meant it. I couldn't let them take off walking." She wiped her nose with the tail of her apron and sniffed.

His hand trembled as he took the envelope. He cursed Flair for doing this to him. He didn't want to take the note. He didn't want to know what it said. Dammit, what was wrong with her? She knew he loved her. She knew he was going to work something out about the will and Douglas. Why didn't she trust him to take care of *everything*? Why would she leave after last night, after what they said to each other, after what they meant to each other?

"Thank you, Bernie. I'm sure she explained everything in this letter."

"You are going after her, aren't you, Mr. Maxwell? You're not going to let her just leave like that and take your son are you?"

Going after her? Hell no! But as soon as he thought that, he didn't know it to be true. He was angry. Damn, he didn't know what to think. If she cared so little for his feelings, maybe he didn't want to go after her. Caden rubbed his forehead. His stomach roiled again. He just didn't know what he was going to do right now. He needed to be alone where he could think.

"Ask someone to take care of my horse. I'll be in my office if you need me."

"Yes sir," she answered softly and stepped out of his way so he could go inside.

Caden stepped into the foyer and knew immediately they were gone. The house was too big, too silent, too lonely. He threw his hat on the foyer table, then walked straight to his office and poured himself a generous portion of Scotch. He drank the first one without stopping for breath. The fiery liquid burned all the way down to his empty stomach and made it cramp. He coughed several times, then poured himself another before shutting the door and sitting down at his desk.

He turned the envelope over in his hand. If Flair cared so little for him that she'd leave without talking to him, did he really want to know what she had to say? *Hell no!*

He sipped the Scotch several more times before bringing the glass down from his mouth. His stomach burned and cramped uncomfortably but he no longer cared. His head felt heavy and a ringing started in his ears. With no food in his stomach the liquor had gone straight to his head. It wasn't smart to drink when he hadn't eaten anything, but at the moment, he just didn't care.

Maybe he should forget about Flair. Once before he had been able to put her out of his mind. It'd taken him a long time to forget about the golden-haired girl with the sky blue eyes who'd become his wife, but he had. And he could do it again. Who the hell did she think she was to treat him so shabbily?

His hand closed round the envelope. It seemed to sear his skin. Slowly he worked his fingers around it, folding, wrinkling, mutilating the paper until it formed a small round ball in his hand, and still he continued to roll it around in his closed hand.

"Hell no!" he cursed again and threw the ball of letter across the room. It hit a crystal candlestick that sat on a table and knocked it over. The candle fell out and the piece of crystal rolled off the table and fell to the floor breaking into several pieces.

Flair and Rich sat at the table of a grouchy old man and a snippy old woman. Surely there were friendlier people who would entertain the idea of hosting an inn and way station for the stagecoach line.

After a few moments at the table of the bickering couple Flair knew why the driver had taken his meal in the barn where he'd be sleeping. He obviously didn't want to hear the old couple's continuous picking at each other.

The stage had bumped and jarred them all afternoon until she was sore from being thrown from one side of the cabin to the other. The train would have been the better choice, but after Benny had dropped her off at the depot she realized she didn't have enough money for their fare and for food. The station master had told her riding the stage would take longer, but cost less, so they'd walked down the street to the stagecoach office. She had enough money to get them tickets home. They wouldn't have much left to eat on along the way, but if she were frugal they would make it.

Since she and Rich were the only passengers on the stage and they had little luggage between them, the team of horses had covered a lot of ground before stopping for the night at this way station.

Their first stop took them five hours and forty miles from Caden's farm. They rested while the horses were changed, then rode another two hours before darkness fell and they'd stopped at this house for the night. She'd been upstairs and checked their room. It was small but clean.

"You get it if you want more coffee. Why should I wait on you when I'm as tired as you are?"

The straggly haired woman's loud voice broke into Flair's musing and she looked up at the embittered face. She wondered if too many years of hard work had stolen the woman's charm or if she'd always been abrasive?

"Cause that's one of your jobs, old woman," her unkempt husband retorted. He scratched his chin beneath the graying beard. "Our guest might want more coffee, too."

Flair glanced over at the woman and quickly shook her head. "No, I'm fine thank you."

"See, I knew she didn't want any. Her cup is half full as it is."

Flair pushed the squabbling of the man and woman to the back of her mind and gave her attention to her son. She watched him play in his bowl of stew. With money so tight she wished he'd eat more of his dinner. By the end of the trip she might not be able to afford more than bread. But she couldn't force him to eat any more than she could force herself. Her bowl wasn't any emptier than his.

Rich wasn't happy and that tore at her heart, causing her great pain. She'd never forget his pleas to let him stay with Caden. If only she could make him understand how much she'd wanted to stay, too. How could she explain that Caden had done enough for them and it was time she gave something back to him. And his inheritance was the only thing she had any control over.

Rich had been sullen the entire afternoon. She understood why he hadn't wanted to leave, but what else could she do? Was it right for her to sacrifice Caden's inheritance for Rich's happiness? For her happiness? All his life she'd loved her son more than anyone on earth and in a way that was still true, but—now there was Caden, and his rights and his happiness were of equal importance to her. Her greatest fear in leaving Caden was the thought that she hadn't managed to make anyone happy.

Rich looked up and noticed her staring at him. "I'm tired. Can I go up to bed?"

"Of course," she answered as she rose from the table. She didn't have the heart to correct his grammar this time. When they reached home there was time enough to get him back into his school work. "I'm finished. I'll take you up and get you settled in."

He hopped off his chair. "I can do it by myself," he said, and without looking back hurried out of the kitchen ahead of her.

Feeling hurt by the rebuff, Flair turned back to her hosts who had stopped talking and were staring up at her. Apparently they'd never seen a young boy claim his independence. She braced her wounded feelings, smiled at the couple, and said, "Dinner was very good. Thank you."

A knock sounded on the back door as she gathered her reticule and short cape. The old man rose and shuffled over to the door and opened it. She heard the driver telling the innkeeper that another rider was joining them and needed a bed for the night. She started to leave the room, but something made her stay. The crabby old man stepped aside and Douglas walked into the room. He took off his hat and smiled at her.

Flair bit her bottom lip to stifle her scream of denial. How had Douglas found them? Why? Was she never to be free of this man?

"Good evening, Flair. What a pleasant surprise finding you here."

"You two know each other?" the whiskery old man asked as he shut the door.

Douglas glanced over at him, still grinning triumphantly. "Yes, we're old friends."

"Will you be wanting a bowl of stew, mister?" the woman asked as she rose from her chair and picked up her empty dinnerware.

"Sounds good to me. You aren't through, are you, Flair? Surely you'll join me."

She swallowed hard, the bit of supper she'd eaten making her feel sick inside. What was she going to do to make Douglas see she had no interest in him? "No," she answered in a whispery voice. "I was just leaving." She whirled out of the room. She heard him ask her to wait but she didn't, wanting only to get as far away from him as possible. She couldn't keep him from following her, but she didn't have to spend any time talking to him.

"Flair, wait," he called again. He caught her by the arm at the bottom of the stairs and forced her to turn and face him. "Wait a minute. Don't run out on me like that. I want to talk to you."

"You still want that supper, mister?" the woman asked following him out of the kitchen and into the wide center hallway.

He threw a glance over his shoulder. "Yes, go back into the kitchen and hold it for me please. I'll be there in a minute."

Douglas's fingers dug into her arm. His touch burned and violated her. His very presence mocked her and infuriated her. She yanked her arm away from him and said, "If you touch me again I'll scream this house down."

His face reddened, but he had the good sense to step back and hold his hands up in the air. "No need to do that. I merely wanted to speak with you. You really should do something about your temper, Flair."

She was too tired, too distraught, too broken-hearted over leaving Caden for this. The last thing she wanted to have to contend with on her journey home was this man. "Douglas, what in God's name are you doing here?"

A muscle quivered in his neck. His eyes

searched her face. "Following you." His voice was calm, honest.

She knew that had to be the case just as he'd followed her to Virginia. "Following me? Why? Nothing between us has changed. It won't change."

His eyes narrowed. "You're wrong. Your divorce changes everything. Rich is my son, and I have every right to see him."

"How dare you think such a thing." Flair felt as if a hand grabbed hold of her heart and squeezed. "You have no rights. You gave up those rights years ago." She took a step toward him and pointed her finger at his face. "Stay away from my son." Her voice was firm, steady, confident. "I will hurt you before I'll let you hurt him."

Douglas jerked his head back away from her pointing finger. He gave her a cold stare. "I don't want to hurt him. I want to be his father."

"Never! He has a father and it isn't you." She picked up her skirts and hurried up the stairs, wishing she could run back to the safety of Caden's arms, but knowing what she was doing was the best thing for him.

Upstairs she rushed inside the bedroom and shut the door and locked it. The only light in the room came from an oil lamp on the small bedside table. Rich huddled fast asleep on one side of the bed, still dressed in his shoes and clothes. Seeing him sleeping so peacefully calmed her. She picked up a side chair and fitted it tightly underneath the door handle. But even with the extra precaution against an intrusion from Douglas, Flair knew she would have difficulty falling asleep tonight.

She walked over to the bed and gently loosened Rich's boots and took them off. She didn't have the heart to wake him to put on his nightshirt. Watching him sleep reminded her of the day he fell off the horse and she'd taken off his shoes. Lamp light flickered on his cheek showing a light patch of freckles. His chest rose and fell in a steady rhythm of rest. Her love for him spilled over from her heart and warmed her as she watched him sleep. How she loved him.

Without effort, her thoughts turned to Caden. She loved him and missed him already. She wondered what he was doing at this very minute. How had he taken the news that she'd left? It would be so easy to hope that he'd thrown the note aside and rode after her. But that wasn't what was best for Caden. And she wanted what was best for him. Flair squeezed her eyes tightly shut to keep her tears at bay. The decision she'd made wasn't an easy one, but it was the right one. She had to keep telling herself that.

After taking off her own shoes and her bonnet, she lay down on the bed beside Rich, but her thoughts were on her husband.

The next morning Flair, Rich, and Douglas rode the bumping, tossing stage southward. They had awakened to dark gray clouds. Thunder, lightning, and a light rain hampered their early morning journey. The driver had insisted they start out and try to make the first way station which was forty miles away. He assured them the roads would only become impassable after hours of rain had soaked the hard packed ground. He seemed sure they had time to make their first stop. If luck was with them, he'd promised, as the day wore on, the rain would move away from them and bring clear skies, a cool breeze, and dry roads.

Even though she was uneasy about the weather, Flair agreed to board the stage, reassuring herself every mile would put them closer to home. Douglas had spoken to her but she'd managed only a slight nod of her head. When Rich had first seen Douglas he'd grabbed hold of her hand. She'd assured her son that Douglas meant them no harm and that he was merely a passenger just like they were.

Shortly after they took off, Douglas made several attempts at drawing her and Rich into a conversation, but when they both continued to ignore him he grew quiet.

Later in the day a heavy rain slashed against the leather-covered windows. Lightning flashed through the cracks in the windows and thunder rumbled loudly. She expected the driver to stop the coach and join them inside until the storm let up, but being a man who'd obviously weathered a few storms, he kept the horses traveling at a brisk pace.

The ride was especially bumpy. Occasionally she'd hear the driver yell to the team, then she'd hear the whip crack above the animals' heads. The rain, thunder, and lightning continued, and soon the inside of the carriage became damp and hot. Water puddled at her feet as it found its way into the cabin.

After more than an hour in the stuffy cabin Rich became irritable and Flair allowed him to take off his jacket and roll up the sleeves of his shirt.

"I think that's a good idea you have there. It's hot as July in here." Douglas looked over at Flair. "You don't mind if I take my jacket off and roll up my sleeves, do you?"

It shocked her that he was actually polite

enough to ask. And even though it was on the tip of her tongue to deny his request, she couldn't. She was hot, too, having already shed her cape. "No, of course not," she answered.

Rich reached into the pocket of his breeches and brought out five or six colorful marbles. He cupped them in his palm, turning them over with a fingertip and inspecting each one of them. She recognized the orbs as the ones Caden had given Rich when he was so sick. Her heart wrenched in her chest as she realized that Rich loved Caden, too. Not only was he sad about leaving the farm, he was sad about leaving Caden.

Flair looked up into the handsomely chiseled face of Douglas. He had a large farm but he was a nothing of a man, always thinking only of himself and what he wanted. Caden was a kind, loving man who thought of what others needed and wanted. He loved his uncle's farm, but he loved her more. *He loved her!* How could she have left him? If she loved Caden and Rich loved Caden wasn't that more important than all the land in Virginia? Hadn't she told herself that night in his arms that love conquered all things? All of a sudden she knew she'd been wrong to leave. Why was she running away from the man who loved her? The man she and her son loved. If Caden said he'd find a way to work things out so they could stay married, then why hadn't she trusted him to do that? Why was she trying to tell him what he wanted, what he needed? Caden was a man who could think for himself. He wouldn't do anything he didn't want to do.

Peace settled over her and she smiled. She and Rich were getting off this stagecoach at the next stop and waiting for one that would take them back to Maxwell Farms.

They started up an incline and the stage jerked and bounced horribly. Douglas loosened the leather strap and stuck his head out the window and hollered up to the driver, "What's the problem?" He held his hat on his head but it did little to keep the rain from pelting his face and drenching his shirt and jacket.

"We're traveling up a steep cliff," she heard the man shout back above the downpour. "It's a bit slippery because of the mud. The horses are skittish from the lightning. Don't worry. Everything will be all right."

"I think you should stop the coach!" Douglas yelled.

"Not yet!" the man returned.

Flair wasn't so sure everything was going to be all right, and she noticed, neither was Douglas as he refastened the leather curtain over the window. Rich moved a little closer to her.

"Damn fool!" Douglas muttered. "He'll end up getting us all killed." He took a handkerchief out of his pocket and wiped the water off his face.

"I'm sure he knows what he's doing," Flair said as much to comfort herself as her son. "Put your marbles away before you lose them," she told Rich.

All of a sudden, the stage bounced and lurched to the left slinging Flair against the door. Rich caught himself with the armrest and avoided a fall.

"Goddammit! I'm telling that fool to stop before he kills us!" Douglas yelled.

Flair heard the driver let out a fearful yell. The stage jerked and started moving sideways. In a glance she saw fear in Rich's and Douglas's eyes. The horses screamed in protest as the coach rattled back and forth.

"No!" she screamed trying to raise up but the pull of the falling stage leaning sideways kept her off balance. She struggled to sit up and regain her footing.

Douglas kicked the door open and yelled, "Give me your hand!"

Flair stretched out her arm but knew she couldn't reach Douglas in time. Her only hope was to try to save her son. "Rich, jump! Jump!" she screamed.

She saw Douglas grab hold of Rich's arm and in a burst of raw strength he lifted himself up, and holding tightly to Rich's arm he dove out the doorway just as the stage toppled sideways.

Screaming again, Flair wrapped her hands and arms about her head to try to cushion the blows as she was thrown about the cabin. The stage toppled end over end down the side of a cliff. A sharp pain struck her arm and somehow her foot twisted beneath her. Her skirt and petticoats flew over her head. She grabbed them and covered her face to cushion her head. Flair heard wood splintering, horses screaming, thunder rolling, and lightning cracking. The coach hit bottom with a jarring jolt. A shooting pain hit the side of her head and thankfully everything went dark.

Eighteen

Rich stood in the doorway of the stage-coach smiling and waving to her. Why was he waving? She didn't want him to go away. She tried to call to him but she couldn't get the words out. Her mouth moved but there was no sound. Her throat was too dry. She hurt but didn't know where. Rich was in danger. She sensed it. Why was he smiling? Douglas's face rose up over Rich's shoulder. Douglas was smiling, too—that triumphant grin that made her blood run cold. She had to get Rich away from Douglas. She ran toward them but came no closer to them. They were getting farther and farther away from her. She tried to call out again but the only thing that reached her ears was silence.

Flair felt the water hitting her face. She tried to turn her face away from the stinging little pellets, but she couldn't move her head, and she didn't know why. She tried to call out to Caden, to Rich, but neither of them answered her. Where were they? Why didn't they help her?

It was raining again. She wanted the rain to stop. She hurt. The stagecoach. Falling. She was falling. It rained. Rich and Douglas stood in the doorway smiling at her, waving. She had to protect Rich. Rich!

"No!" she screamed.

"Calm down. Calm down, everything's going to be all right. You're safe."

A man's voice crooned softly in her ear. Without opening her eyes, Flair realized she was awake. She was held in warm arms against a hard chest. The voice didn't belong to Caden or Douglas. She didn't recognize it. Her chest hurt every time she breathed in. Her foot hurt. Her head hurt. She hurt so badly she knew she had to be alive. And thank God she no longer lay underneath the rubble of the wrecked stagecoach. Her breathing calmed a little, lessening the pain in her chest.

"Everything's going to be all right," the man said again, smoothing her hair against her neck and patting her back affectionately.

She tried to focus, to remember where she was. But she couldn't seem to focus long enough to put her thoughts together correctly. Taking a deep breath, she tried to clear her fuzzy mind. Suddenly she remembered seeing Douglas and Rich jumping from the stagecoach just before it toppled over and slid down the cliff.

Coming fully awake, Flair pushed away from the arms that held her and scrambled to the head of the bed. A sharp pain shot up her leg and she winced loudly and mumbled an oath. The quick movement made her head pound with a dull ache. Her breath grew shallow from the pain in her side, and her foot was killing her where she'd tried to use it to shove herself forward and away from the stranger.

In the clear light of day her eyes grew wide as she tried to take in the whole scene at once. In front of her she saw a large, bearded man sitting on the side of the bed. He was clean, but his long beard and bushy hair and eyebrows gave him a frightening appearance. Not only was he large boned and husky, he was downright heavy. His stomach fell over the waistband of his breeches and the buttons on his cotton shirt gaped. His fat arms strained the material of his shirtsleeves.

"Don't be frightened. I'm not going to hurt you."

For a big man he had a soft and gentle voice. His eyes were small, squinty looking, and almost hidden among all the hair surrounding his face. "W-who are you?" Her gravelly voice sounded strange at first. She cleared her throat and tried again. "Who are you and where am I?"

"Name's Jewel. Right now you're in my cabin and that's my bed you've been sleeping in the past two days."

There was nothing in his voice, his eyes, or his manner to make her fear him, still she did. He was a stranger. She put her hand to her side where it hurt so badly and was shocked to find someone had taken off her corset. She looked down at herself and realized she wore only her chemise and underdrawers. Fear loomed at the back of her mind as she clutched her hands together at the base of her throat.

"Your wife?" she immediately asked.

He smiled and chuckled a little, showing a good set of teeth. "Laurie May is in town for a few days. I had to undress you to check your injuries. Don't worry. I tried to be as proper as possible. I knew by your clothes you were a real lady." He brushed his hand down his beard and continued. "As best I can tell you have a couple of cracked ribs. You complained a lot about your side hurting, foot, too. It didn't feel like anything was broken. Same with your ankle. It's swollen big as any I've ever seen, but it seems to be moving properly, so I don't think it's broken anywhere in there. That knot on your forehead is already looking better."

She nodded and her hand automatically went to the tender rise of flesh at her hairline. She wasn't happy this man had undressed her, but maybe it was best not to say anything. After all, he'd obviously saved her life. She was very lucky.

"I found you two days ago underneath the seat of a broken up stagecoach. I guess the storm caused the wreck."

Yes, she remembered the stuffy cabin of the stage. She looked at the man. Suddenly she stiffened as the shock of what happened registered on her. "Rich. Where's Rich?" she asked, pulling her feet up and underneath her chemise, trying to cover herself.

"If you're talking about the driver, he didn't make it. Had to bury him."

Flair brushed her hair away from her face, still trying to sort everything out in her mind. "No. No, Rich. My son. A young boy. Nine years old."

The man rose, his weight causing the bed to shake. He looked down at her and shook his head. "All I found was you and the driver." He scratched his bearded neck. "But it must have been a day or two after the accident before I came across you. The ground was already drying around the stage. I looked for tracks, but didn't find any. If the boy wandered off he could be most anywhere by now."

She groaned from the pain, from the thought of her son wandering around by himself, from the foolishness of leaving Caden. What had she done?

Jewel picked up a cup from the night table and held it to her. "Here, drink this. It will take that headache away."

"No," she mumbled. Fear welled up in her chest cutting off her breath, tears welled up in her eyes cutting off her vision. "I need to find Rich. I need to find my son."

"Don't worry now, if he's out there, I'll find him for you. Now drink this. You'll feel better when you wake up in a little while."

His voice was so soothing she couldn't help but feel calmer. She took the cup from his hand and sipped the tea. The bitter brew actually felt good going down her dry throat. "Douglas," she said, only able to remember pieces of the past at a time. "There was a man named Douglas with Rich. He wore fancy clothes. Did you find him?"

He shook his head again. "Nobody but you and the driver. If you say there were two others, they probably saw you were in a bad way and went for help. If that's true, they should be back with help in a day or two. The nearest town is about twenty or twenty-five miles away."

"Thank God," she whispered, realizing Douglas and Rich must have managed to jump free of the falling stagecoach.

She finished off the tea and wiped her mouth with the back of her hand. The tea was foul tasting but she'd drink anything to stop the pounding in her head, the pain in her side, and the ache in her foot.

"H-how far are we from the wreckage?"

"Not more than two miles as the crow flies, but unless someone knew my cabin was up here they'd never find it nestled in the crook of this hill the way it is."

Her head was already feeling better, but her ears started ringing. Whatever was in the tea worked fast. "Well how will they find me? I need to go back to the wreck and wait for them."

He took the cup from her and pulled up the sheet. "All you need to do is lay down and rest, sleep. I'll keep an eye on the wreck site. If they come back, I'll know it."

The drink made her sleepy. Her eyes were heavy so she scooted down on the pillow. "What if they don't find me?" she mumbled.

"Don't worry about that now, Laurie May. If we don't hear from them in a day or two when you get better, we saddle my horse and

I'll take you into town and find out what's going on. You just sleep."

"Yes," she whispered, closing her eyes. "That's a good idea. We'll ride into town. A-after I s-sleep." She wanted to ask him why he thought her name was Laurie May, but she was too tired, too sleepy.

Caden stood spread legged in the middle of Douglas's parlor waiting for him to come downstairs. He'd been to Flair's farm and Booker and Samp told him they hadn't seen her, but they'd heard Mr. Eagerton had returned from a trip and brought a youngster with him. The boy had to be Rich. But where was Flair? Either Booker and Samp truly didn't know or they wanted Eagerton to tell him where Flair had gone.

Rubbing his neck with one hand and holding tight to his hat with the other he looked around the expensively decorated room. A large painting of an older man who resembled Douglas hung on the wall over the fireplace and a baroque-style mirror with matching candle sconces hung on another. Caden tapped his foot. He didn't want to look at the damn house. He wanted to see Flair and Rich.

After Flair left it had taken him a couple of days to come to his senses and realize she had no way of knowing he'd found a way to get around the will. He should have told her what he planned to do before he went to see Rutherford. It had been his fault she left.

Caden walked over to a window which looked out over the front porch. Seeing the flowering shrubs made him remember what had made him go in search of the little ball of paper he'd thrown across the room.

He didn't remember much at all about the first night. Like a fool he'd started drinking on an empty stomach and it hadn't taken long before the liquor had him roaring drunk, and then he finally fell asleep. If he remembered correctly, he fired everybody that night, but thank goodness everyone was forgiving and back at work the next morning. Still, over the next two days he found himself doing everything possible to make anyone he came in contact with miserable. He was mean, harsh, and condescending: a real jackass. Just like Shelton. But then Bernie came into his office on the third night bearing a gift.

He closed his eyes and remembered his conversation with the housekeeper as clearly as if it were happening all over again. His mind went back in time.

"Mr. Maxwell, may I come in?" Bernie had asked from the doorway of his office.

Scowling, Caden had looked up at the old

woman. "No, I'm busy. I'll talk to you tomorrow."

"All right, but I have something I'd like to leave with you."

Caden watched her start toward him. Bernie was a brave woman to walk into his office after he'd told her he'd talk to her tomorrow. He scowled at her again, but she didn't blink an eye. She'd always been too presumptuous.

He was about to reprimand her when he noticed she held something in her hands that looked like an old book. She laid the book down on the desk in front of him. The leather-bound cover was worn thin, and the edges were tattered. His breath caught in his throat as his eyes caught sight of the faded gold lettering across the front. His chest tightened as he read the word inscribed in fancy English script. *Holy Bible*.

His eyes widened as he looked up at his housekeeper. A warm glow seemed to circle her face. Her smile was as sweet as an angel's and her eyes teared.

"Where? How?" he managed to ask as his hand snaked out and opened the cover. In a faded but fancy script was written the name Pearson Maxwell. It was his father's Bible. Shelton said he'd thrown it away.

"Shelton gave it to me years ago and told me to burn it, but I couldn't destroy the

Good Book. Anyway, I knew it was meant for you, not him. It's been hidden in the attic all these years. I've been waiting for the right time to give it to you. I think you need it now. I don't want to see you turn out like your uncle. Maybe this will help you remember your papa. He was a good man, a gentle man."

"Thank you," he whispered as she walked out, closing the door behind her. He'd been a bastard the last few days and he'd known why. Flair. It didn't take him long to figure out what Bernie was trying to tell him. Shelton had lost the woman he loved to Pearson and he'd let it turn him into a bitter, unyielding old man. Bernie was trying to show him that he was about to do the same thing. Pearson had given up his right to Maxwell Farms for the woman he loved, and Caden could do it, too. He realized the sacrifice was his to make, not Flair's.

Caden rose from his desk and hurried to the other side of the room. He searched along the baseboard, looked underneath the sideboard and behind the mahogany chest, eventually finding what he was looking for in a brass dish beside the Bible on top of his desk. Bernie had saved that for him, too. With trembling fingers and shallow breath he uncurled the wadded paper and read Flair's letter.

Dear Caden,

It pains me to leave you, but I know it's what is best for you. I love you too much to let you give up your inheritance for me. I've sent Rutherford a note asking him to let me know when the divorce papers are final. I will sign them promptly, so that you can remarry and claim what is rightfully yours. Please respect my wishes and don't make this harder on any of us by following me.

"Like hell," he'd muttered to himself.

The sound of footsteps on the staircase brought Caden back to the present. He shook his head and rubbed his eyes. Damn, he was tired, but he knew he couldn't rest until he found Flair and Rich.

Douglas walked jauntily into the parlor, but stopped mid-stride when he saw Caden. "Oh, it's you," he said in a nonchalant voice. "I should have known you'd show up sooner or later. What can I do for you?"

"Where's Flair?"

Douglas's eyebrows rose a fraction. "You haven't heard. I thought that must be why you were here."

"Heard what?" His hands tightened on his hat as he walked away from the window to the center of the room.

Douglas faced him and looked him in the eyes. "I hate to be the bearer of bad news, Maxwell, but your wife is dead."

Caden felt as if a fist had hit him in the gut and sucked all the air from his lungs. For a moment he was speechless as he tried to let what the man said register. He expected the man to lie, but not this. Caden's right hand automatically folded into a fist. "You best be lying, Eagerton."

His face remained passive. "Really, Maxwell, is this the sort of thing a person lies about?" He walked over to the doorway and leaned out into the hallway and called, "Rich? Rich, come down here."

Caden's heart felt as if it might beat out of his chest. This news was so shocking he didn't think he could move. It had to be a lie. It had to be. If Rich was alive, Flair had to be alive, too. He could kill Eagerton for saying such a thing.

He heard little steps on the stairs and watched the doorway. Rich walked in with his head hanging down, but as soon as he looked up and saw Caden his eyes brightened and a big smile flashed across his face. "Cade!" He yelled and started running toward Caden.

Douglas stuck out his hand and caught Rich's arm, pulling him up short.

"Hey, wait a minute there, young fellow." Douglas grabbed hold of Rich's shoulders and positioned him in front of him, keeping a tight grip on him.

Caden didn't like the way Douglas handled Rich, but he waited to do anything about it. He had to find out about Flair first.

Douglas looked up at Caden. "Ask the boy about his mother. All three of us were riding the stage when it turned over."

Stage? "You're lying. Benny said she took the train."

"Yes, he let her off at the train station, but she and the boy walked down to the stage line."

"Mama didn't have enough money for the tickets so we had to take the stagecoach because it was cheaper," Rich offered as explanation.

No, no! his mind screamed with rejection. He wouldn't believe Flair was dead. He wouldn't.

"What happened?" he managed to ask in a hoarse voice.

"We got caught in the middle of a bad thunderstorm. We had a crazy driver who wouldn't stop. We don't really know what happened except that one minute we were riding and the next we were sliding. I kicked the door open and grabbed Rich by the arm and we jumped just before the stage slipped over a cliff and broke up into several pieces. No one could have survived that fall. Rich will tell you the same story."

His chest hurting with the pressing weight of fear, Caden looked at his son. Rich's bottom lip quivered. His eyes filled with tears. Goddammit! Could Douglas be telling the truth? A devastating feeling of emptiness washed over Caden. He wanted to break something, but knew he had to keep control of himself for Rich.

"Did you see her after the accident?" he asked in a cold tone.

"What? You mean after the stage toppled down the cliff? It was storming and neither Rich nor I could have made it down the side of that cliff and back up again. We waited around for a few minutes hoping we'd see some sign of life from her or the driver, but when the rain slacked and there was no movement from below we started walking. We didn't make it to town until the next day. We told the sheriff about the accident and left it up to him to ride out to the wreckage. We didn't wait around for them to recover her body. I thought it was best to get Rich away from there as soon as possible. No use in the boy seeing her."

Caden cringed at Douglas's choice of words. As long as Douglas hadn't seen Flair dead there was a chance she lived. He wouldn't, couldn't think about any other possibility.

Caden dropped down to one knee and held his hands out to Rich. He twisted away from Douglas's grip and ran into Caden's outstretched arms. Caden wrapped his arms around the little shaking body. Rich buried his face in Caden's neck. He heard a soft sniffle. How would he make it up to Rich if he'd lost his mother? How would he live with himself for not following her immediately and bringing her back home?

Holding his son tighter, Caden said, "It's all right, Rich. I'm going to take care of you. You won't be alone. We'll go back and find your mother."

The click of a hammer being pulled back caught Caden's attention and he looked over Rich's shoulder. Douglas held a pistol on him. Dammit! Why had he let his guard down? He knew Douglas to be a man without principle.

Caden slowly patted Rich on the back before gently pushing him away. "Go back upstairs, son, I have something to settle with Douglas."

"You won't leave me here, will you, Cade?"

"No, I'll call you when it's time to go. Now go get your things together so you'll be ready."

Rich turned to leave, but seeing the gun trained on Caden, he stopped and slowly backed up against Caden's legs.

"I knew it'd come down to this," Douglas said. "With Flair out of the way, both of us wanting the boy."

"You have no claim to Rich." Caden's voice was dangerously low. At his side his hand opened, closed, then opened again.

"Obviously you don't know the whole story of Rich's parentage."

"I know."

"Then you know he's my son. I intend to keep him here with me."

Caden felt Rich stiffen. "You're wrong. He's my son. I won't let you try to lay claim to him."

"I already have. I've been telling folks around here Flair and I were going to get married after her divorce, and that she would want the boy to live with me."

Caden didn't know how much longer he could hold onto his temper. He wanted to smash Douglas's face in. "His name is Rich and he goes with me. We're going to find Flair."

Douglas leveled the pistol at Caden's chest. "This gun says different. You either ride out of here alone, or I pull the trigger and tell the sheriff you were trying to kidnap the boy."

"Do you think the sheriff will believe that? I'm his father."

"I'll take my chances."

"No!" Rich yelled and made a mad dash for Douglas, catching him around his knees. The pistol fired, the bullet landed harmlessly in the far wall.

Caden rushed Douglas and landed a hard right to the center of his chin, snapping his head back, knocking him off balance. Douglas stumbled and fell to the floor. Caden rushed over and put one foot on Douglas's wrist that held the gun and jammed his other foot against Douglas's throat. Reaching down he grabbed the gun from Douglas's hand and threw it to the far side of the room. Douglas grappled with Caden's foot.

Gasping for breath, Caden looked up at Rich's frightened little face. He didn't want to hurt Rich more, but he needed to know how dangerous it was for him to rush a man holding a gun. "That was a damn fool thing to do, Rich."

His bottom lip trembled. "I couldn't let him shoot you, Cade. You're my pa."

Caden gave him a short nod of approval. They'd have a long talk later.

He would have liked to take the time to beat the everlasting hell out of Douglas, but he was too worried about Flair. It didn't surprise him that Douglas left without trying to rescue her. He clung to the hope that the stage line had rushed someone right out to the wreckage and found her alive.

Caden looked down at Douglas. His face was beet red and his eyes bulged from the pressure of Caden's boot. He bent over the sorry excuse for a man and said, "I swear to God I'll kill you if you ever come near my son again." He pressed his foot tighter against his throat and Douglas strangled and gasped for air. "Are you listening to me? Do we understand each other?"

A frantic nod from Douglas's head made Caden lift his foot a little.

"Is there anything upstairs you want?" he asked Rich.

Rich reached into his pocket and pulled out a handful of marbles. He looked at them, then put them back in his pocket. "I have all my things. Are we going to look for Mama?"

Caden swallowed hard. "Do you think she's dead?"

"No sir."

"I don't either."

"He wouldn't let me go down the cliff and see about her," he said.

"You can go with me." He looked back down at Douglas and took his foot off his throat. Douglas coughed and hacked like he was gasping for his last breath.

"You almost killed me, I couldn't breathe."

"I might decide to do that yet. Now tell me where the accident happened and the name of the town closest to it."

"I have no idea where the accident happened. We were out in the middle of nowhere. I don't remember the name of the town. I swear," he hurried to add as he clutched his reddened throat. "It was a small town just this side of South Carolina about a hundred miles outside Richmond. You can't miss it, it's the only one within twenty miles of the border."

Caden started to give Douglas a sucker punch for all the things he'd done to Flair over the years, but decided that wouldn't be a good example for Rich. Instead, he said, "I'm taking a horse for Rich to ride into town. It's the least you can do for him for not checking on the condition of his mother. I'll leave it at the train station. Do you have a problem with that?"

"No." Douglas coughed again. "Just get the hell out of here."

Nineteen

Over the next few days Flair did more sleeping than anything else. Every time she woke, Jewel was beside her, soothing her fears with soft words and urging her to drink the broth and bitter tea he made for her. She'd finally gotten clear-headed enough not to drink all the tea the night before. She had awakened feeling better.

She was thankful to find that Jewel wasn't in the room with her. In the early morning light she lay in the bed and tried to rationalize what had happened to her. She didn't know how many days she'd been at Jewel's house, but thought it was close to a week. Her head didn't hurt so much anymore and breathing came easier. She tested her ankle by moving it around a few times. Her foot felt better, too.

It was time to stop drinking the drug-laced tea and get herself together. She sat up in bed for a few minutes and stretched. Even though she was sore all over, the exercise felt good to her bruised and unused muscles.

After swinging her legs over the side of the bed for a minute or two she tested her injured ankle. It felt tight as she applied weight to it, but the pain wasn't unbearable. After using the chamber pot in the far corner of the small bedroom she looked around the room. The single bed stood between two small drapeless windows. A small table sat beside the bed and a tall chest with a shaving mirror on top of it stood against the far wall. The only chair in the room sat on the other side of the bed. When she finished, she hobbled over to the water stand and poured a generous amount into the basin. She splashed water on her face, her neck, and under her arms. The tepid water felt wonderful. She relished the feel of it on her dry skin as she wet her face again, letting the water trickle down her neck. As she squeezed her eyes shut she thought of Rich and Caden and how desperately she wanted to see them.

While the water dried on her face she exercised her foot and her mind. Every time she woke up, Jewel told her everything was going to be fine, then gave her the tea to drink. The first thing she planned to do was *not* drink any more of that tea. She needed a clear head. If Douglas and Rich had made it to a town, they should have returned with help by now. Something was wrong. If they couldn't find her, she had to find them.

The good Lord had seen fit to let her live through the stagecoach crash and she didn't intend to waste another minute of the life He saved.

She walked around the room several times, knowing she had to build up her strength. She was weak and out of breath but kept going. The longer she walked, the clearer her mind seemed to function. After several laps around the room she was tired and hobbled back to the bed to rest. As much as she hated to admit it, she was beginning to think Douglas didn't intend to return for her. She knew he wanted her son for himself, but she didn't want to believe he was mean enough to leave her to die at the bottom of that cliff.

Flair combed through her hair with her fingers and wondered if Jewel was still sleeping or if he had gone out. She was about to get up and look around when she heard him walking around in the next room. She smelled coffee and the scent of some kind of meat burning. Her stomach contracted. She didn't know how long it'd been since she'd eaten solid food. Maybe Jewel was planning to bring her something other than tea and broth today. But, her hopes were dashed a few minutes later when the door opened and Jewel came in carrying a tray with two cups on it.

He looked surprised to see her sitting up, but quickly hid it behind a smile. "Good morning. You must be feeling better."

She brushed her hair back with her hand and pulled the sheet up around her neck. "Yes, thank you. I'm much better."

"Good. I brought your tea."

Flair looked at the cup. "No, thank you. I don't believe I'd care for any this morning. I'm—I was hoping I might have solid food so that I can get my strength back."

A concerned expression crossed his face. "I don't think that's a good idea just yet. You've been too sick. I don't think food will sit well on your stomach. Better stay with the tea and broth a few more days."

She swallowed hard. She suddenly had a real fear that this man was going to try to keep her here as long as possible. "I'd like to try, if you don't mind. And I'd like my clothes back please."

He squinted his eyes so tight she couldn't see them. "You're not thinking on trying to leave, are you?"

Panic welled up inside her. Could she lie with a straight face? Her life could very well depend on it. She had to. "No, no," she smiled. "Not only can I barely walk on my foot, but I'm waiting for Douglas and Rich to send someone after me." Mentioning Rich's name calmed her and reminded her she would do whatever was necessary in order to get away from this man and find her son. "I can't believe they haven't found me. I—I don't know what's keeping them."

"I've been thinking about that," he said peering down at her, an eerie faraway expression on his face. "I think they probably think you're dead by now."

She felt as if a fist closed around her heart. No! she screamed inside. "Why? What makes you think that? It's only been a few days, hasn't it? Not more than a week. I'm sure they're still looking for me. You said we're not far from the wreckage, didn't you?" she asked, hoping to pin him down on exactly where they were in relation to the stagecoach.

"About two miles."

"Well," she hedged. "Maybe they're looking north, and we're south of the wreck, aren't we?" She had to know in which direction to go when she managed to get away.

"East," he answered. "But the stage line men have already been out looking for you. I told them I buried the driver. Showed them the grave."

Flair held to her temper, her panic. "What about me? Didn't you tell them about me?

That I was here." It was useless to try to hide her fear. She knew it was written all over her face.

He wiped his large beefy hand down his beard. "I showed them your grave, too."

Flair started shaking, which started her chest to hurting and caused her breath to grow shallow. "I—I—my grave?" Light dawned. He'd wanted them to think she had died, too. She was right. He had no intentions of ever letting her leave this place. She couldn't panic, not now. She had to keep control of herself or she'd never get away from this man. "I don't understand. Why would you do that?"

"I'm taking care of you now. You don't need them anymore. You'll be just fine here with me."

The man was mad. No wonder he lived away from civilization. "Yes, I thank you for s-saving my life and f-for taking care of me." She hoped she was saying the right things to him. She couldn't have him watching her every minute or she'd never get away from him. She had to make him think she was prepared to stay with him. "I think I'll drink that tea now," she said, wanting him to leave so she could be alone and think.

His smile told her she'd managed to fool him for now. He handed her the tea and she returned his smile. She took a very small sip but made it look like a big one. He knew that as long as she drank the tea she wouldn't be capable of going anywhere.

Jewel nodded to her. "I'll cook up a big pot of rabbit stew. That'll be just what you need after your rest."

"Yes, that sounds good. I'd like that, but I'll sleep awhile first." She put the cup to her lips again and tilted it, but didn't let the bitter brew enter her mouth. She had to keep a clear head for making plans.

Obviously thinking she would drain the cup as usual, Jewel walked out of the room. A few minutes later when she heard him go out the front door she rose from the bed and hobbled over to the chamber pot. She poured the tea into the pot and added water from the basin until it was the color of urine. She prayed to God Jewel wouldn't notice when he emptied the waste. As fast as her injured ankle would let her she hurried back to the bed. She had a lot of planning to do.

Jewel was a soft spoken, kind man but he was also touched. He'd brought her clothes to wear but they weren't her own. They had belonged to another woman. And instead of calling her Flair, he called her Laurie May.

Flair had decided to play along with him in hopes of tricking him into taking her into town. But every time she mentioned the idea he always had a reason why it wasn't a good time for them to go. He had to reshoe the horse, or it looked like rain, or he had to hunt rabbit or squirrel for supper. Flair continued to go along with him while she regained her strength and full use of her foot. Trying to escape before she could walk well would be foolish. And when she tried, she intended to make it.

She knew it was time to make her move when he'd entered the bedroom and lay down on the bed beside her late one night. She'd remained perfectly still, pretending to sleep. He hadn't tried to touch her, but she was afraid the next time he came to her bed in the middle of the night he might. And with his size there was no way she could fight him off.

He usually went hunting every other day. And she was in luck that this morning was his day to hunt. While he was gone, she intended to saddle the horse and ride east. Surely she'd find a town or a house sooner or later.

Flair could only guess that the stage had taken them roughly one hundred miles from Richmond. Caden was closer than Alabama, but if Douglas and Rich had managed to jump free of the crashing stagecoach she was sure Douglas had taken Rich to his home. And that was where she was heading.

It was late into the morning and he still hadn't left. Flair thought she'd go crazy with an attack of nerves. She tried so hard to appear normal that she knew she was being edgy. Finally she had to ask for her tea and to go lie down. Soon after she'd poured the tea into the chamber pot he came in and told her he was going hunting. She tried to appear drowsy so he'd think the tea had taken effect.

Flair counted to sixty fifteen times then headed for the barn. Jewel had had plenty of time to get away from the house.

Stacked neatly in one corner of the make-shift barn she saw her trunks. She couldn't resist the chance to go through them quickly to see if Jewel had disturbed her things. She opened first one and then the other. If Jewel hadn't been through them, someone else had. At the bottom of one she found her reticule and her heart skipped a beat. Quickly she opened it and breathed a sigh of relief when she saw her money was still there. If she was lucky, it would be enough to buy a train ticket home. She quickly stuffed the reticule in the pocket of her brown skirt.

Flair watched the door of the barn while she saddled the horse. It wasn't easy reaching under his belly and pulling the cinch tight. She didn't have as much strength as she thought she had. At last she had the leather tight enough and she took hold of the reins and walked the horse out into the open. She looked around and saw nothing but barren land and blue sky.

Thinking she was home free, Flair stepped her uninjured foot into the stirrup. As she swung up a hand caught her leg and slung her off the horse. She screamed and landed in the dirt on her hip with a hard thud. Flair quickly used her heels to scramble and scoot on her backside away from Jewel. She'd worry about the pain in her foot and her hip later. Right now she had to worry about her life, and screaming wouldn't help her. No one was around but Jewel.

"I thought you were going to try something like this. You were mighty nervous this morning, Laurie May. Didn't think I'd remember how you acted before the last time you ran away, did you? I remember how you did it."

Flair had to replace her fear with strength or she'd never see Rich or Caden again. She remained quiet.

"I told you once before I'd never let you leave again." He squinted his eyes. "Didn't you believe me? Looks like I'm going to have to chain you to keep you here."

"No!" She'd let Douglas force her into something against her will, and she vowed that would never happen again. And it wouldn't. But what was she going to do? There was a large, angry man between her and the horse that would take her to freedom.

He took a step toward her. "You don't have a choice anymore, Laurie May. I can't let you leave me again."

Flair knew of only one thing that would take the man to his knees. She had to be quick for it to work. While she'd been recuperating, her fingernails had grown long. She dug in the hard ground as he talked, cupping a pile of earth under each palm.

Jewel reached down for her and Flair flung the dirt at his face. He yelled and rubbed his eyes. Flair jumped to her feet and caught Jewel with a hard kick between the legs with her booted foot. His eyes widened larger than she'd ever seen them as he grabbed his groin and fell to his knees. Swinging wide and away from him she ran past him. With a racing heart and trembling hands she swung herself into the saddle. A hand closed around her injured ankle, shooting pain up her leg. She cried out.

She looked down and saw Jewel trying to

pull himself up with her leg. Frightened she wasn't going to get away, she took the excess reins and started beating him about the head with the leather strips. Blood appeared on his forehead but still he held on. He tugged harder on her leg, nearly stripping her from the saddle. In a burst of strength she didn't know she possessed, Flair dug her heels into the horse's flanks and the horse took off, dragging Jewel with him.

Flair felt herself sliding from the saddle as the horse raced. Her heart hammered as if it would beat out of her chest. Just when she thought she could hold on no longer, Jewel hit a tree stump and was jerked free. Her foot wrenched backward in her boot and she cried out, but the horse kept galloping. She looked back and saw Jewel up and running after her. She settled her seat into the saddle and let the horse have his head. Fear forced her to keep looking backward until Jewel was a mere dot on the horizon.

Twenty

Inside Booker smiled as he wolfed down his second helping of boiled peas, potatoes, roasted chicken, and patties of fried cornbread. It was the best food he'd ever eaten. Not even Miss Flair's sweet bread came close to tasting the way his Parthina could cook a meal.

Thoughts of Miss Flair caused a pang in Booker's chest and he slowed his chewing. He hoped that what Mr. Eagerton had said wasn't true and that Mr. Caden and Rich could find her without any problems. If Mr. Caden would have let him, he would have gone with them to look for her. She had to be all right.

Booker had a good mind to go over and punch Mr. Eagerton in the nose for not scampering down that mountain side to see about Miss Flair before he high-tailed it to town with Rich. According to Rich, Mr. Caden had put the fear of God in the seat of Mr. Eagerton's breeches.

He lifted a spoonful of potatoes into his mouth and looked up from his plate. His new wife watched him. She smiled at him and his heart felt as if it melted in his chest like butter in the hot summer sun. She was the prettiest woman he'd ever seen. He winked and smiled back at her before glancing over at Samp to see if his father had noticed their romantic exchange. Satisfied Samp had been too busy with his supper to pay them any attention, Booker continued eating the delicious food and watching his new wife.

It had taken him more than a month to convince Parthina to marry him after he started courting her. He understood that she had to make up her mind about him and he tried not to rush her, but he was eager. Booker knew she was the one for him the first time he saw her in town months ago and couldn't stop thinking about her. Later when he met her at the church, he knew he couldn't let any other man have her. He would have done anything to win her hand, but all he had to do was talk to her, smile at her, and tell her how much he wanted her to be his woman. He looked over at her again. He'd make her proud she decided to marry him.

He'd waited two more weeks to marry her after she'd agreed. When the field work was finished each day he and Samp worked until darkness fell to get an extra room built onto their small house. He wanted the privacy of his own bedroom before he brought his bride home. There were some things a man and woman didn't do with someone else in the room. He and Samp had enough money saved to buy the materials they needed, but at the back of his mind he'd worried a bit that Miss Flair might not approve of the marriage or the new room.

He felt better about the project after Mr. Caden had approved of the addition to the house when he and Rich arrived to tell them about the stagecoach accident.

Booker started to dig into his chicken again when he heard something that sounded like someone calling his name. The voice sounded like Miss Flair's. Booker tensed and stopped chewing. Could that be? Mr. Caden told him Mr. Eagerton said she was dead, although Mr. Caden and Rich didn't believe it. That's why they had gone looking for her.

The front door was standing wide open to let in the cool air of the late afternoon. Booker's eyes were trained on the open doorway. He held still and listened. Someone *was* calling his name. He swallowed hard. Either it *was* Miss Flair he heard or her ghost, and Booker didn't like thinking about ghosts.

Lowering his spoon to the table he pushed back his chair and rose. Saying nothing, he walked toward the door.

"What's wrong? Where you going in the middle of your supper?" Samp asked.

"I hear something," he said without looking back at his father. "Someone's calling me. Listen." He stopped at the doorway and looked out. Miss Flair was hobbling up the pathway leading to the house. She didn't look like a ghost. She called his name and waved. She didn't sound like a ghost.

"Booker!" she called to him breathlessly. "I'm so glad to see a familiar face."

Thank God she was alive! Collecting his wits, Booker jumped down the steps and ran to meet her. "Miss Flair!" he answered. "What happened to you? Where have you been all these weeks?"

They met in the clearing of his front yard. He took hold of her arms and helped her to stand while she labored to catch her breath.

"Mr. Eagerton thought you were dead. He told us you were. But we didn't believe him. We knew you weren't dead." Deep joyous laughter bubbled from his chest.

Almost bent double from the pain in her side, Flair had trouble breathing. When she had found her house locked up as tight as the day she'd left, she panicked, thinking no one was around to help her. She'd hoped and prayed she'd find Rich there. It was sweet relief seeing Booker appear in the doorway. It didn't surprise her Douglas thought she'd died in that accident.

"No, I'm alive," she whispered, looking up into his dark brown eyes and friendly smile. "Do you know anything about Rich? Is he all right? Have you seen him?"

"Yes, ma'am. Don't worry about him. He's been here with Mr. Caden. They left two days ago on their way to find you. They didn't believe Mr. Eagerton when he said you died in that stagecoach wreck. We didn't none of us believe that," he insisted again.

Flair felt relief and a terrible sense of loss at the same time. Rich was safe and that was reason enough to be thankful, but despondency over missing him and Caden by two days struck her like a backhand to the face. Her mind reeled. What was she to do? Should she travel to Maxwell Farms or stay in Alabama and send word that she was alive and waiting for them? Should she go back to the town nearest where she'd been held captive and try to find them? If she left, would she always be two days behind them? A soft moan escaped her lips. All of a sudden, her nonstop traveling caught up with her and her legs turned weak. If not for Booker holding her, she would have collapsed.

"You needs to sit down, Miss Flair. Come inside and rest before you go back home."

"No, I'm fine. I—tell me how did Caden get Rich? He was with Douglas the last time I saw him."

"Mr. Eagerton brought him back here, sure enough. He stayed over there until Mr. Caden got here. Then Mr.—"

"Miss Flair, how did you get back here?" Samp asked interrupting Booker, rushing to her other side to help Booker hold her. A wide smile split his face. "I knowed you weren't dead. That Mr. Eagerton is a sorry soul."

"Samp, it's so good to see you—" Flair stopped. From over Samp's shoulder, standing in the doorway Flair saw the dark face of a beautiful young woman. Parthina smiled at her.

"Oh, Miss Flair, this is my wife," Booker said. "Parthina. Come on down here, honey, and meet her. Miss Flair won't hurt you. She's the nicest white woman I know."

The woman continued to smile shyly at Flair. Tired, but pleased for Booker, Flair returned the smile and said, "I'm very happy for both of you."

"Yes, ma'am. I figured you would be."
Pleasure sounded in his voice.

"Stop this yakking, Booker, and let's get
her inside. She's about to faint on us," Samp
grumbled, and they started moving again.
"Parthina, fix her a plate of those potatoes
and chicken. She looks like she could use a
good meal. Fix her something to drink, too."

"Papa's right, Miss Flair. I'll tell you everything I know while you have something to
eat. Parthina can go down and open up the
house for you and get your bed ready. We're
so glad you're alive."

Depressed over having missed Rich and Caden by only a couple of days, Flair allowed
Booker and Samp to lead her into their
house. Her legs were weak and her side hurt
from the running. Even her ankle was giving
her trouble again.

She was too tired to think, but knew she
had to. After she'd eaten and rested she
could decide what would be the best thing to
do. Should she send a telegram and wait here
for Caden and Rich to return, or immediately
travel back to Virginia to find them?

Knowing Rich was safe with Caden took a
lot of worry off her mind, but it didn't keep
her from wanting to see them, to hold them,
and tell them how much she loved them.

Caden. She needed to talk to him, to tell him

she was sorry for leaving him. She needed to find out if he still wanted her. She needed him to wrap her in his arms and tell her everything was going to be all right. She needed him to tell her he'd find a way they could be together—one that didn't cost him Maxwell Farms.

Doubts set in and ate away at her conviction. Did he want to see her? After the way she'd left him, could he forgive her? What if he'd decided he wanted the farm instead of her? What would she do without him in her life?

Flair stepped into the coolness of her workers' house and a peace settled over her. She knew what she had to do. She was the one who'd left him. It was her responsibility to return.

Sweat rolled down the sides of Caden's face. His shirt stuck to his shoulders. The hot, stuffy barn wasn't the only thing that had Caden in a sweat. As much as he hated to do it, Caden knew he had to leave Rich at the farm. He'd talked with the sheriff that Douglas and Rich had found after the accident and had ridden out to the wreckage. Flair's grave was empty. The sheriff told him about the bushy-haired man who'd shown him the two grave sites near the wreck. Caden decided to bring Rich back to Maxwell Farms before going after Flair *and* the mountain man. He could travel faster without Rich. Bernie and Benny would take care of Rich until he returned.

He wouldn't allow himself to believe she'd died, but he didn't want to believe she'd been abducted by a crazy man, either.

Caden walked around his horse to tighten the cinch on the saddle. It was already mid-afternoon and he needed to talk to Rich before he left. He'd thought about leaving without telling Rich what he was doing, but decided he wouldn't want to be treated that way and he couldn't do it to Rich. Caden knew the youngster wouldn't be happy he couldn't go along. He had to help him understand why he had to stay behind this time.

A shadow appeared in the open doorway of the barn. From the corner of his eye Caden saw Jake walk a few steps inside and take a stance.

"What's up? You just rode in. Now it looks like you're preparing to leave again."

"What I do isn't any of your business?"

Jake grunted. "Until your divorce is final everything you do concerns me."

"Like hell!" Caden wasn't in a mood to put up with Jake. He was trying hard not to believe Flair was dead and worrying about what all this would do to Rich if she was. One thing he wasn't going to do was put up with this bastard giving him a hard time. He threw his saddlebags on top of the saddle and looked at Jake, a black silhouette against the bright opening.

"Rutherford said the divorce will be final in a couple of months. Why don't you do us both a favor and take the money and the horses Shelton left you and get out of here."

Jake chuckled and stuck his thumbs behind his wide belt. "You don't think I trust you, do you?"

"You don't have to trust me. Rutherford would tell you if I didn't go through with the divorce. He's not loyal to me like he was to Shelton."

"I know that, but the farm isn't the only reason I'm sticking around." He shifted. "I figure if I can't have the farm, I'll take the next best thing. The woman."

Caden tensed. He eyed the foreman warily. "What are you getting at?"

"Who else but Flair." A cunning grin appeared on his lips. "She's a beautiful woman. Once you divorce her, she's free. The way I figure it we can put the horses and money I get from Shelton with her farm in Alabama and we'll have a pretty good spread. I think she'll take to the idea, don't you?"

The fine hairs on the back of Caden's neck bristled. His eyes narrowed. "Don't go near her."

"Don't tell me what to do." His manner changed from wiliness to anger. "It's plain and simple. If you don't want her, I do."

Caden took a step toward him. Jake had always known his hot button. Always. "I'll kill you if you touch her."

"Is that what you did to Eagerton? Kill him? Damn, what a high and mighty bastard he was?"

A chill passed over Caden. "How do you know about Douglas?"

"I overheard some talk, so I sent for him. He was real happy to hear you and Flair were getting a divorce."

Rage lit inside Caden. He should have guessed that Jake was at the bottom of Douglas's appearance. "You bastard. You eavesdropped on my conversation with Flair. I should smear your face on the ground."

"That's big talk, Cade, but then, you always did like to best me. You've made your choice. You want Maxwell Farms. Fine. Divorce Flair and take it, but goddammit don't tell me I can't be there waiting for the woman when you get through with her."

Forgetting his own vow to stay quiet until the divorce was final, Caden said, "It won't do you any good because I'm going to remarry her."

Jake relaxed and laughed again. "You can't. There's the little matter of the will, remember. We were just talking about it. The will states—"

"The will states only that I must remarry," Caden said loudly to overcome Jake's voice. "Not *who* I should marry."

"That's not true." The smile was gone. A snarl edged Jake's mouth. He shifted restlessly before resuming a stance.

"Pay a visit to Rutherford and read the will if you don't believe me. You're wrong. We were all wrong in thinking I had to marry *another* woman. The will doesn't say that. It only states that I must marry a woman of social standing in the community." He took another step closer. "Flair *is* a woman of social standing."

A guttural sound forced past Jake's tightly closed lips. "You're trying to pull a fast one over on me, and I'm not going to let you."

The look in Jake's eyes told Caden that Jake believed him. The foreman knew he'd lost, but whether he accepted it was yet to be seen. "You have no choice. Rutherford has already talked with the judge about it and he's concurred. Maxwell Farms will be mine as soon as Flair and I remarry."

With a yell of anger Jake rushed Caden, hitting him in the stomach with his shoulder and knocking him to the ground. Caden's tailbone hit the hard-packed dirt and he grunted when shooting spirals of pain shot up his back. Stunned by the force of the blow, Caden didn't see the fist that connected with his jaw and snapped his head to the side. He quickly rolled over in the dirt and jumped to his feet. Crouching low, he looked for the enemy.

Jake lunged for him again and Caden caught him with an uppercut under the chin, sending him stumbling backward. Jake regained his footing. Caden siezed the advantage and landed two quick punches to Jake's mid-section. The foreman grunted and doubled over. Caden pulled Jake up by the neck of his shirt and slammed him into the barn wall. Jake's hand found the handle of an axe and he grabbed it. He swung the blade at Caden, narrowly missing his chest.

He swung again. Caden ducked. The axe blade embedded in a support beam splintering the wood. A hard blow to the left eye staggered Jake. Caden grabbed hold of his arm and pinned it behind his back. He shoved Jake's face into the roughened barn wall and held it there with the heel of his palm.

"Because of that damned will, I can't run you off, but I can make your life miserable." Caden applied pressure to the side of Jake's head. "Why don't you be good to yourself and take my offer."

"I'll see you in hell first."

Caden shoved harder, grinding Jake's cheek into the barn wood. "I'm prepared to send you. Don't be a fool, Jake. This is our last fight. You can't win this one. Take the offer and go."

Jake hesitated, but finally nodded his consent.

Her head throbbed with pain as she flicked the reins and made the horse pulling her carriage go faster. Flair hadn't wanted to wait the three hours it was going to take the livery man to be free so he could drive her to Maxwell Farms. She chose to rent the small one-man buggy and drive herself rather than wait. It had been too many days already since she'd seen Rich and Caden.

The gentle rolling hills of Virginia were so beautiful. Light blue sky blazed with late afternoon sunshine. The ribbon of her bonnet had loosened and it had fallen to dangle down her back. She hadn't wanted to take the time to stop and put it back on her head.

It had been easy to tell herself Caden wanted her back when she was with Jewel, and later when she'd returned to Alabama looking for Rich. She'd easily convinced herself they could find a way to be together, but now, as she rode the last few miles to Caden's house she wondered if she'd fooled herself.

With good reason the farm meant a great deal to Caden. It belonged to him. How could his uncle have been so cold and calculating as to tie Caden's personal life to Maxwell Farms? Again doubts assailed her. Was she doing the right thing in returning and forcing Caden to make a decision between her and the farm? And what would she do if it was no longer up to her? What if Caden had already made a decision, and she wasn't part of it.

She tensed when she saw a lone man riding toward her. For a moment he frightened her, and she wondered how close she was to Maxwell Farms? As the rider came closer Flair pulled on the reins and stopped the horse. She blinked against the bright sunshine. It was Caden riding toward her. She was sure of it. Her heart started pounding wildly. *He was coming for her.* Caden must somehow have known she was on her way to him.

Flair closed her eyes and smiled with a squeal of delight as she clasped her hands to her chest. She opened her eyes and saw that he had turned and was riding away from her. Her heartbeat increased. Where was he going? Surely he recognized her.

She rose to her feet, waving and calling his name. The horse took him farther and farther away with each gallop. He must have seen her carriage. He must have recognized her. But no, she realized. The sun would have been shining in his eyes.

Flair plopped back down on the seat and grabbed the reins. She gave the horse a hard flap on the rump with the reins and he took off. The jerk of the carriage threw her backward but she regained her seating and held on. She hit the horse again and again, making him use all his muscle and strength to take her to Caden. She didn't know where he was going, only that she intended to catch him.

Dust kicked up by the horse's wild running flew into her face choking her. She coughed and sputtered, trying to clear her throat of the dirt-filled air. The ribbon from her bonnet tightened around her neck as the wind whipped the hat and made it fly behind her. At first her heart sagged because it didn't appear they were gaining on the horse and rider, but slowly she saw they were making progress.

Long before she knew he could hear her she started calling, "Caden! Caden!" The dust choked her and stung her eyes. The carriage bumped and jarred her until her teeth rattled together, still she whipped the horse and called to Caden.

Then, without warning, he turned around in the saddle and looked back as he reined in his horse. He pushed his hat back on his forehead. He sat there for a moment as if trying to figure out who was making the mad dash toward him.

Flair slowed the horse and stuffed the reins in one hand. She waved as she called, "Caden, it's me. Flair."

Her shoulders relaxed when she saw him spur his horse and gallop toward her. Flair pulled back on the reins and slowly stopped the horse. She threw the brake handle and, lifting her skirts, jumped down from the carriage. Her ankle cried out in pain as she started running toward Caden.

"Flair!"

A few feet from her Caden stopped his horse and jumped down to meet her. He caught her up in his arms and swung her around several times until she was out of breath. She buried her face in his neck, crying from joy and happiness.

They hugged.

They kissed.

"I was so afraid, Flair," he whispered against her ear. He held her tightly, completely wrapping his arms around her and pulling her close to his chest. "So afraid you were dead."

"No," she soothed, rubbing the back of his head, loving the feel of his hair against her palm. "I'm alive, and I'm so happy to see you."

"Thank God! You don't know how worried I've been."

"How's Rich?" she asked, thrilling to the joy of looking into his eyes, of touching him.

Caden slid his hands around to her face and cupped her cheeks. "He's fine. He's going to be one happy little boy when you get home." *Home.* She liked the sound of that.

"Rich never believed Douglas when he told him you were dead."

"How did you get him away from Douglas?"

His hands trembled. "I'll tell you all about Douglas later. Tell me what happened to you. Where have you been? I've been through hell worrying about you."

"I have so much to tell you. A man—Jewel saved my life. But then he wouldn't let me leave." Pain shot through her ankle and Flair shuddered. For a moment she felt as if Jewel had hold of her foot again.

"Never mind. We can talk about that later. I need to get you home."

Flair took a step and faltered on her injured ankle. Caden caught her up in his arms and she clung to him. Tears of happiness stung her eyes. She never wanted to be separated from Caden again. She wanted to protest when he left her in the carriage to go back for his horse, but within a couple of minutes he had tied his horse to the back of the buggy and pulled himself up beside her. Flair went into his arms and he held her. She didn't want to stop touching him.

"I love you," she whispered, still breathless.

"I love you, Flair," he answered, and kissed the top of her head. "You must have been badly hurt in the accident. You still have a bad bruise on your forehead and you're limping."

"It was horrible, but I'm all right now."

"Damn, I wish I could have been there for you."

"You were. You were always in my heart. I knew I had to get back to you and Rich. I'm sorry I left you, Caden," she whispered into the warmth of his neck. "At the time it seemed the right thing to do. I didn't think I could let you give up your farm for me. I didn't believe it was right to do that." She raised her head and looked into his understanding eyes. "But I don't want to live without you. I know it's selfish, but—"

"Shhh—you don't have to live without me."

"But is it right to ask you to give up Maxwell Farms for me? Will you hate me one day for it?"

Caden smiled. He lifted her bonnet and placed it back on her head. "Your nose is getting sunburned. I don't have to give up anything," he said as he retied the ribbon under her chin. "I've worked everything out, Flair. It was all in the wording of the will."

"What are you talking about?"

He took her hand in his. "I'll give you all the details later. In short, we still have to get the divorce, but we can remarry the next day. The will didn't say I had to marry a different woman. Only that I remarry a woman of social standing—and you, my love, are the woman I want."

Her eyes searched his face. She was afraid to believe him. "Are you sure about this?"

Caden reached down and kissed her lightly on the lips. "Very sure. I'd gone to speak to Rutherford the morning you left. I told you I would find a way for us to be together."

"I know. I was a fool for not trusting you."

"No. Not a fool. Just a woman who is used

to taking care of herself and her son, and doing a fine job of it."

His praise pleased her greatly, uplifting her. She returned his smile.

"Rutherford and the judge have agreed that after the divorce we can remarry, and full title of Maxwell Farms goes to me."

"What about Jake?"

"Jake's gone. I paid him his money. He picked up his horses and rode out of here with them an hour ago."

Relief was sweet. Wonderful. "Oh, Caden," she whispered, throwing her arms around his neck and holding him close. "I love you so much and I missed you terribly."

"I missed you, too. I thought I'd die when Douglas told me you'd gone over the cliff with that stage."

"I was so frightened, so worried I wouldn't get away, but now I'm so happy to be in your arms again."

"Don't ever leave me again, Flair," he murmured softly.

"No, never again," she answered.

Caden lowered his lips to hers and kissed her hungrily before letting her go and picking up the reins. "We better go. I know a little boy who's worrying himself sick about you."

Flair swallowed hard. "Yes. I'm desperate

to see Rich and hold him in my arms. There were so many times I didn't think I'd see either of you again. Caden, I'm so glad to be home." Flair lowered her head.

He dropped the reins in his lap. "Those aren't tears I see in your eyes are they?" he asked, lifting her chin with his fingertips.

"I have to tell him, don't I?"

Caden remained quiet, his gaze sweeping across her face. "It's your decision, Flair. There's a chance Rich will never find out about Douglas."

She inhaled deeply. "And there's always the chance he will. I think I should tell him."

Smiling, Caden pulled her to him and held her close. "I agree."

Flair snuggled into his shoulder. "Do you think he'll understand?"

Caden nodded. "You've raised him right. He's a smart young man. I'll make it clear to him that even though Douglas fathered him, I'm his papa. He'll understand."

Feeling content with her decision, Flair looked up at the darkening late afternoon sky. A dull pain throbbed in her ankle. *Thank God* she'd gotten away from Jewel. She shivered. Caden placed the reins in one hand and wrapped his other arm around Flair.

"You'll feel better once you get home and see Rich."

"I already feel better just having your arms around me."

They rode in silence for a few minutes, then Flair raised her head and looked at Caden. "What are you thinking about?" she asked.

He glanced her way and grinned. "I'm thinking about how much better I'm going to feel after a night of loving you. I can't think of anything I'd rather do."

Flair smiled. "Neither can I."

PASSIONATE NIGHTS FROM

PENELOPE NERI

DESERT CAPTIVE   (2447, $3.95/$4.95)
Kidnapped from her French Foreign Legion escort, indignant Alexandria had every reason to despise her nomad prince captor. But as they traveled to his isolated mountain kingdom, she found her hate melting into desire . . .

FOREVER AND BEYOND   (3115, $4.95/$5.95)
Haunted by dreams of an Indian warrior, Kelly found his touch more than intimate—it was oddly familiar. He seemed to be calling her back to another time, to a place where they would find love again . . .

FOREVER IN HIS ARMS   (3385, $4.95/$5.95)
Whispers of war between the North and South were riding the wind the summer Jenny Delaney fell in love with Tyler Mackenzie. Time was fast running out for secret trysts and lovers' dreams, and she would have to choose between the life she held so dear and the man whose passion made her burn as brightly as the evening star . . .

MIDNIGHT CAPTIVE   (2593, $3.95/$4.95)
After a poor, ragged girlhood with her gypsy kinfolk, Krissoula knew that all she wanted from life was her share of riches. There was only one way for the penniless temptress to earn a cent: fake interest in a man, drug him, and pocket everything he had! Then the seductress met dashing Esteban and unquenchable passion seared her soul . . .

SEA JEWEL   (3013, $4.50/$5.50)
Hot-tempered Alaric had long planned the humiliation of Freya, the daughter of the most hated foe. He'd make the wench from across the ocean his lowly bedchamber slave—but he never suspected she would become the mistress of his heart, his treasured sea jewel . . .

Available wherever paperbacks are sold, or order direct from the Publisher. Send cover price plus 50¢ per copy for mailing and handling to Penguin USA, P.O. Box 999, c/o Dept. 17109, Bergenfield, NJ 07621. Residents of New York and Tennessee must include sales tax. DO NOT SEND CASH.

SURRENDER TO THE SPLENDOR OF THE ROMANCES OF F. ROSANNE BITTNER!

CARESS	(3791, $5.99/$6.99)
COMANCHE SUNSET	(3568, $4.99/$5.99)
HEARTS SURRENDER	(2945, $4.50/$5.50)
LAWLESS LOVE	(3877, $4.50/$5.50)
PRAIRIE EMBRACE	(3160, $4.50/$5.50)
RAPTURE'S GOLD	(3879, $4.50/$5.50)
SHAMELESS	(4056, $5.99/$6.99)

Available wherever paperbacks are sold, or order direct from the Publisher. Send cover price plus 50¢ per copy for mailing and handling to Penguin USA, P.O. Box 999, c/o Dept. 17109, Bergenfield, NJ 07621. Residents of New York and Tennessee must include sales tax. DO NOT SEND CASH.